VENGEANCE IS MINE

Marsh Rauser

ISBN: 978-0-6151-6072-6

Book cover designed by artist D. Cociuba
Bothell, WA

Also by Marsh Rauser

HIGH-LEVEL SECURITY

Acknowledgments

I want to thank the many friends and the naggers who contributed to the writing and publishing of my book. Yes, you naggers, you know who you are. Without your loving support, confidence building, and nagging, I would have given up years ago.

Special thanks to my sister, Norma Lightner, who told me while the book was still in its first draft that it was the "best book she had ever read."

To the critiquing group—Sheila Dwyer, Chana Madsen, Sandy Verlindin, Michael Hobbs, Frank Kirby, Trish Mitchell, and Joan Roggenkamp—your input was a valuable asset, as was your honest assessment.

To the cheerleaders—Ellen Sullivan, Phyllis Wilborn, Gail Penn, Kathy Vanderford, and Alexa Brydges—I feel blessed to have so many good friends.

I dedicate this book to all of you.

Introduction

In the annals of world history, World War II will go down as the largest conflict the world had ever witnessed. Although there were many heroic campaigns, one in particular stands out: the Sicilian Invasion called *HUSKY*.

Dates: July 10, 1943–July 31, 1943

Mission: Operation *HUSKY*. A plan devised in February 1943 by President Franklin D. Roosevelt and the Prime Minister of Great Britain, Sir Winston Churchill.

Execution: Orchestrated, jointly, between General Dwight D. Eisenhower and Sir Harold Alexander.

Strategy: To destroy the line of communications between Africa and Italy and secure the Mediterranean.

Purpose: To defeat Italy and bring down "Il Duce" better known as Benito Mussolini, the Italian prime minister.

Obstacle: German forces had arrived prior to the invasion. Germany and Italy were allies.

PART 1

July 7, 1943

Chapter 1

Nineteen-year-old Thomas Callahan, better known as TC, boarded the 227-C47 aircraft from New York City. TC was on his way to Italy to take part in a campaign called *HUSKY*. Orchestrated by two world powers, Great Britain and the United States joined forces on the operation, doubling their military strength. This included the navy, the air force, and the army and its paratroopers. TC was one of those paratroopers chosen for this military coup d'état.

The realization of the danger involved had occurred to him. This was TC's first European mission and he was terrified. He decided to take his mind off the realization that he could be killed so far away from home.

I'm as patriotic as the next person, but I'm young and I've got my whole life ahead of me. I wonder if the person who said, "War is hell," had any concept of how scary hell is? You never know if today will be the day and you'll come back in a pine box. Jesus, my mother will freak out if I don't come home. And then there's my wife, Anna Marie. I promised her I'd come back. I have to. Damn it, I'm scaring the hell out of myself. For some reason, I have this horrible feeling that this is it, that I won't be on the return flight home. I wonder if these guys feel the same?

I decided not to think of the present and just think about what my life had been like before I was drafted, before I decided to become a paratrooper. I smiled when I thought about my family and a life that was secure and predictable. And that was how I liked my life—planned out and organized.

Who would have thought that I'd be going to Italy? Tom Callahan from Philly. Most of my friends never even got as far as New York City. They were happy just to hang in the neighborhood. I'm also a home boy, but I still wanted to see the world. I had a hankering to see different places. In fact, I always wanted to go to Italy. Who wouldn't? Beautiful women, good food, seeing old stuff—but on a vacation, not by putting my ass on the line.

I was born with the map of Ireland all over my face: blue eyes, red hair, and freckles. Can you get more Irish than that? Dad was the one with the blue eyes and red hair (Mom called it rust). I was brought up Catholic to an Irish clan in Philadelphia.

I'm just one of four kids born to Thomas John Callahan and Loretta Mary Callahan. I have two brothers, Patrick, eighteen, and Devin, sixteen. They look more like Mom, with the dark hair and green eyes. And then there's my little sister, Blair. She's fourteen years old and looks like Dad and me. One time I heard my Dad say, "Thank God she came along." Dad thought Mom would have never stopped wanting kids until she got her girl.

I'm the oldest, so I was named after my old man. That's why everyone calls me TC. My old man is a cop, second generation, and I want to follow in his footsteps and keep up the tradition. After all, I'm his namesake. A lot of the cops in Philly are second generation, and some are even third. I'm going to make the old man proud. Someday, I'm going to be the chief of police right in our neighborhood precinct. They all know me, and no one knows that part of town better than me. They also know I'm tough. I won't put up with any crap in my part of town.

My brothers want to go to college, though they're still not sure what they want to be when they graduate from high school. They only know that they don't want to be cops. Without an education, the only other options would be the mill or the mines. They have this highfalutin idea that they want to be "big shots." And everyone knows you have to go to college to be rich. To me, the chief of police is a "big shot."

Besides I'm the only one that wants to get married and have some kids. Annie. Beautiful Anna Marie Cassandra, the love of my life. I've known Anna

Marie since we were kids. Carmine, Annie's brother, is my best friend. He's a homeboy and a number one ace. We hung around together all through grammar school and high school. She was always following us around. We thought she was a pain in the ass.

Carmine's old lady would always rag on him. "Carmine, get in here and watch out for the baby." Or, "Carmine, take the baby with you." The only time we could get away from the brat was when we played at my house or in the schoolyard.

This one day, I was over at Carmine's house (I was about sixteen), and I noticed that Anna Marie looked different. For one thing, she was all dressed up in a party dress. Carmine said she was going to a friend's birthday party. She had on this dress that kind of hugged her body. She looked different. She didn't look like a kid anymore. For the first time, I noticed that Anna Marie had these big black eyes and hair so black it shined silver in the sun. I was also surprised that for a fourteen-year-old, her boobs were really starting to develop. Man, was she stacked! She was no longer Carmine's kid sister, but a beautiful babe. *"Madone."* That's what Carmine always said when he saw something he liked. It was Italian.

From that time on, Annie and I were like two peas in a pod. I really had the hots for her. I think Carmine was a little jealous. He didn't like his kid sister following us around. Me, on the other hand, I preferred it. After a couple of years, Annie and me started going steady. Before we knew it, we started talk-ing about getting hitched right after she graduated from high school.

I was graduating in June, and in two years, she would follow. Our plan was that I'd get a job, any job I could get. I would go to night school. I'd take a couple of courses in law and police science. Then, when I was twenty-one, I would join the police force. We would live in the same neighborhood as our folks. We even planned how many kids we'd have; we would have two kids, a boys and a girl. Life would be good.

So when I got my draft notice two weeks before graduation, I freaked out. Annie and my old lady cried, and my Dad—you know Dads, "I'm proud of you, son. You go over there and show them what us Irish Yanks are made of."

I told him, "Yeah sure, I'll win this war all by myself. Are you nuts? I can get killed!"

"You won't get killed if you don't act like a jerk and take too many chances. For once in your life, learn how to take orders."

I got the impression that my old man thought that going to war was going to make a man out of me. And Annie, she decided that she wanted to get married now. She wanted us to elope and not tell anyone until the war was over. I told her it wouldn't be right. She was too young and she needed to finish high school. And what if something happened to me? No, we'd have to wait however long it took. Besides, we were both young and we had the rest of our lives. I told her, "I'll do what I have to do, and when the war is over, we'll get married."

I usually caved in when Annie started to pout or cry, but this time I was sticking to my guns. The only problem was that she was one of those good Catholic girls—no sex before marriage, and I was sick of waiting. The Church and her Mother convinced her it was a mortal sin to have sex before marriage. I tried to persuade her that it wasn't a sin if we were in love, but she wouldn't buy it.

She actually thought I was going to wait for her to be the first. She wasn't. I felt what she didn't know wouldn't hurt her. I wanted her, body and soul. The other girls were just practice. Besides, "practice makes perfect," and I wanted to be perfect for her.

The night before I left for Fort Dix, my folks gave me a graduation and send-off party at the Elks Club. I think half the town showed up. After living in this neighborhood all my life, as did my parents before me, you get to know everyone on the block. My old man even invited the guys in his precinct.

6

I wasn't the only kid who was drafted. A couple of guys from the neighborhood got their notices too. Carmine didn't, and he was pissed.

"How come you get drafted and not me?"

That idiot actually thought this was some sort of honor that the government was bestowing on me because I was special.

"Carmine, don't sweat the small stuff. My number came up and yours will too. And why the hell do you want to risk your life fighting a war we're not sure we can win? You lucked out."

As usual, Carmine didn't get it. He just looked at me with this wild stare and stated, "Because you got asked first. You get everything first."

"Carmine, just for once, get your head out of your ass. Being drafted is not an honor."

He looked surprised and then he laughed. Then I laughed.

"You know, Carmine, I'm going to miss you, you grease ball."

"I'll be missing you too, you dirty mick."

After the party was over, I drove Annie home, begging her all the way.

"Let's do it. I'm leaving tomorrow. Who knows when you'll see me again? I might even get killed."

She looked up at me, and she started to cry.

"Holy shit, Annie, I'm sorry. I was just kidding. I won't get killed. You can't get rid of me that fast. Besides, sweetheart, I'll be back to collect what you have been holding back for two years."

She finally smiled. We kissed, we touched, and we did everything but go all the way. It was tearing up my insides.

She couldn't help it. It was that old religion thing. God will punish you. Only bad girls have sex before marriage. And the dumbest of all, after you give in, your boyfriend will tell everyone and give you a bad reputation. What a bunch of crap! But what the hell could I do? I love this girl.

After I dropped Annie off at her house, I started thinking. There is no way out of this draft situation, so if I have to do this, I'm going to do it right. I'm going to be a freaking hero who will bring honor to my love, my family, and the whole damn town. But first, I have to go home and pack.

Chapter 2

At six o'clock in the morning, me and the other local guys took the bus to Fort Dix, New Jersey. The bus ride was as hot as hell, but we all knew we weren't going on a picnic.

Basic Training—Six weeks/Ft. Dix, NJ: As soon as we arrived in Fort Dix, we went to a hospital for our physical. They were pretty thorough. We were all so young. Only a couple of guys didn't pass, but most of us had no problem. Of course, not passing didn't mean they got to go home. They found them desk jobs instead.

While in line at the hospital, I met this straight shooter. A guy from Baltimore named Jerry, Jerry Stein. And it just so happened we wound up in the same barrack. We soon became good buddies.

Basic training—it was everything I thought it would be and more. I wasn't sure I would survive, especially the lousy discipline. But I was determined to make good. My self-imposed commitment was to get noticed and to at least make sergeant before getting out.

At first, they made it easy. They started us out with three weekly six-mile runs for fewer than fifty minutes. Then there was the twenty-five-mile march, wearing all of our gear, which weighed a hundred pounds; then a forty-eight-mile march in eighteen hours. And this was besides all the other crap we had to do like marksmanship, dismantling artillery and putting it back together, climbing walls, and doing calisthenics.

I survived my six weeks of basic training and signed up for Airborne School, and so did my buddy Jerry. No way we wanted to be foot soldiers. This also meant we had to go for another physical and instead of going to Signal Training, we would be transferred to Airborne Training Camp.

It's said that paratroopers are the best-trained and physically fit troops in the army. Expectations are that you're to perform under extreme conditions.

I passed the physical and called Mom to tell her the good news.

"Guess what, Mom. I'm going to be a paratrooper."

She was obviously not impressed.

"That's nice. When are they going to let you come home?"

"I'll be coming home in a few months. Right now, I'm being transferred to Fort Benning, Georgia."

"What do you mean? You have to go to Georgia before coming home? Why can't you come home first and then go to Georgia?"

"Because if I do that, I'll be locked up for desertion. Your son is going to be a paratrooper! You should be proud. Not everyone made the grade."

"Did I say I wasn't proud of you? I just want to know when you're coming home on a furlough."

"That's what I'm trying to tell you if you would let me get a word in. I can't come home now. First, I have to go for paratrooper training, and after training I get to go home for a while. And then I'm being sent overseas."

"Where are they sending you?"

"I don't know where. And even if I did, I can't tell you; it's top secret."

"You can't even tell your own mother? Remember, I'm the one that brought you into this world."

"Do we have to discuss this now? Look, Mom, I've got to go. I'll talk to you later. Other guys want to use the phone. Bye. I can't hear you. Bye. Oh, Mom, tell Annie I'll see her in a couple of months. And I'll write."

I finally hung up. Holy shit, she was making me a nervous wreck! I know how she feels. I'm her son, but she didn't have to get so emotional. And to top it off, my idiot brother Pat enlisted in the navy. Now Mom is afraid she might lose two of her sons.

Chapter 3

Airborne Training—Six weeks—Fort Benning, GA: It wasn't long before we were on a train to Fort Benning, Georgia. When our group arrived, they assigned us to the 505th division. Surprise! Surprise! Being we were the new recruits, Jerry's first assignment was KP duty and I got to clean the latrines, not the best job in the world, especially for a guy who didn't even know how to make his bed before he was drafted. Jerry's job was cooking and scrubbing the pots and pans. Also, during the day, there were push-ups, running, and training.

After several weeks of KP duty, we started Airborne School. It was a six-week training program. I didn't think I would make it after the first week, but after a while, I got the hang of it.

At first we jumped the thirty-four-foot towers. We jumped during the day, five days a week with one day off, and they threw in a couple of nights. It took a lot of practice to figure out how to maneuver the parachutes, and it was harder yet, learning how to hit your targeted area.

After three weeks, we graduated to the Douglas C-47 transport. My first night plane jump scared the hell out of me. Mostly, it was the flames shooting out of the engine. I was so scared my chute would catch on fire. It took several nights of jumping to get oriented and be able to distinguish and maneuver within a perimeter on the ground.

Jerry almost got himself killed. He pulled the ripcord and nothing happened. He must have panicked because he never thought to pull the reserve until it was almost too late. We all watched in horror. Finally, it opened. What a relief! It sure scared the shit out of him. I mean, literally. He stunk so bad that all the guys razzed him. He was embarrassed. I told him not to sweat the small stuff. He lived. That was the main thing.

In order to graduate, you have to advance from a single jumper in the door to jumping with five men. Then you have to jump with all the guys, using both the doors. Some of the guys couldn't hack it and backed out, Jerry and I stuck it out. We wanted our wings.

Annie wrote to me every day. Without those letters, there would have been nothing to look forward to. She was eagerly awaiting me being furloughed. I still couldn't give her a date. There was no way they would let us leave before we completed our training, and that could take weeks or even months.

Finally, graduation day! After six weeks of training, I finally got my jump wings during a graduation ceremony. General Marshall himself pinned on my jump wings. He stood back, saluted, and said, "Welcome aboard, Soldier. You are now airborne."

Oh man, what a day! This was great; I could now go home before going overseas. But my excitement was soon shot down. Sergeant Cox walked up to Jerry and me while we were in the mess hall and informed us that some of the men in our unit were being reassigned in two days. All the others would be taking their furlough. Jerry and me were on the roster to be moved to Fort Bragg's 82nd Airborne Division for special training. Shit!

Chapter 4

Special Training—Six weeks at Ft. Bragg, NC: The training at Fort Bragg was grueling. Rumor had it we were being trained for a special mission. You needed a lot of strength to carry one hundred pounds of equipment. We carried our parachute, reserve chute, two-day rations, a small shovel, four grenades, an M-1 rifle, several clips of ammo, a change of underwear, and a gas mask. For stamina, we were made to march for twenty-five miles, wearing all of our gear.

Preparedness is vital to our survival. We are trained to prepare for hunger, fatigue, and severe weather. They handed out all those conditions. We were also trained to have quick responses and make fast decisions. Timing is essential when you land in enemy territory. We practiced day and night: practice jumps, night maneuvers, hand-to-hand fighting, and foxhole digging. We learned how to use not only American weapons, but the enemy's weapons as well. Some of us were also trained in machine gun maintenance. We trained six days a week, which left little time to worry about what our tour of duty or what our next assignment might be. All we wanted was a couple of days off, but there is no time-out in the military.

On March 10, they finally let us go home. They gave us a two-week furlough. We were told that when we got back, we would be going overseas. Where or when was top secret. At that moment, I didn't give a shit. I just wanted to go home. I called the folks and told them I had my train tickets and I should be pulling into the Pennsylvania station at around five p.m. I asked Mom to call Carmine and Anna Marie to let them know I was on my way home.

* * *

I couldn't believe it. When I got off the train, the whole family was standing there just waiting for me to arrive, that is, everyone except my brother Pat. He was at the naval station at Norfolk, Virginia. To tell the truth, I got a little choked up. I didn't realize how much I'd missed them, and they obviously missed me. Of course, Mom was crying, Dad was smiling, and Anna Marie, well, she was a sight for sore eyes. Yes, Tommy, you are one lucky guy. You've got a good family and a beautiful girlfriend. It's funny how you don't realize what you have until you don't have it anymore.

I was really surprised to see how my kid sister had changed in the short amount of time I'd been gone. She went from a little girl to a beautiful teenager. I started thinking about how those horny guys in school had better keep their mitts off her. Or they'll have to answer to me. What is it about being a big brother? You don't mind screwing someone else's sister. You just don't want anyone to screw yours. And why am I even thinking of something like that at a time like this?

All of a sudden, I saw Carmine running toward us. Good old Carmine, a friend till the end. But Carmine didn't look too good; he didn't look healthy. He looked kind of thin and scrawny. We all hugged, we kissed, and then we all went to my folk's house. Mom said she made a special dish for me, my favorite, corned beef and cabbage. You would have thought that by now she would have known that I hated corned beef and cabbage. It was my brother Devin who liked corned beef. I liked steak. What the hell, she meant well.

I kissed her on the cheek and thanked her. "You know, Ma, I thought about your cooking the whole time I've been gone."

She smiled and kissed me. "I know, Tommy. There is nothing like a mother's home cooking."

We ate, drank, and laughed. They started catching me up on all the local gossip—like who got married, who died, who got pregnant.

I said, "As long as it wasn't Annie, I couldn't care less."

Both Annie and Mom darted me a look that could have killed. I guess I was out of line. I laughed anyway.

My mother gave me another look and blasted me.

"What's wrong with you? That remark was so disrespectful to Anna Marie."

"I was kidding. I was only kidding. I'm sorry. I guess I had too much beer." It was getting late and everyone was getting drunk, so we decided to call it a night.

Carmine said his good-byes and announced that he would take Annie home.

I said, "No, you don't. Thanks just the same, but I want to be alone with my girl."

Dad threw me the keys to his car, a 1940 black Ford sedan. Once we were in the car, I noticed how quiet Annie was, she hardly said a word the whole time I was driving her home.

"What's up, doll? You haven't said a word since we got in the car."

"I can't believe you, Tommy. How could you show such disrespect for me in front of your family?"

"I'm sorry. It just came out wrong. What I meant was I didn't care to have to listen to who got pregnant. I don't care about that. You're right. It was a stupid remark. I'm sorry. Do you still love me? Or have you already found someone else?"

"Did I stop loving you? No, there is no one else. There will never be anyone else for me."

I didn't say another word. We were at her house. I stopped the car. This was what I was waiting for, what I dreamed of: Annie and me alone in the car, necking and making out and, of course, her hand pushing my hand away. Same old stuff, but it sure felt good. After fifteen minutes into all this good stuff,

Mrs. Cassandra appeared at the door. She yelled for Annie to come into the house. She then yelled at me.

"Hi, Tom. Welcome home! Why don't you stop at the house tomorrow? Anna Marie has to come in now."

"Hi, Mrs. Cassandra," I yelled back. "OK, I will."

Annie started laughing. "Good-bye, Tommy. See you tomorrow."

I didn't think it was so damn funny. I gave her one final French kiss before opening the door for her. Annie's old lady was still watching, and I wanted her to know how polite her future son-in-law was. When I got home, everyone was in the living room listening to the radio. I excused myself. I was tired with all that traveling and excitement. I'm sure the beer helped.

I didn't realize how much I missed home, my room, and my own space until I walked in the front door. Everything in my room was exactly the way I'd left it except for Pat. Pat and I shared this room. I used to hate sharing a room with him. I wanted my own space. But now I would have given anything to see him again.

I started thinking about us as kids, fighting over the radio, fighting over when we would turn out the lights, even fighting over each other's toys. When any kids picked on us, though, we joined forces. You couldn't take on just one of us; you had to be ready to take on both of us. After all, we're brothers. Many a time, we beat the crap out of some kid. Sometimes it was a couple of kids. And many a time, they beat the crap out of us.

I must have been a little drunk. I started talking to him like he was in the room.

"I miss you, Pat. I wish you were here to see me before I go overseas, but we'll have a lot to talk about when I get home . . . if I get home. To tell you the truth, brother, I'm no hero. I'm scared. I'm scared to death. But that's just our secret. Don't tell Dad. I guess I'm not as tough as everyone thinks I am or as tough as Dad expects me to be. When Annie and me get married, you'll be my best man. Come home alive, brother."

It didn't take me long to get back into the swing of things. I visited everyone I knew and then some. The hero had returned (some hero). I even went to visit my high school teachers. I figured I had to wait for Annie to get out at three o'clock anyway, so I walked around and talked to all my old teachers. I couldn't believe how fast the time had passed since I had walked these halls. I felt like I had grown up. I didn't belong there anymore.

Almost every night, I would meet up with Carmine; Carmine's girlfriend, Louise; and my girl at Tony's Pizza and Fine Foods. Sometimes we would even have dinner there—like pizza, a calzone, or some pasta and then shoot some pool. Carmine and me would drink beer, and the girls had their cherry Cokes. Most of my buddies from school had been drafted. But the locals always stopped in to have a beer before going home. Dad's cronies also stopped in after their shifts. That's what I liked, a neighborhood where everyone knew everyone. There was always someone to bullshit with.

On the Thursday of that first week, we were at the table drinking, eating, and clowning around. Carmine and Louise played the jukebox and got up to dance. They played the new song "As Time Goes By" from the movie *Casablanca*. Annie and I saw it three times.

I told her, "If I could be like any movie star, I would want to be Bogie."

I asked Annie if she wanted to dance and she said no.

"I want to talk to you alone."

"Alone? We're always alone."

She glared at me. "We are never alone. You always have a crowd around you. When are we ever alone?"

I flipped my mouth off. "Maybe that's because you never want to do what I want. And you know what I mean." I relented. "OK, what do you want to talk about?"

Her dark eyes shone as black as the night, and out of that beautiful mouth came, "I want to get married."

"I know. So do I, and we'll get married as soon as the war is over."

Again, she looked me straight in the eye. "No, Tommy. I want to get married now. I want to get married before you go overseas."

"What? Are you crazy? What if I don't come back? And what about school? You only have one more year to go. And most of all, your parents will flip their gourd. No, this discussion is over."

She started to cry. Christ, I can't stand to see a woman cry, especially my woman.

She then started in on, "You don't love me."

"I don't love you? It's because I love you, I want to wait and do the right thing. You're all I ever think about."

"Then marry me. Let's elope. We can go to Elkton, Maryland. In Elkton, you can get married at sixteen, without your parent's consent."

"Sweetheart, this doesn't make any sense. What about the Church? We won't be legally married in the eyes of the Church."

"I thought about that too. We can keep it a secret until you get back, and then we'll redo our vows and have a real wedding in the church."

I tried to reason with her. "Annie, think about what you're saying. I say we wait."

"No. I love you, and I want to marry you before you go overseas. I have it all planned. Tomorrow is Friday. Pick me up after school. I'll tell my mother that I'm sleeping over at Louise's house. She'll cover for me. We'll be back on Saturday night, and no one will know the difference. Think of it, TC, you and me, sleeping overnight at a hotel together. Isn't that what you've been waiting for?"

I must admit that the "sleeping together" part made perfect sense. "OK, OK. I'll tell Carmine."

"No. You can't tell Carmine. He has a big mouth, and he'll tell my parents. I'll make Louise swear to God to keep her mouth shut. Which means she won't be able to see Carmine tomorrow night. I know she'll do it. She already thinks it's so romantic."

"OK, sweetheart. Here's looking at you."

We both laughed. I made a lousy Bogie.

When I got up the next morning, Mom made me a big breakfast of ham, eggs, and toast with a lot of butter smeared on the toast. She knows the way I like it. She was really spoiling me, and she was also trying to fatten me up. I couldn't help but feel good and it showed.

Mom was smiling when she asked, "What's up with you? Why are you so happy this morning?"

"Why not? It's cold but sunny, and I'm having breakfast with my beautiful mother who is trying to get her son fat. Mom, if you don't stop feeding me, I won't be able to get through the door of the airplane."

She laughed.

"You got so skinny. You need some beef on those bones. People will think I don't feed you."

It's always been what people think. I wondered what they'd think if they found out that Annie and me got hitched. *Well, at least they won't know for a while. I'll worry about the fallout later on.*

"Oh, Mom, by the way, I won't be home tonight. I'm going to Pittsburgh to meet a buddy of mine. I met him in training."

"What buddy?"

"Come on, Mom. You wouldn't know him if I told you. I met him in Fort Dix."

"What's his name?"

"God. Mom. Do you also want his telephone number? Come on, I'm nineteen and I'm a soldier for Christ's sake."

"All right, Tommy. But what did I tell you about swearing in this house? Especially taking the lord's name in vain."

"I'm sorry, Mom. I'm really sorry."

She smiled and gave me a big hug. I could always charm her.

"I love you, Tommy. This war scares me. Please take care of yourself."

"I love you too, Mom. And don't forget to tell Pop I'm taking the car for the weekend." She started to frown.

"He's not going to like that."

"I know. But he'll get over it."

First, I had to pick up a few things from the store before three o'clock. The first thing I did was go to a jewelry store that was outside the neighborhood. I wanted to surprise Annie and get her a wedding ring. I couldn't afford much, so I bought her a plain band that she could easily hide, but it was real gold. And I also needed to pick up some rubbers. There is no way I wanted her to get pregnant.

By three o'clock, I was waiting in front of the school. As soon as she saw me, her face lit up. She and Louise ran to the car. Louise was crying.

"A-yo, Louise. What happened? Did someone say something to hurt you? Point him out. I'll beat the crap out of him."

"No, TC. Stop being so stupid. I'm crying because this is so romantic. You guys running away to get married. I wish it was me and Carmine."

"OK, Louise, now stop blubbering. And remember, don't tell anyone about us getting hitched. Especially Carmine."

As we drove away, I started to feel a knot in the pit of my stomach. It wasn't that I didn't love Annie. I just felt like I was taking advantage of her. You know, not doing right by her. You're supposed to protect women. They're so fragile, so vulnerable, and she's so young and beautiful. What if I didn't make it back? She'd be a young widow, and she's much too young to be pining over me.

Annie must have guessed what I was thinking. She could read me like a book. If I was quiet, I was thinking.

"Stop dwelling on this, Tommy," she said. "I want this. I really want this. Do you think you're the only married man going overseas? There are thousands, maybe even a million."

"Yeah, sure. But they're probably already married and not taking the plunge and risking—"

Before I could finish, she interrupted me. "Stop it. I don't want to hear this. It's my decision. I want to be Mrs. Thomas John Callahan, the second. It has a nice ring to it. Besides, now you can't fool around on me. You wouldn't, would you, Tommy?"

"Are you kidding? You know me."

What a damn liar I am, except that those girls never meant anything to me. So why hurt her on our wedding day? Besides, I wasn't married when I screwed around.

"What about you, Annie? Would you ever fool around on me?" I asked.

"Never. Never. I will wait like any wife should. And when you get home, we can retake our vows at St. Jude's. No one need ever know. Just us, Louise, and of course, God."

We laughed, we held hands, and we kissed at all the traffic lights.

It only took an hour and a half to get to Elkton, Maryland. We listened to the radio, and when the news of the war came on, we changed the station. We sang all the way to Maryland to songs like "I've Heard That Song Before," "Don't Get Around Much Anymore," and "All or Nothing at All"—all the songs that were on the *Hit Parade*. But when "As Time Goes By" came on, Annie started to cry.

"Hey, baby, what's the matter with you? You cry every time you hear that song. This is your wedding day, and it was just a movie." I did my Bogie routine. "Here's looking at you, kid."

She started laughing.

We finally hit Elkton, Maryland, the eloping capital of the East Coast. I checked around for a florist and found one on the corner of West Main Street. I stopped the car, ran in, and bought Annie a gardenia corsage. I asked the girl at the counter if she knew where we could get married. She gave me directions to this little white house where the sign read: *Justice of the Peace.* And believe it or not, it had a white picket fence around it. We laughed. This was just like in the movies.

I rang the bell. This middle-aged man opened the door and asked, "Can I help you?"

I said, "Yeah, we want to get married."

"You look awfully young. Are you sure?"

"Yeah, we're sure. We're not as young as we look. I'm nineteen and Annie here is seventeen."

He smiled.

"Oh, you're that old? I would never have known."

He was a tall, thin, wasp-looking guy, about six foot two with light brown hair that was starting to recede. He called to his wife.

"Honey, we have company."

This older woman came running in with her apron still on.

"Sorry, folks," she stated. "I was just cleaning up in the kitchen."

She looked at us and asked the same thing as her husband.

"Aren't you both too young to be getting married? I assume you're here to get married?"

"No, darling," he remarked. "He's nineteen and she's seventeen."

They both laughed.

I was starting to get pissed. I felt like they were laughing at us. But Annie said I was too sensitive. I told them our story. How I was going overseas and how Annie and me had been sweethearts since we were kids. I explained that

22

we were both Catholic and that we planned on getting married again in the Catholic Church just as soon as I came home.

The guy smiled. He told me his name was Larry Jones.

His wife, Margaret, was the total opposite of him. She was short, pudgy, and her blonde hair was in a bun on top of her head.

We followed Larry and Margaret into a room they called the chapel. It looked more like their living room with its lace curtains. The only thing that set it apart was the altar. There was a fancy white lace cloth hanging halfway down. On the top of the altar were two brass candlesticks on each side of a large white Bible. In the corner near a window was an organ. On the wall behind the organ were pictures of about a hundred couples. The only other furniture in the room was a flowered couch with a coffee table in front of it. It was easy to assume that the pictures were of all the couples that they had married. I stood there, looking at all the smiling faces.

Larry came over and pointed to a picture on the wall that was way up in the far left corner.

"They were the first couple we married."

I looked at the picture and thought, *They're probably old and have kids by now.* Also neatly framed was his justice of the peace license. I guess he was legitimate.

Larry handed Annie and me some papers to fill out. He said it was a Maryland state requirement. While I was filling out the papers, Margaret lit the candles on the altar. As soon as we finished, Annie went into the bathroom to comb her hair and change into the new dress that she'd had stashed into her overnight bag.

When she came out, she looked like a movie star. Her dress was pink with a full skirt that swayed when she walked. I handed her the box with the gardenias. Rather than pin them on her dress, she chose to hold them, as if it were a bouquet.

Margaret was now sitting at the organ. She asked us if we had a request.

I looked at Annie and then at Margaret. "Do you know 'As Time Goes By'?"

"It just so happens I do," she replied. "But that's not the kind of song you play at a wedding."

"I know. But that's our song. In a couple of days, I'll be going overseas. I want to remember this day as the day I think about when things get rough."

Gee whiz. Annie started to cry, and Margaret looked like she was going to blubber at any moment. Women. Margaret never said another word. She put her pudgy hands on the keyboard and started playing our song. *You must remember this: a kiss is still a kiss . . .* I don't think the ceremony took more than five minutes. When I put the ring on Annie's finger, Larry said, "Until death do you part."

I kind of got a lump in my throat. I guess it was because I knew that the possibility of my death did exist. Our kiss was long, passionate, and embarrassing. We finally let go of each other. It was done. It was legal. We were married.

We asked the Joneses if they knew of a hotel in the area where we could spend our honeymoon. They recommended a boarding house that was called The Elkton Love Nest. And if we hurried, Mavis, the owner, might still be serving dinner. That sounded good to me. I was starving.

I wasn't keen on sleeping in some stranger's house. Annie deserved better. She deserved the bridal suite at the Ritz or at least Howard Johnson's. Maybe a hotel with a great restaurant and dancing would be good. We both knew how to jitterbug and do the two-step. Larry assured us that the only decent hotel was in Baltimore, but we were too tired to make the trip.

Larry gave us the directions on how to get to the Love Nest. He and Margaret wished us well and took our picture to join the other newlyweds on the wall. This whole wedding thing seemed a little weird. But I knew within the next hour or so came the part I'd been waiting for. We would finally make love.

The Love Nest was just a few blocks away. As soon as we pulled into the driveway, the door of the house opened and there stood this woman who was almost as wide as she was tall. She had short blonde curls, rosy cheeks, and the friendliest smile I'd ever seen.

"Come on, loves, come on. I have dinner waiting for you."

We were so taken by surprise that for a few seconds we just stood there staring at her.

As I walked through the door, I had this warm feeling.

"This is a real nice place, isn't it, Annie?"

She shook her head and smiled. She seemed almost embarrassed—not scared, just shy.

The woman introduced herself as Mavis Abbott. Mavis had an English accent. She explained that Larry had called, told her we were coming, and asked her to take good care of us.

"He also said you were hungry."

I thought, *good old Larry*.

"How about some dinner, darlings? You must be famished. I have chicken, mashed potatoes, gravy, string beans, and apple pie for dessert. Is that all right?"

"All right?" I answered. "That sounds swell."

"First off," she said. "How about a nice hot cup of tea?"

Annie said, "Tea would be nice."

I don't drink tea, so I asked Mavis if she had any coffee.

"No, dearee. Sorry. I never keep the stuff in the house. Bad for the nerves, you see. But I do have a bottle of brandy I keep around for medicinal purposes or for special occasions. I would say this is a special occasion."

Mavis ran into the kitchen to get the bottle of brandy and pour me half of a jelly glass full.

"Sorry about the jelly glass, darling, but my crystal stemware broke on the way over to the States."

"When did you come to the United States?" I asked. "And how long have you had the Elkton Love Nest?"

"Well, love, I guess you could say I was a war bride. I met my Jimmy in London in 1940, right before the war broke out. Jimmy was in London on some sort of banking business. I worked for the Bank of England and handled his company's account. He seemed like such a nice chap and good looking too. So when he asked me to have dinner with him that evening, I accepted. He waited for me in the lobby of the bank until I got off work. We walked to a pub that was close by, and right away we hit it off.

"We saw each other every night while he was in England. And like they say, 'all good things must come to an end.' He finished his business and went back to the States. Shortly after, we started writing to each other and became very good friends. I was very fond of him. Then one day, Jimmy wrote and said he was going to enlist in the United States Navy. I thought I would never see him again. You know how that is, long-distance romances and all. We kept up the correspondence and before you know it, we knew we had fallen in love. Then out of the blue, I get a letter from Jimmy, asking me to visit the colonies. He had a two-week holiday, and he wanted me to meet his mum. I told him that was too short a time to make preparations and that I was sorry, but I couldn't afford to go.

"A week later, he was knocking at the door of my flat. I nearly fell over. What a bloke! He picked me up in his arms, danced me around the room, and told me I was a sight for sore eyes. And then he asked me to marry him. The rest is history. We got married in a small chapel in London. We had a wonderful two-week honeymoon before he left for Hawaii. His mum called me and invited me to come to the States. She was a widower and said she would love the company, that we could wait together for Jimmy to come home. I did and surprisingly it wasn't difficult getting a visa, being that I was married to a Yank. His mum lived here in this house, and I've been here ever since."

Mavis's voice and facial expression had changed; reliving her story was obviously painful. I asked where her husband was now stationed and when she thought he would be coming home.

"No, love," she sadly replied, "he's not coming home. My poor Jimmy is dead. He was stationed in Pearl Harbor. His mum died shortly after from a broken heart. When she passed on, she left me the house. I needed some income and I love company, so I turned the house into a bed and breakfast, a love nest for newly married couples just like you. You should see this place in the summer. Not a room to be had. That's enough of me. You must be exhausted. Let me show you to your room."

We both got up and followed Mavis to our room.

The minute we hit the room, Annie pushed me on the bed and said, "Just watch and don't say a word."

There was no shyness, no fear or apprehension on her part. I was totally flabbergasted. This girl who held me at arm's length for years was doing a striptease. First, she took off her dress and danced around. Then she removed her slip and more dancing. I was shocked. Annie, with her strict Catholic upbringing, was not shy at all. She was dancing, bumping and grinding like she was Gypsy Rose Lee.

I laughed until I thought I would piss my pants. This was definitely worth waiting for! What a babe. It wasn't until she took off her bra and panties that I realized Annie was no longer a girl. She was a woman.

I motioned for her to join me in bed. I removed all my clothes. She curled up in my arms then put her lips to mine and gave me the most passionate kiss I've ever had. Our tongues met. Our breathing was heavy. I have never felt such love or happiness as I did at that moment. Her body was soft, her kisses moist. This was not the kid I fell in love with. We had come full circle.

We made love for the first time. I tried being gentle, but the passion was so overwhelming, I couldn't catch my breath.

Her breathing was also labored, and then she started to moan, "Oh, Tommy. Oh, Tommy."

Talk about seeing stars!

When it was over, I told her I was glad we got married not so much for me, but for her. I knew there would never have been a honeymoon for Annie without the wedding.

We fell asleep, hanging on to each other for dear life. I awoke in the middle of the night. The moon was full, and it lit up our room. I looked over at Annie. She was sound asleep, and she looked so beautiful. Her skin was moist, her face flushed, and her long black hair was tousled.

I whispered, "I love you. I love you, Annie Callahan."

She opened her eyes, looked up at me, and whispered, "Mrs. Callahan to you."

We kissed and then turned our bodies to spoon. I never wanted to let her go. We fell back to sleep.

I awoke around seven o'clock in the morning and realized that I never used the rubbers I'd brought with me for protection. *My God, what if she got pregnant?* How would she explain it to her folks? No, you can't get pregnant doing it just once. Isn't that what I always told Annie? We'll have to be careful from now on.

I finally fell back to sleep only to wake up startled. I felt something crawling on my chest and slowly going to my thigh. I opened my eyes. It was Annie (propped up in bed) watching me sleep. Her fingers started at my chest then slowly to my stomach, and then on to my Johnson. Obviously, the most sensitive parts of my body reacted.

"Annie!" I laughed. "I created a monster. Hey, promise me that while I'm away you'll stay away from all those pimple-faced kids in your class."

"Tommy, not to worry. I'm yours, body and soul."

I laughed. "Hey, wasn't there a movie like that?"

We fooled around and made love again. This time, I used a rubber. It wasn't as good, but it was better than nothing. Again, she got so excited, I could hardly stop her from yelling.

"Honey, please, Mavis will think I'm beating you."

At first, she laughed, and then she got very serious.

"Tommy, I'm scared."

"Of what, baby? Are you afraid your folks will find out?"

"No, I'm worried about you going into combat. I'm afraid that something will go wrong and you won't be coming home."

"Come on, Annie, you're scaring me. I'm coming home. Look, I'm not going to take any more chances than I have to. Don't worry, honey. I'm coming home."

"Then how come you can't tell me where you're going?"

"Because it's such a top secret, they didn't even tell me. Look, Annie, this day, at this time is the best day of my life, and I wish it would never end. I don't want to even think about going back."

It wasn't until we went to shower that I realized what a cool room we were in. It was a little too feminine for my taste, but I guess it fit the occasion. I figured it was called the bridal suite.

Annie squealed, "How beautiful! Tommy, look how pretty this room is. I want us to have a bedroom as beautiful as this when we get married. I mean, when we get a house."

"Sure, honey, anything you want."

I was starting to get scared. I was too happy. Everything I'd ever dreamed of was coming true. I had to be careful not to tempt fate.

When we came down the stairs, Mavis was smiling.

"Good morning, my darlings. How did you like your room?"

Annie gushed. "It was beautiful, Mavis. Was that the bridal suite?"

"No, my dear. They're all the bridal suites. But I gave you the best of the bunch.

"I thought I would make breakfast for you before you leave."

"Sounds great," I replied. "I'm really hungry."

Annie agreed. "Me too. That was some workout."

I couldn't believe she said that.

Mavis remarked, "What did you say, love?"

"Oh, I meant that we like to exercise before breakfast. I read that exercise is really good for you."

Mavis laughed. "Well, love, you can call it whatever you like."

We all burst out laughing.

Mavis gave us eggs, bacon, and these things she called scones with marmalade. It was good—different but good. She said she enjoyed having us stay with her. This was usually their off season for weddings and she sometimes got lonely.

Annie went over and hugged Mavis. She told her, "If it's all right with you, I'd like to call you from time to time."

"Oh, my dear, that would be ever so nice. You are such a charming young couple."

Mavis insisted on only taking twenty dollars for the room and the meals.

She said, "You should save your money for that grand wedding you'll be having when you return from the war."

We kissed her and thanked her.

When we got in the car, I asked Annie, "What do you say as soon as the war is over, we come back and stay in our old room?"

"Oh, Tommy, that would be so neat."

30

We were kind of quiet on our way home. Neither one of us wanted to separate and go back to our parents' homes. I dropped Annie off at the corner of her street and kissed my wife good-bye. I reminded her to take off her wedding band. She took it off, kissed it, looked at me with that silly little grin, and put it in her bra. Although the temptation to retrieve it was great, I forced myself to drive home.

As usual, my mother was in the kitchen.

I yelled, "I'm home!"

She yelled back. "Good. I'm making your favorite dinner: corned beef and cabbage."

Madone!

That night, I couldn't fall asleep. My mind reenacted our first night together over and over again. And then it hit me. Carmine and me—we're not only good friends, now we're related. He's my brother-in-law. We're family. I started to think about Carmine. I felt kind of bad for him. He confided in me that he got his draft notice soon after I left for Fort Dix. He didn't pass the physical, it seems. Carmine had diabetes and needed to take insulin shots on a daily basis. No wonder he looked so unhappy. I tried to cheer him up. I told him he was a lucky son of a bitch, but he didn't buy it. All of our friends were drafted, or they enlisted. He felt alone. Here he was, a guy stuck here with all the women.

The day finally came that my leave was over. It was time for me to go back to my base. Saying good-bye was the hardest thing I ever had to do. It was bad enough leaving my folks, but leaving my wife was even harder. We had so little time to be together. We saw each other, but not like a married couple. We had sex in the backseat of the car. It was just getting laid and not making love. There was no holding, no quiet conversation or spooning. At least, I made sure I was careful about not getting her pregnant.

When it was time for me to say good-bye, I felt like it was for the last time. I figured every soldier felt the risk and realized the odds. Deep down in the pit of my stomach, this seemed different. I knew I wasn't coming back. Stupid fears. I was a survivor, and I knew how to take care of myself. I told no one about my feelings. It's not very manly to be afraid, so I put on a very brave front. I was cocky at times, hiding behind my fears. This way, no one would need to worry about me.

I remembered that when I was just a kid, if I cried that someone beat me up or whined, my father would say, "Act like a man. Men don't cry."

I wasn't a man. I was a kid. I made up my mind that I would never say those words to my son. It made me feel weak; worse than that, I thought my old man thought I was weak, so I turned into a bully and kept everything inside. I pretended I was a big man. I now felt kind of bad for the kids I beat up and made fun of for no reason at all.

I never saw my dad cry, not even at Grandma's funeral. I thought he didn't care. But Mom said he did. He just has a hard time showing his emotions. I guess that's why he made a good cop; he never showed or acted like he gave a shit. But I wanted to be a cop too.

Everyone that was there to greet me came to say good-bye, except that this time Annie's mom came to support her daughter. Annie made no bones about being upset.

As the train started to move, I put my head out the window and yelled. "See you next year. Pray for me."

Why the hell did I say that? I sounded weak and scared. I hope my old man didn't think I was scared.

Chapter 5

Camp Edwards, MA: Just before leaving, I had received my orders. I was to meet my regiment for extensive training for a secret mission they called *HUSKY*. On April 28, 1943, the 525th Division would leave New York. Ten top jumpers would stay behind for more briefing. And then, five out of the ten would get to go on this mission. How they would be picked depended on their survival and jumping skills. They would then join the 505th on May 10th in Casablanca for their orders.

The five chosen jumpers would also go to New York, the point of embarkation for North Africa. That date had already been chosen. We would practice jumping the terrain near Koradji, Morocco. If we survived, five of us would jump, along with the other paratroopers for the 505th's mission. Except we would jump first at a designated area. The specifics wouldn't be given out until the last minute.

None of us had an idea what the mission was. Briefing would come when the five men were picked. I soon found out I was not only one of the men picked, to my surprise I was promoted to corporal and second in command. I was glad my buddy Jerry also made the cut. Lieutenant Harvey Bradshaw would lead the group.

OK, TC, that's enough daydreaming. You're aboard the 227-C-47 aircraft, and you will have to make the best of it. It had just dawned on me how quiet everyone was. Usually, we're yakking up a storm. You could have heard a pin drop. I felt like I was going to puke. It took every bit of guts I had to board this plane.

Us paratroopers that are on this special mission are to be dropped southwest of Palermo. There we were to meet with the head of the underground. We were to rendezvous with Mario Moretti at a secret meeting place. With the exception of the pilot, none of us knew where that would be. Our lieutenant would hand off the information after boarding the plane.

Mario and his band of Nazi- and Fascist-haters would show us where the German headquarters and their strongholds were. They also knew the terrain and the times the enemy were most vulnerable.

Mario said the Italian army would be easier to conquer. Their weapons were old and they lacked training. The band also knew where they had their headquarters and their weapons storage facility. Once we had this information, we would radio our commanding officer and tell him where to drop the rest of the paratroopers and station the ground troops. It was risky but worth it. We would then meet with the rest of the 505th and liberate the Italian people, whether they wanted it or not. We assumed they did. Mussolini was not a popular dictator.

Most important, knowing this information could save a lot of lives. Our mission was to defeat Italy and bring down Mussolini. That would open the Mediterranean Sea route. If we had waited much longer, the Germans would have beefed up their strength in that region. The way it was now, we outmanned the Germans stationed in Sicily.

All but five of the paratroopers would be dropped at Caltagirone. The infantry would invade the beaches at Gila. We (five paratroopers) would be dropped in Palermo on the outskirts of town. Once we radioed the information we gathered from Mario's partisans, we would meet our ground forces. We had forty-eight hours to complete our mission.

The five of us that parachuted out first were to get as close to southwest Palermo as possible. The five chosen were Harvey, Leon, Jerry, Ralph, and me.

The time finally came for us to jump. It was as dark as hell, and we didn't know if we would be landing on the ground or in a tree. The saving grace was that we were expected, so the underground guided us by flashlight. Once we were down and accounted for, they took our parachutes and buried them in the woods.

This band had six men and two women, eight in all. They put their hands over their mouths to show us not to speak until it was safe. The Germans patrolled the area with large spotlights. It wasn't until we reached this farmhouse that we actually saw who it was that was guiding us. It was still dim, just candlelight on an old wooden table, but at least we could see their faces.

Mario was the leader, all right. You could tell by his stance and the way he ordered everyone around. I thought this was probably how Bonaparte must have looked and acted. You know, small man, loudmouth mentality. He was much younger than I had expected. He looked to me like he was in his early twenties with short, black curly hair, bushy eyebrows, and a quick smile (that was actually a smirk). His eyes were so dark, they went right through me. At least he knew how to speak and understand English. All this time, I was worried about how we would communicate. In fact, he had a slight English accent. I assumed that was why he was picked for this particular assignment.

Only three of the eight could speak or understand, English, so there was a lot of interpreting. One of the women in the group was called Angelina. I thought the name suited her. She looked like an angel. She must have been about eighteen. She had blonde hair that she tied in a bun on the top of her head, and she was tall for a woman, maybe five feet eight inches. She was slim and in the candlelight, her skin looked like the color of milk. *Holy shit. TC, calm down, you're married and you're here on a mission. Jesus, forgive me for my thoughts.*

I was glad that Harvey was in command. He's a good man, smart and not a glory boy. I'm so not about that. Never mind the medals. His motto was, "Let's get this war over with and go the hell home." That was to my way of thinking.

As we sat around the table looking at the maps, one of the other women, named Mary, brought out some wine, cheese, and bread, apologizing that there wasn't more. It seemed that when the Germans marched in, they cleaned out the town and took most of the food. If it weren't for some of the farmers in the area who were helping the underground, they would have no food at all.

We told them not to worry about us. We brought rations and we would be glad to share with them. They became indignant. No, we were their guests. Shit, this was no time for protocol. I must say they really had a handle on this mission. They knew where and when to strike.

Mario said, "You should rest now. At dawn, we go to the Cathedral Monreale by foot. There, we will meet up with ten more of my men and women. They will help you by mapping out where the Germans hide their trucks, tanks, ammo, and ships."

I reminded him that our mission was to cut all lines of communication.

Mario was quick to answer. "I know that, soldier. The others will show you where the lines are and where the Italian military is."

They all laughed when he said "Italian military."

Lieutenant Bradshaw asked, "What's so funny? Let us in on your little joke."

The only ones who knew what Harvey asked were Mario and Angelina.

Angelina laughed as she explained in broken English, "Mario made a joke when he said Italian Army. All they have is light tanks, motorcycles, horses, bicycles, and mules. If it weren't for the Germans, they would have nothing to fight with."

We were all laughing now. But inside, I knew it was still a dangerous mission and it wasn't going to be a piece of cake. I was getting real tired. I assumed the rest of the guys were too. We had been up for eighteen hours, and the wine didn't help.

Mario led us to cots and showed us where the outhouse was, with its pile of newspaper in case we needed it. And then he said, *"Ciao."*

We all felt very uneasy about this band of partisans. Maybe it was because of the language barrier? But what it came down to was that we didn't trust them. Maybe war makes you paranoid?

I got up early the next morning. When I went to the can, I all but threw up. What a filthy rat hole. I decided to go into the wooded area surrounding the farmhouse. I had just taken a piss when I heard someone coming toward me. It was kind of hazy and not quite light out.

I drew my gun and said, "Hold it. I've got a gun."

I heard a voice say, "Cowboy, American cowboy, don't you know when you hear the bushes rustle you're supposed to hide and surprise the enemy. You're going to get yourself killed if you stand there shouting. 'I've got a gun!' You would have made a good target. You would have been killed."

She was right. I was trained to think like a soldier, but I acted like a green-horn kid. Angelina came toward me, smiling.

I said, "Hi. What are you doing out here this early?"

"It is not early, Yank. You forget; I'm part of this group. There is no time to sleep. We have too much to do. I, too, cannot stand the smell of that filthy outhouse. And like you, I went into the woods. But unlike you, I do not stink because I took a bath in the brook that's a few kilometers from here."

"Are you always this miserable in the morning? Or is it that you just don't like Americans?"

"I love Americans. I just don't like arrogant men."

I couldn't help but laugh, and when I did, she did.

She was beautiful. I noticed in the light what I hadn't noticed at night. Her eyes were green. *I'll be damned, a blonde and green-eyed Italian.* She must have read my mind by the way I was giving her the once-over.

"Northern Italy," she said. "My parents are from northern Italy. Blonde hair and light eyes are not so uncommon."

"How did you learn to speak English?"

"We learned from Mario. Mario went to school in England."

She looked about fifteen, but she told me she was nineteen. She also told me that a few months ago her best friend, Rosemarie, was raped and killed by "fascist Italian pigs" and that she'll do whatever it takes to avenge her death.

I reminded her that there was a chance that could also be her fate.

"Why don't you go home and wait to be liberated? That's why we're here."

That really pissed her off.

"Why don't you go back to where you came from, Yank? This is my country, and I want to be part of saving it."

"Wait a minute. Boy, you've got some temper. You remind me of my wife, Annie. She also has a hot Italian temper."

She responded, "At least you made a good choice in picking a wife. If you are married, why aren't you home with her?"

"I guess you haven't heard about the draft." I quickly changed the subject. "Hey, Angelina, where is that brook you were talking about? You're right; I do stink."

She started down a path and I followed.

"Come, I will show you. But be careful, there might be snipers. So far, we have been safe here, but you never know."

I swear it was like a picture postcard, the babbling brook and morning mist. The hillside was becoming ablaze with the morning sunrise. I started taking off my gear and my clothes. Her eyes never left my body.

"Hey, Angelina, turn your head. You wouldn't want me staring at you, would you?"

She laughed. "You have nothing I haven't seen before."

"Oh yeah? Tell me more."

She giggled.

"No. What I mean is, I have a husband and a brother. My husband is much bigger than you."

With that remark, I lost my footing and slipped on one of the slippery stones.

"That's a low blow, lady. And I'm going to get you for that remark."

The water felt good and clean. For a minute, I felt like a kid again.

Angelina never stopped looking at me and kept on laughing as I made a complete fool of myself. I poured water on my head, pretending I was swimming in three feet of water.

I got dressed, ran up to her, and said, "Now, you're going to get it."

She made a mad dash for the woods, but I tackled her to the ground. We were laughing and out of breath when, all of a sudden, we were kissing. Strangers with different lives thrust into a war neither one of us wanted. Knowing today could be our last day on Earth, the passion was overwhelming and we couldn't stop if we wanted to. We were tearing off each other's clothes like animals. When it was over, I started to shake.

"Oh my God, Annie. Annie, forgive me."

Angelina put her arms around me and whispered, "It's OK, cowboy. It's OK. God will forgive us this sin and our few minutes of pleasure."

We got dressed, brushed the leaves from our clothes, and went back to the house in silence, like nothing ever happened. When we walked in, the lieutenant asked me, "Where the hell were you? I thought you were my first casualty. Don't you ever leave without telling us where you're going! You could have gotten us all killed. We have a mission we have to work on. Where the hell were you?" He stared at me and then at Angelina. "Have you gone mad?" he asked.

Leon and Jerry cut in. "Come on, Lieutenant, He's here, he's OK, and nothing happened. Let's get back to what we came here to do."

Lieutenant Bradshaw reluctantly agreed and walked away.

I told the other guys, "Harvey was right. I should have said something. But everyone was sleeping, and I knew this was going to be a long day, so I said nothing. I was wrong. I'm sorry."

Lieutenant Bradshaw turned to look at me when he heard me talking to the guys and reprimanded us all.

"Let me make this perfectly clear. Nobody takes a shit without telling me. Understood?"

We all spoke in unison. "Understood, Lieutenant."

Mario broke the silence. "Let's go. Let's get out of here. We have a long walk to the church."

Lieutenant Bradshaw asked Mario, "How long will it take? How many miles is it to the church?"

"I don't know miles. It's about twenty-four kilometers." He asked, "Do you know, Angelina?"

Angelina spoke for the first time since we got back. "I think it's about fifteen miles."

Mario handed us some clothes.

"Here, take off your uniforms and put these clothes on. We're going to town. You can't go to town in your American uniforms. I have some clothes here for all of you. Leave your uniforms here. You can pick them up when you rejoin your troops."

At the time, it seemed to make sense. We took off our uniforms, put on the clothes, rolled up our gear and our weapons, and started walking. I started thinking about the five of us being out here all by ourselves. We couldn't risk radio contact and no one from the 505th knew where we were. I was starting to feel spooked. What did we really *know* about these people?

I asked Mario, "What's the name of that church again?"

"The Cathedral of Monreale. 'Our Lady.' King William II, son of William the Conqueror, built the cathedral and dedicated it to 'Our Lady' in the year 1172."

"Holy shit, that's old," Jerry said.

I said, "You know, Jerry, you really have a way with words. Have some respect."

Mario decided to join in. "That's the trouble with all you Americans. You have no respect for anyone."

Mario's remark pissed off the lieutenant. "Hey, wait just a minute, Mario. We're here risking our ass to save yours. You have some respect."

Mario apologized. "You are right, of course. Forgive me."

He then went back to telling us about the history of the Cathedral of Monreale.

"Monreale is a small city in the province of Palermo. Palermo is old and, like any old town, the buildings and roads have shown some wear and tear. It's still beautiful. You will see."

After ten miles, we had to rest and take a drink. It was getting hot. Although we were tracking through the woods, we had to keep our voices down and our eyes and ears opened.

Mario was the one who kept us going.

"Come on, come on, we have to meet with the rest of the group. Five minutes, only five minutes to rest."

I'll give them that. They knew the area inside and out. We never saw a Kraut or any Italian soldiers. We seemed to be the only ones in the forest. We were one tired ragbag of an army.

Leon asked Mario, "How much longer before we get there?"

"Not long," he replied. "Maybe another couple of hours."

Finally, we came to Palermo. But what we saw made us realize that without the guidance of Mario and his men, we could have easily wandered into a trap. We saw a lot of German and Italian soldiers, patrolling the area.

Mario was cautious. "We will wait for darkness and then make a run for the church. There, we will be safe."

He was right. There was a lot of activity going on in town. It made good sense to be careful and wait it out.

As far as I could see from this distance, I understood what Mario was talking about. The town was old world. In fact, it looked pretty much like a picture postcard. I started thinking of Annie. I bet she would like it here. Maybe we should go to Sicily on our honeymoon. I can't wait to tell the folks back home. Too bad I can't get any postcards.

Angelina and I didn't look at each other all day. We both felt guilty. At least I know I did. Most of all, we were working now. There was no time to let our guard down.

It finally started to get dark. The streets were emptying out, and everyone was going home or to the bars. I guessed they were mostly going home for dinner. In groups of two, we made mad dashes to the steps of the church and then to a door on the side of the church but only when the area was clear. Every once in a while, we would see a truckload of Italian soldiers go by. Other than that, the streets were empty. I thought that was strange, not seeing a person walking or wandering around. But then, this was war. I imagined there was a curfew.

Even Lieutenant Bradshaw questioned the silence. "Where the hell did everyone go?"

Ralph put in his two cents. "Probably home to have dinner to be with their families. This is war, man. Anyone who has a brain should stay indoors."

Finally, we were all inside the church, and we were all out of breath. The stairs leading to the church left us open and vulnerable. At least now we were in a place that looked like an old cellar. It was damp and musty and smelled of mold. There were cobwebs all over the place. The good thing was there was a wine rack filled with wine.

Mario opened the first bottle.

"Come on, everyone, drink up. Our food will be here soon."

Food, I hadn't thought about food all day. I was really hungry. Just then we heard a door open from the top of the stairs. We all cocked our guns. It was a priest. He was introduced to us as Father Michael Ferrenti. I got up off the barrel I was sitting on.

He said, "No, no, please sit."

He was a man who looked to be in his mid-sixties. He had gray hair and stood about five foot nine. Somewhat portly around the middle, he had the kindest, smoothest face I have ever seen on a man of his age. His English wasn't great, but he spoke and understood some. What he didn't understand, Mario interpreted. He asked us to rest.

"I will have my housekeeper, Louisa, bring you some food. You must be hungry. We have pasta, wine, bread, and cheese. Enjoy."

I called out to Father Ferrenti, "Father, would you have time for my confession before Mario's men get here?"

"Yes, my son. I will be glad to hear your confession."

I could see and feel Angelina's eyes burning a hole in me.

I shook my head. She understood and smiled. I knew I would have to leave that chapter out. She had to live here. The priest knew her and her husband. I couldn't do that to her. I was just a passerby.

Soon after, Louisa came in from the same side door we'd arrived in, carrying a big bowl of pasta. It smelled like heaven. She smiled and announced in Italian, "I will be back."

Angelina and Mary offered to help.

Louisa told them, "No. It could be dangerous. The soldiers are used to me coming and going. I don't want to raise any suspicion."

"Why?" asked Angelina. "It's natural for women to be carrying food into the church."

They went with Louisa anyway and came back with what looked like a feast. We ate like it was our last meal. I was stuffed. Between the food and the wine, I was actually feeling good. I think we all were.

The lieutenant asked Mario. "What time do you expect your men to be here? We only have forty-eight hours to complete this mission and we've already used up twenty-four."

Mario looked at his watch. "Let's see, it's six forty-five. They should be here at seven thirty sharp. You can be sure of that."

Again, Lieutenant Bradshaw asked, "I assume they will meet us down here?"

Father Ferrenti interrupted, "No, no, we will meet them in the rectory. I locked the doors to the cathedral. Don't worry, you'll be safe."

We started to let our guard down. We all started talking but still making sure that we kept our voices low. Actually, it was Angelina who started the conversation. She started by asking us questions about the United States. She wanted to know about the Statue of Liberty, what New York City was like, and did we ever go to the Grand Canyon? We all put in our two cents when answering her questions. It felt good talking about home until we heard a noise coming from above us inside the cathedral.

Mario told us to keep quiet and to stay where we were.

"I think it's my men getting here a little early. Let me go up and make sure."

Father Ferrenti whispered, "I bolted the door. How did they get in?"

We became very silent.

Mario went slowly up the stairs, barely opening the door before he shouted, "It's OK to come up now. It's just one of my men."

We all went up the stairs quietly. When we opened the door, there was Mario and another man pointing their guns at us.

Lieutenant Bradshaw asked, "What the hell is this? What the fuck is going on here?"

The five of us went for our weapons.

Mario shouted, "I wouldn't do that if I were you. Everyone, drop your weapons."

His fellow partisans stared in disbelief. He repeated, "All of you."

Angelina and the others yelled at him in Italian. He just smirked.

"OK, so now what?" I asked. "We're prisoners of war?"

Mario's eyes met mine. "No, Yank. We take no prisoners."

Father Ferrenti, the last one up the stairs, walked in front of us as if to protect us.

"What is the meaning of this? Have you gone crazy?" he asked in broken English and Italian. Mario turned his gun on him.

Father Ferrenti got very angry. "Get out of my church, you devil. This is a sanctuary. You cannot kill anyone in a church. It is a mortal sin."

Mario and the other man looked at him and laughed. Then Mario said in a voice that sounded like the devil himself, "Get out of my way, Father, or you will be the first to go."

Man, that priest sure had guts. He turned his back on Mario and walked to the altar, lit the candles, and started praying.

Mario became flustered and started shouting, "Everyone move closer to the front of the church. Move. Hurry up!"

I walked to the where the priest was. In broken English, he said, "May God have mercy on your soul."

Mario and the man he called Antonio opened fire on all of us Americans first. I remember falling to the ground. Father Ferrenti tried to break my fall but couldn't. I knew I'd been shot, but I felt nothing—no pain, no fear, nothing. I looked up at the ceiling and saw Jesus looking down at me. He looked sad and in pain, and I could have sworn I saw tears in his eyes. I figured I must be dead. Then I remembered I was in the church and had fallen to the floor right beneath this large crucifix. I couldn't move. I could only see and hear.

I then saw Mario standing in front of Angelina.

She was screaming at him, "You traitor! You Nazi lover! You are as evil as Hitler. Did you get your three pieces of silver? Traitor, I spit on you. God will make you pay."

I heard two shots and saw Angelina fall to the floor. And then there was silence.

What's that smell? What the hell is that smell? My God it smells like corned beef and cabbage.

And then I saw her, my mother. She was setting the table. She looked straight at me and dropped the glass that was in her hand.

"Oh my God, Mom. Help me. I'm dying."

Vengeance Is Mine

The German and Italian forces surrendered in May 1943. Dictator Benito Mussolini attempted to escape by hiding in a German convoy truck on its way to the Alps. The partisans found and imprisoned him. They executed him and fifteen leading Fascists on April 29, 1945.

Those who aided Mussolini's regime were considered traitors. They were shunned and some were killed by their own people.

Most Sicilians saw us for what we were, liberators saving them from German occupation and a tyrannical dictator. Although, the HUSKY campaign was successful, many lives were lost.

PART 2

June 12, 2006

Chapter 6

Hotel Marlowe—Cambridge, MA

Startled and with my heart pounding, I awoke from a nightmare that has plagued me since childhood. To my mind as a child and now as an adult, it made no sense to me at all.

I'm running through the woods. I'm with a man, a soldier, but I can't see his face. We're running as fast as we can toward a church. I don't know where the hell it is. The church looks old. The church doors are closed, so we start pounding on these huge bronze doors, "Open the door! Let us in! Open the door!"

One door opens and a priest says, "Come in and close the door." We rush in and close the door behind us. And then the man pulls out a gun and raises it as if to shoot the priest, but he doesn't. The gun looks like an old Colt pistol. The priest ignores us and goes over to the pulpit to light some candles. He never looks back at us.

He asks, "Why are you here?"

The man says, "Revenge."

With that, a crucifix that's on the wall adjacent to the pulpit crashes to the floor, starting a chain reaction. The whole building starts to shake as though in an earthquake.

And I can't get out. The door is locked.

That's when I awake, shaking and sweating.

My mother always thought that I was re-creating a movie that I must have seen as a kid. I had seen some old war movies, but they had movie stars in them. If I re-created a movie, wouldn't the same actors be in the dream? Besides, I don't ever remember seeing a movie like that. But then how else would I know what a Colt pistol looked like? I don't know, but I'm not going to let it upset me on this day.

Today is my last day in Boston, and it is also one of the top ten days of my life. Today is a nine because today is graduation day. I'm graduating from Harvard University with a law degree in hand and a job waiting for me in Manhattan. The folks are so proud. I'm the first attorney in the family. Hell, I'm proud of me. It was tough going for a while, but I finally did it. Now all I need is to pass the bar. I'll worry about that when the time comes.

I sat up in bed, beating my chest like Tarzan. I'm the man. Yeah, I'm the man. Today is my day. I have to get my mind off that dream. If anything, it seems to be occurring more often now than when I was a kid. You would think I'd be used to it by now. One of these days, I'm going to see a shrink, but not until I have insurance and I'm collecting a paycheck. My education has put me in the hole for a hundred thousand dollars, but it would have been a lot more if my father hadn't helped me out.

My dad has worked hard his whole life. I'm sure he makes a decent living. I've never heard him complain about money matters, and he's very secretive about how much he's really worth. All I know is that he's been generous to all of his three children. He never claimed that the money he gave me was a gift, so as soon as I'm able, I'll pay him back every dime I owe him.

Graduating from one of the oldest and most prestigious law schools in the country has already landed me a job with the law firm of Mark Moran, Mark Moran Junior, and Associates. It's not the largest firm in New York, but they bill in the millions. Mark Moran, Sr., started the law firm many years ago and is semiretired. I heard he was a shrewd and calculating attorney who rarely ever lost a case. Mr. Moran's sons are now taking over and they have decided to expand. It seemed a good place to get the experience I'll need while starting my climb up that great ladder of success. As Jackie Gleason would say, "How sweet it is." And as much as I'm looking forward to graduation, I'm also looking forward to going back to New Jersey and getting on with my life.

My parents have planned a graduation reception for me at the Marlboro Inn, a local high-end bed and breakfast mansion in New Jersey. History states that The Marlboro was built in 1840 for a Mr. Samuel Holmes. It was then remodeled and the name changed to the Marlboro Inn Bed & Breakfast. The architecture is English Tudor, and it sits on three acres of prime real estate. Upper Montclair is known for its old, beautiful mansions, most of them dating back to the thirties and forties. Many years ago, Upper Montclair was the suburb for the wealthy.

I had been to the Marlboro on several occasions. Uncle Frank had his daughter Robin's bat mitzvah reception at the Marlboro, so I guess my parents thought it was only fitting for me to have my graduation party there. I don't know why they would want to go to all that expense. This place doesn't come cheap.

A house party would have done just as well, but my parents were adamant. Mom said that they were happy and proud of me, and they wanted to share their moment in style with all the people who had endured their constant bragging about their son, the lawyer.

Dad noted, "Especially your Uncle Frank."

Mom looked away. She always looks the other way when anyone mentions Uncle Frank. He's my father's brother and his only sibling. It's so bizarre, you mention Uncle Frank's name to my mother, and the conversation is over. My mother would like to disavow Frank Scarpelli. According to my mother, Uncle Frank has somewhat of a shady past. Rumor has it that he is, or was, in the Mafia. He denies it. Rumor also has it that he helped my dad out by loaning him the money to start his own auto repair shop. Dad started with one shop and now has five Scarpelli's Auto Service Centers. Dad reminded her that he paid back every dime he ever borrowed from Frank. But the loan caused a big argument between my parents. My mother said she didn't want a cent of "Mafia money."

My dad stuck up for his brother and told her in no uncertain terms is she ever to interfere with anything that goes on between him and his brother. And he was *not* in the Mafia.

She cried, "He's a gangster and a bad influence on the children."

My father put his foot down, got mad, and started shouting at her, "Stop it! Stop it, and watch what you say in front of the kids. Frank is a legitimate businessman. You got that? And I will never have this conversation again, Terry. Do you understand me? Never again."

Most of the time, Dad is usually a very kind and easygoing guy, but he also has an excitable nature, so he yells. When he does, we know he's really upset, so we stay cool. We don't want his wrath coming down on us. He doesn't ask for much, and he gives a lot. He's a good man.

Al, my brother, is four years older than me and he's a lot like my dad. They resemble each other physically and have the same temperament. But me, I'm not very emotional and I'm pretty easy going. It takes a lot to get me mad. When I do get mad, I don't get excited. I get nasty and arrogant.

Mom no longer argues with Dad about his brother. She knows how close the family is and to argue would be futile. If it were up to her, she would like never to see Uncle Frank again. But the bond between the two brothers is unbreakable. The truth is none of us knows what my uncle does, including his own daughter.

When confronted, his wife, Dorothy, would say, "It's rumors, just rumors. Would a Mafia guy marry a Jew? Some people are just jealous of us, so they pass on rumors."

Anyhow, that's the story she tells her family and her daughter, who is being raised in the Jewish faith—except on Christmas, Good Friday, and Easter.

Uncle Frank was happy and proud when my dad named me after him. My mother was furious, but Dad held his ground. Even if Uncle Frank had had a son, he would not have had a namesake. In the Jewish religion, you name your children after only deceased family members.

Uncle Frank (his real name is Francis) is older than my dad, so when their mother died of pneumonia, it was my uncle who took care of him. Their father, my grandfather (we all call him Pop), worked day and night, mostly for money and partly because he couldn't stand the loneliness. He never remarried.

Although my uncle is only four years older than my father, Dad told us that it was he who made sure he got up every morning for school and that his clothes were clean and that he had money for lunch. Thanks to his brother, Dad graduated from high school.

But Frank dropped out at sixteen and worked the pool halls, hustling for money. Even as a kid, he spent some and saved some. He had a bank account when he was just sixteen years old and soon learned there was more money in lending than hustling. So he started a loan shark business. That's where he made his big money. It's now a legitimate business. They now call him a venture capitalist, and lately he has been making a killing in real estate.

In the beginning, it was on a small scale. After all, he was still a kid. Uncle Frank is a genius when it comes to finance. He's been taking care of my dad's books since he set him up in business.

He always told my dad, "Never buy what you can't afford. The interest rates will kill you."

When Dad's business started growing, his brother would tell him when and where to buy the buildings for his next auto service.

"If the business goes bust, you lose everything. But if you own the building and the land, you still have an investment."

I always thought that, given the advantages that I had, my uncle would not only have gone to college, he would have graduated with high honors.

As Aunt Dorothy would say, "Go figure, a high school dropout is a mathematical genius."

She's right. My uncle can figure in his head what most people need a calculator for.

I think Uncle Frank favors me a little more than my brother, Al, and my sister, Julia. He treats them great. And me, he's always busting my chops. I'm somewhat like him. I don't need coddling. I can take it because I can give it. I never start fights, but I also never walk away from one either.

Many a time, I came home beaten to a pulp, but I never cried. I figured it was as much my fault for not running away as it was theirs for starting the fight. Actually, I was more afraid of my mother's reaction than I was the kid who was beating me up.

It was my uncle who encouraged me to go to law school. I was just a kid when I knew I wanted to be an attorney. I loved watching trials on television. I found them fascinating. I even watched the old *Perry Mason* reruns. I told my uncle I wanted to be a lawyer when I grew up.

He encouraged me. "Go for it, kid. Go after your dream. Besides, we need an attorney in the family."

I knew that in order to succeed, I would have to keep up my grade point average, so I missed a lot of hanging out with the guys and other after-school activities. When I got a little older, it meant missing out on dates—except when I went to high school. That's when I met Jessie.

Jessica Smith was a cute blonde with classic features and blue eyes. She was taller than most girls. At five nine, she was a popular cheerleader. She looked snooty, but she was really down to earth. Jessie was my steady girlfriend all through Montclair High School. She was full of life and fun to be with. And she liked sex. I guess you could call her my childhood sweetheart.

Right before graduation, I received my acceptance to Harvard. I ran over to Jessie's house to tell her the good news. She didn't think it was good news. I guess she never said anything before because she never thought I'd be accepted. She calmly stated that she was breaking up with me because she did not want to wait six years for me to finish my education.

She had her own agenda. She was going to Montclair State to become a physical education teacher. And after graduation, she would teach at the local grammar school. She also informed me that right after graduation, she intended to get married and have two children, a boy and a girl. She wouldn't and couldn't wait for me to graduate.

Besides, she argued, "You're going to a prestigious school, and you will probably meet your own kind and dump me anyway."

"'My own kind,'?" I said. "My kind is here in Montclair. Yes, I'm going to a good school. I worked hard to get there, and I know it's going to be tough."

"My point exactly, Frank. You should stay in New Jersey and go to one of the local colleges around here. This way, we won't be so far away from each other."

"Are you crazy? I should give up going to Harvard because you're a spoiled brat who's used to getting her own way? I'm so glad you have your life so neatly wrapped up with school, marriage, and babies. But the truth is, right now all I care about is getting my law degree. I don't know what or where I'll be six years from now."

I walked out of her house with my acceptance letter in hand. I can't say I blame her. I cared about Jessie, but nothing was going to deter me from getting my law degree, not even her.

Of course, my mother was heartbroken. She liked Jessie and the idea of my going to a college in New Jersey. Another thing about Italian mothers, they want you married and having babies as soon as possible. They live for grandchildren.

Although I still haven't met "the love of my life," I know now that Jessie and me breaking up was a good thing. I wouldn't have had the time needed for a relationship. I always knew that when I was ready, it would happen. After all, I'm not that hard to look at. I'm six one with black hair, light hazel eyes, and a muscular build. And although I'm Italian, our family has been blessed with small, straight Roman noses.

My father's mother and father are from Naples and my mother's family is from Rome. In fact, my mother's parents live in Rome. At one time, they immigrated to the United States and lived in Verona, New Jersey—the next town over—for twenty-five years before they decided to go back to Italy. By then my mother had met my dad. They married and the rest is history. Mom goes to visit them every three to four years. It was my mother's side, the Santoses, that gave us these small noses. Thank you, God and the Santos family.

When you think of it, I had a charmed life. My only real struggle has been dealing with my nighttime terrors. As they say, "no one goes through life unscathed." I just wish I knew why and how this happened to me. It might be easier to handle. It's a strange thing. Sometimes I'll go for six months and not have the dream. Then, all of a sudden, it will return as if it's reminding me it's not over yet.

When I was a kid, the dreams were not as intense as they are now. It seems the older I get, the longer the dream. It's like watching the same play over and over again, and then one time it's a little different. Subtle differences surface: another actor is added, more dialogue, the scenery is somewhat changed. They're small changes but changes nevertheless.

As soon as I'm settled into my job and find an apartment in New York, I'll start looking for a good psychiatrist. Hopefully, the dreams won't be as difficult to get rid of as I think they will be.

My parents wanted to take me to a psychologist when I was nine. But I was afraid it would get out and the kids in my school would find out and call me crazy. You know how kids are. Not to mention their parents. How would they feel about me playing with their kid, or letting their daughter date someone who is seeing a shrink? So I lied and told my parents it stopped, that I just grew out of it.

My mother is not happy about me moving into my own apartment. She actually wants me to live at home, save my money, and commute. She claims none of the children in the family moved out until they got married.

I reminded her that they all got married before they were twenty-four.

I told her, "It will be better for me if I have my own place. It's more convenient."

I tried to explain that a lot of evenings would be spent in reading briefs and studying to pass the bar. And besides, if I work downtown, I should live downtown and not have to commute. Finally, I can now afford my own place.

The truth is, it's time I start living the life that a young twenty-four-year-old should be living. With my heavy schedule at college, my social life was kept to a minimum. I've been waiting for the day I'd have my own place. It's about time I make up for lost time. After all, in a couple of months, I'll be twenty-five, and I haven't been in a relationship for a long time.

I dated some. There were a lot of smart, great-looking women to choose from, but you can't hang out at the bars, have a relationship, and keep up your grades. I found that out after seeing other guys burning the candle at both ends. They wound up flunking out. I'm a very patient person.

After haggling with my mother over my move, my father finally put in his two cents.

"Terry, enough already. It's enough. Leave him alone. He's a grown man. Leave him be. I want this to be the end of this conversation."

Thank you, Dad.

Chapter 7

Graduation went off without a hitch, except for a minor embarrassment brought on by my grandfather. I was chosen valedictorian and was asked to deliver the farewell address at the commencement ceremony.

As I walked up to the podium, Pop stood up and began clapping and shouting, "That's my grandson! That's my grandson!"

Everyone in the audience laughed. The man is eighty-three. I suppose at eighty-three you can do any damn thing you want. Dad tried to calm him down, but Pop kept right on yelling in his Italian/New Jersey accent.

I really didn't care what anyone thought. I was happy that he was well enough to attend my graduation. Six months ago, he'd had a heart attack and we nearly lost him.

Also attending were my parents; my brother, Al, and his wife, Barbara; my sister, Julia, and her daughter, Katie; and Uncle Frank, Aunt Dorothy, and their daughter, Robin. They were proud of me; I was the first college graduate in the family. And I was proud of them; they all looked great. One thing about the Scarpellis, they know how to dress for an occasion.

Uncle Frank wore a very expensive, brown, tailored suit with a light yellow dress shirt. His tie was brown with gold diagonal stripes, and his shoes were brown Italian leather. He's five ten and in pretty good shape for a man of fifty-two. I imagine an older woman would think he was good looking with his normally dark hair graying on the sides, just enough gray to make him look distinguished. To the world, he looked like the CEO of a large corporation. And if my mother was right in her assumption, he *was* the CEO of a very big corporation.

Aunt Dorothy, Frank's wife, was something else. She has long, reddish brown, curly hair, and in high heels she was about the same height as Uncle Frank. She looked very young for forty. My mother said she's had cosmetic surgery. If she did, you'd never know it. I'm sure she had on more expensive diamonds than any other women there. A little tacky, you might say, but this woman was the salt of the earth and no one could be nicer.

The most remarkable thing about this couple was their relationship. Every time she looked at Uncle Frank, her eyes would shine. She truly loved and worshipped this man. And he felt the same about her. I hope when I find my significant other, we can maintain that same kind of loving connection.

Now take my sister, Julia. She is twenty-seven and came without her husband, William McCray. Everyone calls him Willie for short. Willie is what Italians call a *gavone.* He's a real jerk; he's a drinker and a womanizer. No one knows why Julia loves this idiot.

My dad gave him a job just so he could keep an eye on him. Willie was a wild, good-looking teenager. Standing slim and tall with blond hair and blue eyes, he had the kind of looks any young teenager would go crazy for. My parents went crazy when she brought him home. Julia was the only one of us who didn't go to public school. She went to parochial schools. My parents had big plans for Julia; they wanted her to become a nun. But Julia had her own plans and came home pregnant when she was a junior in high school. I thought my father would kill the bastard. Instead, he told Julia she would have to marry him.

She said, "Great, that's why I got pregnant!"

And so they were married in the chapel at St. Josephs. She was seventeen and her daughter, Katie, was born six months later—premature, of course. Now Mom is happy she didn't become a nun. She now has a grandchild.

Although my brother, Al, has been married for two years, he and Barbara still don't have any kids. So Katie is the only Scarpelli grandchild. Katie is a great kid, and in spite of her stupid father, we're all happy she's here.

Shortly after the graduation ceremony, there was the usual picture taking and congratulatory hand shaking. I was quite surprised when Robert Matthews, the dean, came over to my family and shook everyone's hand.

He then held Pop's hand just a little longer and remarked, "It's OK to be proud, Mr. Scarpelli. You should be. Your grandson is not only smart, but he's also a fine young man. Frank will make an excellent attorney."

I was quite taken aback at his statement. I didn't know he knew that much about me. I don't think we had more than a few words in all the time I'd been at the university.

Although I was happy, I was anxious to get on with the next phase of my life. I started going over my mental list: graduation is over, next my graduation party, and tomorrow, my trip to New York to look for an apartment.

In about six weeks, I start my job, a real job. Luckily, I didn't have to start my job until August first. Mark Moran, Jr., the senior vice president, told me I would need time to get situated. Besides, business was a little slower in the summer months, so it was a good time to start. I thought, *My life is finally on track and I'm a happy man.*

When graduation was over, I was to drive home with Mom and Dad. But first, we were all going to meet for a late lunch. Uncle Frank made our reservations at Anthony's Shack, a popular seafood restaurant. In fact it's one of Boston's landmarks.

I don't know how he managed to get us a reservation on such short notice. I heard this place is booked several months in advance, especially this time of the year.

Uncle Frank was also picking up the tab. He insisted on always going first class. The waiter stayed by us like glue. I guess he knew a mark when he saw one. We ate, drank, and Uncle Frank made the toast. I noticed that during his toast, there were tears in his eyes. When it came to family, he could get very emotional, but I know for a fact he's a shark when it came to business.

After lunch, we all kissed each other good-bye and went to our own cars for the long drive back to New Jersey.

I was in the backseat and decided to rest my eyes. It had been a hell of a day.

I couldn't have been asleep for more than a few minutes when I saw myself running through the woods. At my side was the soldier. I turned to look at him, and this time I saw his face. He looked at me and smiled. We were running so fast, I was getting out of breath. I started breathing hard. He was also running, but he kept looking at me. Although he had on a helmet, I could still see his face. He had freckles all over his face and blue eyes. I was so startled, I woke up; I wasn't frightened—just surprised. This was the first time I saw his face. He had always been a shadow.

My mother asked, "What's the matter with you, Frankie? Your breathing is so heavy. Are you all right?"

"Yeah, Mom, I'm fine. I'm just tired."

"Did you have one of those dreams again?"

"No, Ma, I'm tired and excited. There is nothing for you to worry about."

"Look, you," my mother remarked in a joking tone. "Just because you're a lawyer, don't tell me what to do. It's my job to worry. It's all I've got."

Dad and I laughed, but it was true. She drove us all nuts.

On the trip home, I finally had the time to evaluate my life and my good fortune to be in such a good family. I guess I had had too much wine; I was actually getting emotional and allowing myself to feel something. For so much of my life, like any kid, I took things for granted. And like any kid, I didn't appreciate anything. Everything was about my fun, my friends, my career, and me.

A new phase was about to begin, and I wanted to start by being a little grateful and, yeah, maybe a little humble. Of course, if I were really humble, I would have opted for the prosecutor's office (it was offered to me, but I turned it down) instead of an established, accredited firm. But I truly believed I could be of some good. I'd just get paid more for my services.

I wonder why Uncle Frank never offered to throw me some of his business. He probably thought it would be small potatoes for me and the fees would be too high. If the truth were known, I would work pro bono for him. But then I thought it was best not to mix business and family. What if I screwed up?

After we drove in silence for several miles, my mother asked, "Why so quiet, Frankie?"

"I don't know, Mom. I'm just thinking. I was thinking about Pop. How great he is and that I was so glad he was well enough to make the trip."

"Well," she said, "if you ask me, he was rude. Why did he have to be so loud? He should have kept his mouth shut and showed a little more dignity."

My father did not like that remark. "Like you should, Terry," he said, his voice quiet but deliberate. "You should keep your mouth closed. That man raised two kids on his own, so show him some respect. He's an old man now and he's my old man."

"I know, I know. I'm sorry, Al. I know how sensitive you are about him."

Dad gave her that look, the eye. I call it the evil eye. She got it and changed the subject.

"You know, Frankie, you never asked me who I invited to the party."

"I thought it would be family and some very close friends."

"If I did that," she replied, "I would have had it at home. We've invited two hundred guests."

"Mom, you have to be kidding. You invited two hundred people? Who did you invite?"

My dad finally joined in the conversation. "The whole damn town."

"Like I asked before, Mom, who did you invite?"

"Family," she replied, "and some of your friends, some of your father's friends, my friends, business associates, and of course, your Uncle Frank had to have some of his so-called friends."

Dad looked at her. "Terry, what the hell is wrong with you tonight?"

"I don't know what's wrong. I don't know why I keep aggravating you. I guess I'm just tired and excited about having my boy home again."

Then she jokingly interjected, "Stop complaining. At least we don't have to pay for his wedding."

Dad teased her. "How do you know he wants to get married?"

She started to laugh. "Don't tease me, Al. You know how long I've waited for that day."

"Oh, by the way, Frankie, I invited that nice girl from the neighborhood."

"What girl, Mom?"

"You know, Jessica, Jessica Smith. Well, her name is now Hart. It just so happens she is getting a divorce and she needed a pick-me-up, so I invited her. I don't know why she's getting a divorce. In fact, no one seems to know. Maybe we'll find out at the party."

"Mom, could we please change the subject about Jessie? Why she's getting a divorce is her business; you and your friends shouldn't gossip." But that meant nothing.

She went on and on, so my dad and I kept quiet. We couldn't win. I guess I was away so long, I had forgotten what a nag my mother was. The ride home reinforced my plan to leave the nest as soon as possible

As soon as we got home, I went to my room. I was exhausted and afraid to sleep. I didn't want to ruin my perfect day by having another dream. It was needless to worry. As soon as I hit my pillow, I was out like a light.

Chapter 8

The next morning brought mixed emotions about the party. It's great seeing the family and friends I hadn't seen in a long time, but I thought two hundred of them was going overboard. It was actually embarrassing. What was my mother thinking? There is nothing I can do about it now except maybe skip town, but that's out of the question.

I started thinking about Jessie. I wondered how she was holding up, what had happened and why didn't she tell me she was getting divorced. The last time I saw her was at her wedding. Except for an occasional Christmas and birthday card, we really hadn't kept in touch.

Being at her wedding was rather awkward. I kind of liked the clown she was marrying. At least he seemed nice, a real jock. He was a physical education teacher at the local middle school in Montclair. Not bad looking, if you like that type. Jessie looked beautiful in her wedding gown. She was even better looking than when she was in high school. She was smiling at everyone. Jessie was always smiling; it looked easy for her.

She was a smart, great girl, every man's dream. Then why didn't I fight a little harder to keep her? Was it ego? I guess. After all, she dumped me. My pride was shattered. How could she dump me and marry that jock? I was surprised that I felt jealous and a little bit of resentment, like he was stealing my girl. But she wasn't my girl she was just a friend. We'd broken up years before he came into the picture. She had every right to fall in love. Maybe I was jealous of the fact that she found someone first.

Jessie finally got what she wanted: a husband, kids, and the security of living in the same community she grew up in. And I had chosen my path: a career, leaving the town where I grew up, and putting some distance between my family and myself. Jessie was happy with the same old thing, but I wanted to expand my horizons. I didn't want to be the local family attorney.

The party was starting at 3:00 p.m., so we arrived at 2:45 p.m. to greet our guests and make sure the bar was stocked the way Dad and Uncle Frank liked it. Surprisingly, the guests started arriving on time. I guess they'd never heard of "fashionably late," but then we weren't those kinds of people anyway—no pretense here.

Everyone came up to me, offering congratulations. Some friends and relatives I hadn't seen in years were there, and to my surprise it felt good seeing them again. I felt like I was with my own kind, although I kept waiting for Jessie to show up. I watched the door for fifteen minutes until I got busy with greeting people and shaking hands. Suddenly I felt a tap on my shoulder. I turned and there she was. What a sight! I thought, *Holy shit, this girl is a knockout.* We laughed. We kissed. We hugged. Divorce seemed to agree with her.

"Frankie," she remarked, "you look great. How the hell are you?"

"Frankie? You called me Frankie? No one but my family calls me that."

"Well, that's because I haven't seen you in years."

"Jess, call me shit-head, jerk, whatever, but don't call me 'Frankie.' It sounds so juvenile."

She started laughing. "Look at who's the big man."

I walked right into that. "OK, now please behave yourself."

She laughed and I swear the room lit up, along with the lower extremities of my body. It had been a long time since I had had sex with someone I was really attracted to.

"Hey, Jessie, what's this I hear about you getting a divorce? Is that right?"

She stopped smiling and looked sad. It was stupid of me. I hit a nerve.

"You know, Frank, everyone will be wanting to speak to you. Why don't we discuss this at another time? I'm off for the summer, so give me a call and we can get together when things calm down for you. My phone number is the same, and I'm still living in the house. I'm buying Parker out."

"You know, you're right, this is not the time or place. But stay close by. I want to be able to find you when the music starts."

She smiled. "You got it, Frankie."

My brother finally walked in after being a half hour late. I walked up to him. "Where the hell have you been?"

"What do you mean, Frank. This is your day."

"Thanks a lot, brother. You know how uncomfortable I am with all this attention."

"Well, Frank, you better get used to it. With your high-powered New York job, the ladies will be flocking all over you. It's about time, though, don't you think? It's about time you got laid."

"What the hell is wrong with you? And where is Barbara? Are you drunk? Did something happen? Are you upset with me because of all of this? You know, I didn't want this party."

His voice softened. "No, no that's not it. Yes, I'm drunk. I got drunk before I got here." He then put his arm around my neck and kissed me on the cheek.

"Then what the hell is going on? Why are you acting like a drunken jerk?"

"Frankie, are you insinuating that I'm jealous of you?"

"Why the fuck is everyone calling me that today?"

"We just want to put you in your place, so you don't get a swelled head. It's like, we knew you when you were Frankie. As I was saying, brother (is that better), I'm not jealous, I'm happy for you. In fact, I'm proud of you. All that studying, all that missing out on parties. Not to mention getting laid. You deserve this and more. Give me a hug, brother!" He held out his arms and was coming at me.

I laughed and moved back. "Now get the hell away from me. You're drunk."

"Do you want to know why I'm drunk?"

"Sure, you've probably become a lush since I was away at school. OK, tell me why you're acting like such an ass."

"I'm drunk because this morning Barbara gave me some great news and I didn't want to spring it on the family today because today is your day."

"Tell me the truth, Al. Are you having problems? Is Barbara leaving you?"

"Leaving me? She's not leaving me, you dumb shit. I told you it was good news. We're going to have a baby, a bambino!" Tears were in his eyes.

Al, my big brother, was moved to tears. I haven't seen him cry since he was twelve years old, when a fourteen-year-old kid from down the street beat the shit out of him.

"You see, brother, I'm not jealous of you or anyone. I have everything I have ever wanted. I like working for Dad. I wanted to go into the family business. I have a beautiful wife who loves me and now a baby. I'm the happiest man alive!"

I hugged him and then sat him down on a nearby chair and asked him to stay put until he sobered up."

I found a waiter and asked him to get my brother a very strong cup of black coffee. Barbara saw us from across the room. How would I describe her? She's as cute as they come. She's short, in good shape, with long dark hair and blue eyes—your typical Irish lass. She was beaming when she came over and kissed me.

"Congratulations, Frankie. From the look on your face, Al must have told you the news. He's been blubbering ever since I told him. Can you imagine this big hunk getting so sentimental?"

Here I was worried that Al was feeling left out maybe, even a little jealous of his younger brother. The truth is he now had all he ever wanted—to be just

70

like his father. He loved the business, and he loved working in Montclair. He also knew that some day it would all be his and he deserved it. And now that he's having a family, well, that's like the icing on the cake.

I was the one who was starting to feel a little jealous. *What have I missed out on? Did I miss out?* And then I realized we all make our own choices, and we both made the right ones. I guess it's true. We all hear a different drummer. I kissed my sister-in-law and whispered in her ear, "Thank you for making my big brother so happy."

She giggled. "That was the easy part. The hard part is telling your mother."

"You're right about that. That woman will drive you crazy."

My sister, Julia, noticed we were together and came over. "What's going on here? And what's wrong with Al? What happened?"

"Wouldn't you like to know," I remarked.

With that, she slapped me on the back of my head. I grabbed her hand to stop her from doing it again, and we both started laughing just like the days when we were a couple of kids.

I whispered, "Al will tell you later."

She whined, "No, now. I want to know now."

"You know, Julia, you're still the same pain in the ass you always were." As usual, she gave it back.

"And you, Frankie Scarpelli, think you're the same boss you always thought you were."

Al decided to join in the conversation. "OK, kids, let's not fight." Then he looked at Julia and whispered, "I'm having a baby."

Julia had to have the last word. "You're having a baby? What about Barbara? Does she know?"

My brother slapped her on the back of the head. We all started laughing so hard, my mother gave us a dirty look and Dad walked briskly over to reprimand us.

"What the hell is wrong with you kids? You're all so loud, everyone is looking at you. What the hell is so funny? You kids never grow up!"

I put my arm around my sister and brother. "You know, it's like old times. It's really good to be home."

I walked over to my mother kissed her on the cheek. "Thanks, Mom. This is a great party!"

Chapter 9

I got up early that Monday morning to go into Manhattan to look for an apartment. It was a little too early, so I picked up a newspaper and stopped at a diner for breakfast. I figured it would probably take all day to find something. Actually, the newspaper didn't have much. So I called the few apartments that were listed and some real estate agencies that had several apartments and condos available for lease in Manhattan. I got out my cell phone, a pad, and pen and started making some calls.

Almost every answering machine had the same message: "The apartment that was advertised in the Sunday paper has been taken." All, that is, except for one and that one sounded like a dump. They called it an "efficiency apartment." It had one large room and a bath in a crappy neighborhood. That one was going for two thousand a month.

I left the diner and hit some of the realtors, but I got the same old story. "Nothing on the market." If I leave my name and number, they'll get back to me. A few had subleases that would be available for the summer months only. I finally parked my car at the Port Authority and took a cab to a desirable neighborhood and started walking.

I went from apartment to apartment, looking for something, anything, even if it was just for a year. A year's lease was all I wanted. I found nothing. As I sat on the bench in Central Park, I decided to get a cold soda, go home, and start looking again tomorrow.

I went back three days in a row. The weather was starting to swelter, and I was getting tired and frustrated. I started to think that maybe I should get an apartment in New Jersey and commute but dismissed that plan; that was not what I wanted. I'd have to keep trying. I called several friends and acquaintances and asked if they knew of any apartments for rent. They all said the same thing, that they would keep their ears open and let me know as soon as they heard something.

I was trying to think of what else I could do when I finally called my father. The office was noisy. I shouted, "Hi, Dad. It's me, Frank."

"I know it's you. Why are you yelling? I'm not deaf."

"Oh, sorry. It was so noisy; I didn't think you heard me."

"I hear you. How are you doing, kid?"

"I'm OK, Dad. I just wanted to know if you had any friends or clients who may know of or have an apartment in New York that I can rent."

I knew I was grasping at straws, but my father knew a lot of people. A lot of his clients lived in Montclair on weekends and holidays but stayed in the city during the week for convenience. Maybe someone had a contact. *What the hell,* I thought. *At this point, I'll follow any lead.*

"I'll ask around, kid, but I can't promise you anything. Are you having a hard time finding something?"

"Yeah, Dad. It's impossible."

"Then why don't you live at home until something opens up?"

"No, Dad. I don't want to. I want my own place, and I thought you might know someone who knows someone."

"You know, Frankie, you're so damn stubborn. I can't tell you anything. You're just like your Uncle Francis."

"Thanks anyway, Dad. I'll see you later."

I heard, "Wait, kid." It was my Uncle Frank's voice in the background.

He said, "Let me put you on speaker. I want to talk to you." It clicked over.

"What's the matter, kid? You can't find an apartment? I'll ask around, but in the meantime, you can stay at my place."

"Thanks, Uncle Frank, but I don't want to stay in New Jersey."

"Who said anything about living in New Jersey? My place in New York—I'll let you rent it until you find your own place."

In unison, Dad and I both asked, "You have an apartment in New York?"

"Jesus," he said, "I don't need you two broadcasting it all over town."

I heard my father say, "How come you never mentioned that you had an apartment in York before?"

"Because it's none of your damn business," I heard him say while laughing under his breath.

My first thought was that he was cheating on Aunt Dorothy. Then I thought better of that. They were so much in love. He would be the last person besides my dad to cheat.

My father had no trouble questioning my uncle's loyalty. "What the fuck is wrong with you, Frank? Are you cheating on Dottie?"

For what it was worth, I put in my two cents. "Are you?"

"No! I love my wife. I should kick both of you in your ass for thinking that. I would never cheat on Dottie. Besides, she'd kill me. You guys don't know what a temper my firecracker has when she gets mad. It's a business expense. I entertain my clients there, and sometimes I let them use the place when they're in town. It's actually a condo. I bought it a long time ago."

Again, we both said, "You own it."

"Of course, I own it. What did I tell you about paying rent? It's an investment. I got it because ten years ago, some guy owed me money and couldn't pay it back. He had secured his loan by using the condo. So I took possession and now it's more than doubled in value. Are you both happy now? You know everything. Look, kid, do you want it or not? Take it or leave it."

"Are you kidding? I'll take it. Where is it? What does it look like, and how much rent do you want?"

My uncle interrupted. "We'll get to all that later."

"Uncle Frank, does Aunt Dorothy know you have this condo?"

"Of course she knows. We go there from time to time to rekindle. You have to rekindle. Do you ever rekindle, Al?"

My dad remarked, "There's nothing to rekindle. It's already burned out."

My uncle said, "You are such a romantic son of a bitch, aren't you? I am a romantic. I bet you didn't know that about me."

I broke into the conversation. "Could we please get back to the condo?"

"I don't know how to describe it, kid. It's got furniture, two bedrooms, and overlooks Central Park. It's on Park Avenue."

My dad and I both chimed in again. "Park Avenue?"

"What is it with you two? Is this a comedy routine?"

My father sounded mad. "You never told me!"

"What do you want, Al? I should tell you everything? How about when I take a piss?" They both started laughing. That's how it was with them; they really only busted each other's chops. They never got mad, and they always ended up laughing.

I started to raise my voice so I could be heard above the laughter. "Can we please get back to me now?"

Sudden silence. "OK," my uncle remarked. "Come home now. It's too hot to be in New York today. I'll pick you up at your house on Monday and take you over to look at the place, and I'll tell you how much rent you'll have to pay. There are no free lunches! I'll pick you up around nine o'clock. Be ready. I hate waiting."

He hung up. As long as I could remember, he'd always said, "There are no free lunches." When we kids needed money for something, we would go to Uncle Frank. Not that dad wouldn't have given it to us; it's just that we would have had to listen to a story on how life was when he was a kid. Uncle Frank gave us the money and set a date for payback.

He would ask, "When can you pay me back?"

We'd tell him.

He would write it down and when the time came, he would ask us for it. "Thank you for paying your debt. You have to learn that in this world there are no free lunches," he'd say.

We always found a way to pay him back. If we didn't, we thought he would never loan us money again. We would do dishes, clean our rooms, or my sister would babysit. He taught us a good lesson. When birthdays came around, graduation or Christmas, he was generous to a fault.

I went home, showered, had dinner, and looked forward to calling it a night. I was beat, and tomorrow was going to be a good day. I was taking Jessie out for lunch. We had a lot of catching up to do.

I must have fallen asleep after the eleven o'clock news, and around 2:00 a.m. the nightmare started.

This time I'm running to the church and a few soldiers are behind me. We're all carrying weapons when one of the soldiers shouts, "Hurry, Tom. Hurry up!" I heard someone else shout, "I am. I am." We get to the door of the church and it's locked. Someone is shooting at us. I hear the gunfire behind us. Finally, the door opens and a priest lets us in. He walks over to the pulpit and lights the candles. He says, "Why are you here?" One of the soldiers says, "Revenge." The cross comes down and the building starts to shake and then I wake up in a cold sweat.

When I looked at the clock, it was 2:03 a.m. It was the end of me getting any sleep for the rest of the night. Shit! Tom? Who the hell is Tom? Maybe when I get to the end of this saga, the nightmares will go away. That's wishful thinking. The end of what? This is so bizarre. I think I must be nuts, or I'll go nuts before it stops.

I picked Jessie up at her home. It was the first time I had been to her and Parker's house. When she opened the door, she had a big smile. Still I could see the sadness in her eyes.

She said, "Come on in. I'll be with you in a minute."

She led me into the living room. From what I could see of the house, it was a nice place, an older, midsize home, nicely furnished. It was comfortable, just like her.

She soon appeared in the living room. "Well, Frank, I'm ready to go."

"This is a really nice house, Jessie."

"Thanks. It's a little big for just one person."

I put my arm around her and gave her a big hug. "I'm sorry, Jessie."

"Hey, it happens to marriages over fifty percent of the time. It just wasn't in my plan, but I'll live through it. Now tell me about you, Frank. What are your plans?"

"Well, unlike you, I kind of live from day to day, no long-term plans. But you know that about me." We started walking to the car.

"I wouldn't say that about you, Frank. You have been in school forever. You went to one of the best schools in the country. That took some planning."

"You're right in some respect. I picked a career and I went for it. I didn't plan on going to Harvard. It became an opportunity, and I had to work hard to meet the school's high standards.

"But now that part of my life is over and it's just day to day. I don't say I plan on being married in three years, or I will have two and a half kids in six years and then buy a house in the suburbs, you know what I mean? You never know what life has to offer."

"In a way, you're right, Frank. I had my life all planned out and look what happened."

"I'm sure it wasn't your fault, Jessie."

"How do you know it wasn't my fault?"

"Well," I said, "because to me, you're perfect."

She smiled, leaned over, and kissed me on the cheek. "You have always been a charmer.

"How is it you're not in a great relationship with some smart, great-looking woman from Harvard?"

"Maybe I'm not as smart as you think. And how do you know I'm not?"

She looked me right in my eyes and asked, "Are you?"

I laughed. "No, I'm not. I dated some. I just haven't had the time it takes for a serious relationship, or I just wasn't in the right place at the right time to find Ms. Right."

"Tell me, Frank, how did you get the job you have and what's the name of the firm?"

"It's Mark Moran, Mark Moran Junior, and Associates and I was recruited. It's a midsize company, but they bill in the millions. It's a good place to start. It's not big, but it's not small either. They showed up at the university in March. They asked permission to go through our files and picked out ten graduates of interest. We were asked if any of us would be interested. We all were. Then we all went on interviews. Our first interview was with Camille Powell from human resources and then with Mark Moran, Jr., the president's son."

Jessie added, "And you got the job?"

"Right. I got the job."

"You know, Frank, you've lived a charmed life. Everything comes to you. Look at you, you're handsome, you're smart, you're nice, and you're even modest about your accomplishments. And you're going to be rich. You're every woman's dream."

"That's what you say, lady. You happen to know me. We've been friends for years. All of the things you say about me are flattering, but that's just your opinion. Let's face it. I never had women knocking down my door in school, or for that matter, in any of the schools I went to."

"Do you know why, Frank?"

"No, but I think you're going to tell me."

"You're aloof and you seem disinterested. It's like you're on a mission of some kind and that mission comes first. Women want to come first."

"What's that supposed to mean? What the hell are you talking about? What mission?"

"I don't know, Frank. Only you know that. Maybe when you find Ms. Right, you'll snap out of it."

"And what about you, Jessie? Correct me if I'm wrong, but you had a great home life and good, decent parents. You were popular in school, and you lived the life you wanted. You're the teacher you've always wanted to be. You bought a home exactly where you wanted to live, right in Montclair, right near your family. And you got married. I'm sorry that it didn't work out for you, but you're young and beautiful. Maybe you think I'm spoiled, but you haven't done so badly yourself, so stop with this 'pity me party' you're on. You got almost everything you've ever wanted. As far as I can see, you've lived a charmed life."

Tears rolled down her cheeks, and her nose started running. There she goes, making me feel guilty. Maybe I was hard on her, but damn it, she didn't mind giving it to me.

"I'm sorry, Jessie. I don't mean to hurt your feelings, but if you're going to give it, you should also learn to take it." I reached in my pocket and gave her my hankie.

She wiped her eyes and blew her nose. "You're right, Frank. I'm as spoiled a brat as you are."

We both started to laugh.

We finally arrived at a restaurant called Bon Appetite. I decided to change the subject.

"I hope you like the food here. It's always been one of my favorite restaurants."

"I know, Frank. You've taken me here a couple of times."

"That's right. I did."

Before getting out of the car, we just sat there looking at each other. I started thinking that I wish I could tell Jessie I would like to resume our relationship, but I didn't know how I felt about her and I wasn't sure it was the right time. In fact, I wasn't even sure I loved her. For that matter, I don't even know how she feels about me. I said to myself, *Not a good time to bring this up. First we should get reacquainted.*

"See what I mean, Frank? There goes that reserve."

"What the hell are you talking about? What do you want me to say? Come on, Jessie, give me a break. Are you insinuating that that's why you broke up with me?"

"I broke up with you because when you decided to become an attorney, you also decided not to go to a local college. You opted to go away for six years."

"That's right. I opted to go to a university instead. I don't see that as being irresponsible. I see that as a good career move. The truth is my plans weren't the same as yours. I didn't want to stay in Montclair. I don't want to live next door to my parent's house, and I want to have a career that's challenging."

"I know that, Frank, and I also know that you didn't love me enough. You never told me you loved me."

"Well, Jessie, you've heard the expression 'actions speak louder than words.'" That was my cue.

It was my time to get out of the car, open her door, and walk inside the restaurant. We got a table with a view of New York City and the Hudson Bay. We ordered wine and toasted both our futures. I then asked her about the breakup of her marriage.

"Why are you getting a divorce? The last time I saw you both was at your wedding, and you were so much in love. What was that, two years ago?"

"I guess it was the same thing that happened to us. He fell out of love with me."

"You know, Jessie, I know you're hurting right now. If it makes you feel better, just let it all out. But the reality is we were just kids, childhood sweethearts, with deep feelings for each other, or maybe it was just hormones. Nevertheless, it was you who said you wouldn't wait the six years for me to finish school and now, looking back, I don't blame you. It wasn't part of your plan. But you and Parker were a different story. You were both out of college, more mature. You loved each other. What happened?"

Jessie's eyes welled up with tears, and I felt maybe I had been a little to blunt at a time when she needed sympathy.

She started to explain. "It started with one of his students."

I said, "What?"

"No," she went on, "it's not like it sounds. There was this kid in his class, an eight-year-old boy whose father was a casualty of 9/11; he was killed in one of the towers. You can imagine how this would affect any child, let alone an eight-year-old. It's hard enough to lose a parent, let alone through terrorism. So Parker tried to help. His name is James. Jimmy was nervous, despondent, and he wouldn't go to school. After a couple of months, he finally did show up, but his grades started slipping. If he didn't get the help he needed, he wouldn't pass. Parker stepped in to help the boy. He asked him to help him set up schedules for the games. He brought him in on the strategy sessions with the players. You know, he tried to keep his mind off his problems as much as he could. It became a big brother situation. The family was originally from the Midwest, and they didn't have any relatives in New Jersey. His mother thought about moving back to Kansas but decided to wait. Jim was born in New Jersey, so she thought it would be too traumatic for him to make the move at this particular time."

I said, "That sounds commendable, but how did that break up your marriage? Were you jealous?"

She glared at me. "No. That's not it at all. At first, I was part of it. I wanted to help the boy out as much as Parker did, so I would invite him over for dinner, or we would take him to movies, sometimes a football game. Then Parker started tutoring Jimmy at his home. At first, it was one night a week, then two, and then it seemed to me he was there more than he was at home. I tried to be patient, but then I became suspicious and confronted him. I asked him if he was there for Jimmy or was he more interested in being with Kim, Jimmy's mother? I thought he would say, 'Don't be ridiculous, I'm sorry I've been taking so much time away from home.'

"Instead he said, 'I'm sorry, Jessie, I don't know of an easy or kinder way to say this. I've been having an affair with Kim and I was going to ask you for a divorce, but I was waiting for a better time.'

"I asked him when would have been a better time? I told him to get the fuck out that night and to never step foot in this house again.

"He tried to calm me down, saying, 'You're acting like a child.'

"Can you imagine? How civil can you be when your husband is having an affair with another woman?"

I reached for her hand, and she pulled it away.

"Don't, Frank, I'm very angry right now and I don't want to talk about it anymore."

For a while, we ate in silence.

"When do you start work, Frank?"

"August first," I replied.

"Are you moving to New York?"

"Yes, I already have an apartment."

"When did that happen? I hear it's almost impossible to find an apartment in Manhattan."

I'd promised Uncle Frank not to spill the beans on the apartment, so I lied and said, "Could you believe the luck? A friend of mine is going to Europe for a year, so he said I could sublease his place."

"You see what I mean, Frank? You have a charmed life."

"Don't kid yourself, Jessie. No one goes through life unscathed."

"Frank, do you still have those nightmares?"

"No, not since I was a kid."

"Come on, Frank, save it for someone that doesn't know you so well."

"OK, yes, and it's becoming more frequent since I left college. Before, I could go several months without having an episode, and now it's a couple of times a week."

"Why don't you go for help?"

"I've been wanting to, but it's only now that I'm able to afford it. I can't use my insurance company. The claims will be filed through my job, and then human resources will know that I'm seeing a psychiatrist."

"So what? Everyone I know sees one from time to time."

"Yeah, sure. Would you go to an attorney who's seeing a shrink?"

"You know, that's a stupid statement for such a smart guy. How about hypnosis?"

"I'm not sure that would be a solution. I don't think my nightmares are caused by an actual experience. They take place in what looks like World War II. What did I know about World War II when I was just a kid?"

"Well, you did go to movies. You read books, or maybe a family member talked about their experience?"

"No, that's not it, Jessie. I've racked my brain. It started when I was around nine, and to my knowledge no one in my family was in that war."

"Who knows, Frank? Maybe there's a good explanation."

"What explanation? I just want it to stop."

Jess held up her half-empty glass of wine and smiled. "I guess you're right, Frank, we all have our problems. But you know what? We're going to be OK."

I also raised my glass. "You bet, sweetheart."

We clinked our glasses to toast our endurance and left the restaurant.

On our way to the car, I had a thought. "Hey, Jessie, do you have to go right home?"

"No, why? What did you have in mind?"

"Do you want to go to Verona Park? Remember when a bunch of us used to hang out there when we were kids?"

"Sure. Why not? After that big lunch, I could use a walk."

When we reached the park parking lot, we took off our shoes and walked around the lake holding hands, talking about old times. Kids were playing. Mothers were walking their babies, and the lake was filled with paddleboats. We found this great old oak tree to sit under and we kissed, just as we had done before.

Chapter 10

On Monday morning at 9:00 a.m. sharp, Uncle Frank pulled up to the house. I ran out to meet him, saving him the embarrassment of coming in and having my mother give him that disapproving look—especially today when instead of being grateful that he was helping me, she saw it as interfering in her life by helping her baby move out.

Another new black Cadillac—Uncle Frank bought a new Caddy every two years and always the same color, black.

"Nice car, Uncle Frank. When did you get it?"

"I picked it up last week. You know me, kid; I get the same car, same color every two years. It's my way. This way, I know what to expect."

When I sat on the plush leather seats, I realized it was not such a bad thing. It wasn't my taste. I'd like something sportier, but for a man his age, it was damn nice.

I reiterated my thanks to him for helping me out. "Uncle Frank, this is a godsend. I tried finding my own place, but either the rents were prohibitive, or the place was a dump. I couldn't find anything that was halfway decent in my price range. In fact, I couldn't find anything in any range."

"That's OK, kid. Glad to help out, but as you know, there are no free lunches. You will have to pay me rent."

"Sure, I expect to. I have no problem with that. What do you want for the place?"

"I don't know. Just pay the taxes, the utilities, and the homeowner dues. I'll figure it out. First, you have to see if you like it, and, oh yeah, it comes with two parking spaces in the garage below the building."

Like all the buildings on Park Avenue, the buildings are old but the architecture is stately and timeless.

"We're here!" he stated as he pulled into the garage and parked the car.

We took the elevator up to the eleventh floor and turned right to the door numbered 1103. He opened the door, and I followed him in.

"It probably stinks in here. The windows are closed and I shut the air conditioning off," he said. "Here, give me a hand and let's get the windows open."

I walked into this big, beautiful, modern apartment and over to the window that was overlooking Central Park.

"Uncle Frank, this is cool!"

"It's OK for New York."

"Are you kidding? It's OK for anywhere."

The whole apartment was done in black, white, red, and yellow. All the kitchen appliances were in stainless steel. The kitchen cabinets were black with silver knobs and the countertops were in white marble. I think you might call this decorating style art deco or modern. It looked like something out of *Architectural Digest*. I was shocked. There was this staircase in this large black-and-white marble entranceway. I ran up the stairs; there were two bedrooms. The master was huge. The closet was the size of my room at home. I shouted, "I can't believe this, and certainly I can't afford this!" I ran down the stairs. If I were a kid, I would have slid down the white wood banister, just like I had done in my uncle's house on many occasions.

"Frankie will you please come in the living room and sit yourself down. I don't have all day, and we have to get things straightened out."

"Sure, I'll sit down, but I know I can't afford this place."

"Could you just keep your mouth shut and listen to what I have to say? I might stop in from time to time, but I'll always call first just in case you have company. You know what I mean?"

"OK, Uncle Frank. Now let's talk money because I know my salary will not cover the cost of this place. How much is this going to cost me?"

"I don't know, Frankie. I thought it should come to about eighteen hundred a month."

"Uncle Frank, you know that's not nearly enough for a place like this."

"Look, if I make a profit, I'd have to declare it as income on my taxes. This way, you can save some dough and get your own place once you've been established."

I walked over to shake his hand and then hugged him. "Thanks, Uncle Frank. I really appreciate this."

"Hey, kid, in a minute you're going to bring out my sensitive nature and get me all choked up like a big galoot. Before we go, I just want you to know how proud your aunt and I are of you. A school like Harvard is no piece of cake. You could have taken the easy road and gone into business with your father or me. But you stuck it out, and now you're a lawyer, the first in the family."

I reminded him that I still had to pass the bar.

"Don't sweat it, kid. You'll ace it. You have the brains. You always did.

"Here's the key. You can move in whenever you want."

On the way home, we stopped at a diner to grab a bite to eat. As soon as we walked in, this man came running over and put his arms around my uncle and gave him a hug.

"Welcome, Mr. Scarpelli, my good friend, welcome."

"Vito, I want you to meet my nephew and godson, Frankie."

Vito shook my hand until I thought it would fall off. "Glad to meet you, Frankie, glad to see you. I have a great booth for you."

As we started walking toward the back of the diner, Vito was still talking.

"Your uncle and I go way back. He's a good friend and a good partner."

I looked toward my uncle. "Partner? You're his partner?"

"Yes, I'm his partner!"

"I didn't know you owned this place."

"Only half this place. Vito owns the other half."

"You know, Uncle Frank, there's a lot the family doesn't know about you."

"What's to know, Frankie? Always remember, what you don't know can't hurt you."

"What does that mean?"

He laughed. "It's a joke, kid. Don't be so serious. Can't you take a joke?"

We both laughed.

I couldn't wait to go home and start packing, not that I had a hell of a lot of packing to do. I just had some clothes, trophies, pictures, and some sports equipment. I'd been in college for such a long time that I didn't have the time or the money to accumulate things.

I started thinking about my mother. I felt kind of bad that she was taking this personally. She didn't seem to understand that I was going on twenty-five and that it was time for me to be on my own. I love my family, and I like being with them from time to time, but I don't want to live near them.

I was also afraid that if I stayed at home, I'd be relying on them and not grow into the independent man I wanted to be. I want to be like Uncle Frank. I've always wanted to be like him. He's my mentor. Sure, it's nice having my mother clean my room, cook my meals, and wash my clothes. And boy, could I save a bundle of money. But at what price? Besides, I've been away for six years. You would have thought she would be used to it by now.

I remember what it was like when I first went away to school. I was a little overwhelmed with all the responsibilities of taking care of myself. I now like my independence and making my own decisions, whether they're right or wrong.

As soon as I got home, I told my parents that I was moving out the next day. I also called Jessie and told her that I took the apartment and I was planning on moving in tomorrow. I asked her if she wanted to see the place when I brought my stuff over.

It took no time at all for her to answer, "Yes." She told me she had nothing to do and she would love to go into New York. I told her I'd pick her up at 10:00 a.m. sharp, figuring there should be less traffic going in to New York at that time. I started packing. This was damn exciting. My own place! *Frankie, you are on your way.*

Chapter 11

When I picked Jessie up, she looked so damn cute. Her hair was in a ponytail. She wore tight jean shorts and this little top that didn't cover much. She saw me coming and came running over to the car.

We talked all the way to the apartment, mostly about her job. She loves teaching, and she talked and talked about the kids in her class. She really gets involved. If anyone needed to have kids, it was she. And to tell the truth, I wasn't bored with the conversation. It was nice to hear of her experiences. Besides, most of her stories were so damn funny.

We arrived at the garage, and I parked the car. Jessie helped me with my stuff, and we took the elevator to the eleventh floor. When I opened the apartment door, she said, "Oh my God, this is awesome. Christ, are you lucky."

"I am, but please no lectures on how lucky I am. It sounds like what you really want to say is, 'what a spoiled brat.'"

"You are, you son of a bitch."

It was as hot as hell, so I put on the air conditioning and went to the refrigerator.

"You know, I should have stopped on the way to pick up some beer or soda or something. The only thing I have here is Diet Pepsi and Perrier."

"I'll take the Diet Pepsi, but first I'm going to look around. This is the most beautiful bachelor pad I've ever seen. So tell me, this friend who is letting you stay here, is he single?"

I quickly tried to change the subject. "So tell me, Jessie, how many bachelor pads have you been in?"

She laughed. "Wouldn't you like to know? I don't kiss and tell. Good God, Frank, did you notice the size of that bedroom and it's a loft? Wow, look at that bed!"

"What about the bed?" I shouted.

"It's king size," she yelled. "It's big enough for three people."

"Now there's an idea. Thanks."

I guess she came downstairs when I was preoccupied because before I knew it, she had thrown an ashtray at me. It barely missed my head.

"Hey, you could have killed me with that thing. I thought you were still upstairs."

She started giggling, "Come on, Frank, stop being such a wimp. The ashtray is plastic, for God's sakes. Your carpet is so plush, you didn't even hear me walk down the stairs."

"OK, the drinks are ready. Let's sit on the couch. It just occurred to me that I also forgot to pick up some food. It looks like we have to go out for lunch."

I went to sit beside Jessie, who was sitting on the couch looking out the window. I handed her a glass filled with ice and a can of Pepsi.

She turned to look at me, and her hand hit the can. The soda spilled all over the couch, her legs, and her shorts.

She jumped up, saying, "I'm so sorry. I'll clean it up."

I got a dishtowel from the kitchen and started wiping the couch, her legs, and her shorts.

"That's OK, Frank. I'll do it. It's not a big deal. It'll dry."

She went to stand up while I was leaning over her, and she walked right into my arms.

Before we knew it, we were kissing—long, steaming kisses. She never pulled away, so I started caressing and kissing her body. It was so soft. Then she unzipped my pants. Her cool hands touching my body made me even more excited. I took off her blouse and my shirt and pants. We undressed until we were naked, still kissing and caressing. I leaned her down on the couch.

She whispered, "Not here, Frank. Let's go upstairs."

We held on to each other as we walked up the stairs, intermittently kissing and pressing up against each other's bodies all the way to the bedroom.

It wasn't long before we were on the bed, touching all the places that would excite our senses. We couldn't have stopped if we wanted to. I climbed on top. Our rhythm was in sync, and after a few minutes, the frenzy accelerated. Intertwined in a passion that had been suppressed and was now finally released, we were exhausted and fulfilled. It had been seven years since we had made love. It was obvious we had both matured.

After it was over, she asked, "Did you plan this too?"

"Hell no. Did you?"

We started laughing and hugging. Then all of a sudden, we became very quiet, taking in what we had done, analyzing it. Was this the wrong thing to do at this time?

I asked Jessie what she was thinking.

"I was thinking how much better you are now than when you were seventeen."

"I'll take that as a compliment. And so are you. It seems you've had a lot of practice."

She pretended to blush and put the sheets over her head.

We got up and after she had washed them in the bathroom sink, I put Jessie's pants and underwear in the dryer.

While we waited, we talked about old times and the gang we hung with. We wondered where they were now. We even talked about putting up a Web site to see if we could find them and perhaps get together. We talked about high school and things I hadn't thought about in years.

Finally, I asked, "Aren't you hungry?"

"Yes, I am. After you put your clothes away, why don't we find a deli, get some sandwiches, and walk around the park?"

"Good idea, Jessie. To hell with unpacking, I can do that later on. Let's go, girl."

As we took the elevator down, Jessie asked if I wanted her to stay the night.

"Only if you want to," I replied.

She thought for a while.

"No, I guess not. You can take me home, but later this evening. I'm having too much fun to leave now."

We held hands as we looked for a deli. We didn't have far to go. We found one called Nate's Deli just down the street from my apartment.

We took our lunch to the park and sat on the grass, under an oak tree. Then we walked around Central Park until it got dark.

I took her home around nine that evening. She was a little quiet on the way home. I figured she was tired.

While she was getting out of the car, she looked at me and said, "Frank, on the way home, I was wondering if our making love might have been a mistake. Maybe it shouldn't have happened. You're still not ready for a commitment."

"You're right, Jessie. I'm not and neither are you. You're just getting out of a marriage, and it's too soon for you to make any emotional decisions right now."

She looked at me as if she hadn't expected me to agree with her. Knowing her the way I do, she also didn't like the fact that I pointed out that she wasn't either. Either way, her remark made me feel that maybe I had taken advantage of her. She was vulnerable and I didn't want to hurt her. But I also didn't want her to think it meant more than it did. I told her I was sorry it happened if it was some kind of a commitment test.

"Don't be a nerd, Frank. I'm not a kid. I could have said no. The truth is I wanted it as much as you. Besides, what's better than having good sex with an old friend?"

"Thanks, Jessie. I'm glad you feel that way."

Before she got out of the car, I told her I would give her a call as soon as I settled in. She smiled and kissed me on the cheek and closed the door.

While I was in Montclair, I figured I would stay at my folk's house one last time. When I walked in, they seemed surprised and happy to see me. Dad got me a beer and Mom was smiling.

She said, "I'm surprised you came back tonight. I thought you would be staying in New York."

I told her I had taken Jessie with me to see the apartment.

"I had to drive her home anyway, so I thought I would stop in and say hello and use my room for the last time."

"I like Jessie," she replied. "She would make a great daughter-in-law."

"Good night, Mom and Dad. I'm going to bed now."

I went back the next day to put my clothes away, but on the way down I stocked up on some groceries, toilet stuff, and beer. I never went shopping like that before. I didn't know what the hell I was buying. I just kept picking up food and snacks that I liked. I didn't realize how expensive everything was. It's a good thing I had enough cash on me because I forgot to bring my credit cards.

After I put all my clothes and groceries away, I started looking for a place to put my baseball bat, my mitt, tennis racket, balls, golf clubs, and my suitcases. I noticed that there was a closet under the staircase. I went in to see if there was room for my stuff.

There was room all right. It was narrow and very deep, and it had a light bulb in the middle of the ceiling. I started poking around, looking for the switch when I noticed some cartons that were closed, a locked metal box, boxes full of what looked like ledger books, canceled checks, and some old photos.

I decided to bring the pictures out and take a look at them. I then I noticed the light switch on the left-hand side of the wall, right near the closet door, so I just stood there looking at the pictures. These were pictures I had never seen before. They were pictures of some young men in front of an old church. They were all standing on the steps. They looked about thirteen or so, and a priest was standing on the very top step. They posed in pyramid style. There were ten kids in all. I looked at the faces and tried to see if there was anyone I could recognize. It was impossible.

The pictures were too old to be of my dad and Uncle Frank. The clothes were very old fashioned. The men wore knickers and caps, and the woman wore dresses. *They must be Pop's pictures.* I looked really close, trying to recognize him, when I saw the priest again. I got this uneasy feeling. But I get that feeling with every priest I see, the very reason I try like hell to stay out of church.

Only after I had been threatened with bodily harm did I accompany my family to mass. I don't know why, but I have always felt uneasy walking into a church. I suppose I somehow associate all churches with my nightmares. I believe in God and pray every night, but I always ask God the same questions. *Why did this have to happen to me? What are these nightmares all about?*

There were several pictures, and I kept searching for some familiar landscape, but none of the terrain looked familiar to me. Then it dawned on me. *They must have been taken in Italy where Pop grew up.* There were pictures of a family, a man, a woman, and a boy about eighteen, and a girl around the same age. I checked the back for writing, but the script was in Italian. I couldn't understand anything except the date, 1941.

In another picture, there were five kids about eighteen or so and that same girl. There was also an album that had six pages filled with pictures. It must have been Pop's and my grandmother's pictures. I had only seen a few pictures of my grandmother. Dad had a couple that he kept in his sock drawer. I did see the resemblance between her and my dad. Uncle Frank looks just like Pop.

The next couple of pages were only pictures of Pop, Frank, and Dad that were taken in and around New Jersey, and that was all there was.

This was so interesting that I kept digging into the box. I soon found Pop's immigration papers, dated September 14, 1945. The big shock was that he actually emigrated from Sicily. This couldn't be his. He's not from Sicily. He's from Naples. But there it was, Angelo Michael Scarpelli. *What's up with that?*

I started digging some more and found a rag that was dirty and heavy. It had something in it. I unwrapped it and found a gun, an old German Lugar. My first instinct was to drop it. I hate guns. *What the hell is this doing here? I certainly can't ask Uncle Frank. I'm sure I wasn't supposed to be snooping around. If Pop is really from Sicily, why did he lie about it?* I carefully put everything back in the closet and closed the door.

I wondered if my brother, Al, knew anything about this. I'm going to ask him if he knows anything about Pop emigrating from Sicily. I'm really curious.

That reminded me; the family doesn't have my address and cell phone number. *I'd better give them a call tomorrow.*

After a while, I went up to my bedroom to watch the news before calling it a night. I don't know the time the dream started, but I could bet it was 2:00 a.m. It always started at that time.

I'm running through the woods. I'm with a group of soldiers. We're crouching down. We hear footsteps and artillery fire. We are so still. Then someone speaks. "Quiet, Frank." I look behind me and there's a man in the same uniform as me. He's smiling. I could see his red hair below the helmet and the freckles on his face.

He smiled and repeated. "You have to be quiet."

I was starting to get annoyed. "I am. Can't you see I'm quiet? Who are you?"

"You know me, Frank. It's Tom."

"I don't know you, Tom."

"Yes, you do, Frank."

I asked, "Why am I here?"

"You're here because I need your help."

"Help with what?"

He handed me a gun. "Here, Frank, take this."

"I've seen that gun. It's a German Lugar."

"Remember the gun, Frank."

That's when I opened my eyes. Oh, this is just great! I'm now carrying on a conversation.

This had to be related to me finding that gun in the closet. That's it! I saw a gun and then dreamed about it. The strange thing was, this time I wasn't scared. No rapid heartbeat and no sweating. I looked at the clock. It was 2:03 a.m. I got up, went to get a beer, took a shower, and went back to sleep.

I must admit the couple of months that I've been off were great. I got to be with Jessie on several more occasions. We had great times together. It took her mind off her ex-husband. But after that day in my apartment, we never had sex again. I felt free for the first time in years.

I even got to know some of the people in my building, some a little too high class for my taste, but polite. I also got to know where the best places to eat, drink, and buy groceries were. I jogged in Central Park early in the mornings before the sun came out. I couldn't believe the amount of people who jogged before going to work. And I used the gym that was in the condo complex. I was starting to get in pretty good shape.

Everyone in the family came up to see me. It was great having them all visit me in my digs. Of course, my mother and sister brought all the food. That was the stipulation; you want to see me, bring the food.

I also got a chance to talk to my brother about the pictures and Pop's heritage. He said he had the same information I had. He told me to forget it, that it wasn't a big deal. If it were, we would know about it. I told him he was right and dropped it for now. He just didn't get it.

Chapter 12

The first of August finally arrived, and it was time to quit being a bum and go to work. The day has finally arrived. After all those years of school, it should finally start to pay off. I don't mean just in money, but in the satisfaction that I had reached the first step in the pinnacle of a successful career. I now needed the experience to become one of New York's finest attorneys.

I never thought for one moment that I wouldn't be. If it's one thing I have, it's confidence and faith in my ability to transfer my will into reality. And with my education behind me, I'm not only going to be a good lawyer, but a reputable one.

The word *lawyer* has such bad connotations to a lot of people. *Shyster, crook, leach,* and even *ambulance chaser,* that is until they get in a jam and need help in getting out of it.

I often wondered what I would do if I knew my client was guilty. Would I want to get him off if it was a heinous crime? Would I want to let him out to repeat the same offense? Suppose the crime was murder? But then, on the other hand, we were taught even the guilty deserve a good defense. Isn't that what our country was founded on, "innocent until proven guilty"? I'm thinking way too much. I'll just have to deal with those issues when they come up.

I was very careful in getting dressed for my first day at the office. After all, first impressions mean a lot. I wore my dark navy suit, a light gray shirt, a gray tie with just a hint of red, and my Italian black leather shoes—sharp. I looked good. I even got a haircut. Since college, I'd been wearing it long, kind of hippie style. It was now time to get a new conservative, "I'm a professional who's working downtown" look.

I decided to take the subway to the office. It was easier than driving in all that traffic. I was told to go to human resources to fill out some paperwork and for some kind of orientation. After orientation, I would be shown around the office and eventually wind up with Mark Moran, Jr., who would welcome me and then take me to my office. I was told to be there at 8:00 a.m. I was there at 7:45 a.m.

The guard let me in after I showed him my letter of employment. I sat in human resources and waited for the staff to appear. One by one, they filed in, glancing in my direction but not saying a word.

At eight o'clock, a woman walked in and sat next to me on the black leather couch and smiled. I was kind of surprised that she sat so close to me because there were several other seats surrounding the couch.

I said, "Hello. Is this your first day?"

"Yes, my name is Darlene Banks." She immediately held out her hand for a shake.

I just sat there, staring at her. She must have started to feel uncomfortable; I know I would if someone was staring at me while my hand was outstretched.

"And your name is?" she asked.

"Frank, Frank Scarpelli." I thought she was the most beautiful woman I had ever seen, and I've seen a lot, believe me.

She was about five eight, slender, with her weight in all the right places. She also had curly, midlength, black hair. Good God, she was stunning and that smile . . . I felt stupid and finally shook her hand. I thought if I said anything, I would probably stammer like a sixteen-year-old. I sat still and said nothing.

Again, she tried to make conversation. "I assume you're one of the newly hired attorneys?"

"Yes, your assumption is correct. Today is my first day with the firm. I'm a recent graduate. Is this your first day?"

"Yes, as I said the first time you asked, it is, Frank."

I was chagrined, realizing I asked her the same question twice. I tried to cover. "I sure hope they hired you to be my secretary."

She quickly answered, "What makes you think I'm a secretary, Frank Scarpelli? Is it because I'm a woman, or is it because I'm black?"

Her voice was composed and articulate. I could feel my face getting red with embarrassment.

I finally answered, "I'm sorry. I wasn't thinking. I didn't mean to offend you."

She laughed good-naturedly. "That's OK, Frank, I accept your apology. But answer my question. Was it because I'm a woman or because I'm black?"

I looked her straight in the eye.

"Are you black? Sorry, I didn't notice. But I certainly noticed that you're beautiful and you're a woman. The only thing I can say in my defense is that it was wishful thinking; this way I would get to see you every day all day."

"You know, Frank, you're digging yourself into a hole here. If I were you, I would just leave it alone. But you are amusing. And I'm quite sure you will be seeing me quite often. I'm also one of the new attorneys recently hired. If I had to rate you on how you handled your chauvinistic statement, it would probably be a five. That's just mediocre, and you certainly don't want to be a mediocre attorney."

"You're right, Darlene. I'm going to have to do a lot better if I want to compete with you. The first thing I have to learn is to think before I speak. I guess Harvard never prepared me for that."

"Oh, that's too bad, Frank, because Yale did prepare me for everything."

We both started to laugh.

I was saved when I was called in for orientation. After I filled out all the insurance forms and W-2 forms, I gave Maureen Sylvester, the manger of human resources, my new address and watched a video on safety and disaster protocol. She had me sign up for a course in CPR. I was then escorted to the main lobby that would lead me into the offices.

I guess I shouldn't have been surprised by the ambiance and the quality of the furnishings. I really didn't know what to expect. Coming from a small town in New Jersey, I was used to a small, four-attorney office in Upper Montclair where Dad did his business.

As I passed through the long, wide entranceway with its shiny brass elevators and dark green walls with ornate oak woodwork, I noticed the dark oak parquet floors with the largest Oriental rug I had ever seen. On the walls were three large portraits in wide gold frames. At the bottom of each frame was a brass placard with the names of the people in the portrait. Two were of Mark Moran, the founder. One was when he was about forty, and in the other portrait, he looked to be around sixty. The third was obviously more recent. He was a man in his eighties, and the portrait also included his two sons. Mark Moran, Jr., and his other son, Timothy Moran.

I was surprised that there was little resemblance between father and sons. They both had a much lighter complexion and although their hair was slightly graying, it was much lighter than Mark Moran, Sr.

Senior was gaunt and dark. Although his hair was starting to gray in the one picture and was all white in the other, you could tell it had once been black. But it was his eyes that got me. They were dark and stern. He looked like he could be a real piece of work to work for.

I confided in Maureen that I thought Mark Senior looked cold and condescending and asked her, "How is he to work with?"

She thought that the picture made him look a lot sterner than he was. She'd worked in the firm for ten years and he had always been a very pleasant gentleman to her. And as far as she knew, the rest of the firm felt the same. She looked at me and smiled as we entered the large glass doors leading to the reception area.

"Don't worry, Frank, you will fit in just fine. They only hire the best, and from what I hear, you will be the best as soon as you get your sea legs, so to speak."

I needed that reassurance. I was starting to feel a little uneasy.

I followed Maureen into every office and shook everyone's hand, eight attorneys in all, not counting the CEOs. Finally, she brought me into my office. I was relieved. I thought I would have to see Mark first. Right now, I didn't need the added stress of first-day anxiety.

My office was a nice surprise. I really lucked out, a corner office with two large windows overlooking all of Manhattan. It wasn't too long before Mark Moran, Jr., came into my office. He was friendly and smiling.

He asked, "Well, how do you like your office?"

"Like it?" I replied. "I think it's great, Mr. Moran."

"Frank, you can call me Mark. That is, unless my dad's around, and then you can call me Junior. But I must warn you; if you want to keep your job, that's the only time you call me Junior."

We both smiled and I assured him I got it.

He asked me to follow him. He would show me the rest of the office and introduce me to the staff.

"I assume you had the pleasure of meeting Darlene and the rest of the attorneys?"

"Yes, Mark, I did."

He went on.

"First, I will introduce you to your secretary, Joan, and then to Bea, your right-hand paralegal."

He then informed me that I would be sharing a secretary with Darlene.

"Darlene is also a recent graduate of Yale University, with grades, I might add, that were almost as high as yours. You will be sharing for now because we expect your workload to be light with very little overtime. We realize you both have to pass the bar and this will give you both ample time to study in the evenings."

I thanked him and told him I didn't expect this kind of consideration.

"Well, Frank, we've all been there and you're an investment. If you're treated well, you will make us all a lot of money."

I didn't know what to say to that. I knew they were taking a chance on a recent graduate, and I didn't want to let them or me down, so I said nothing. Of course, I was concerned about their expectations.

So Darlene's grades were as high as mine. No wonder she was insulted when I inferred she was hired to be my secretary. Sometimes I'm such a jerk.

Mark took me to meet my secretary. She was an older woman, about fifty or so, and she had probably been with the company for many years. Mark introduced us.

"Joan, I want you to meet Frank, Frank Scarpelli. You know what to do. He's green and he'll need all the help he can get."

Joan was a little overweight, short, with brown hair, glasses, and impeccably dressed. She held out her hand to shake mine, and I immediately had a good feeling about her; a feeling of relief came over me. *Thank God I won't have to try to impress her; she looks so nice. Better yet, she probably knows more than I do.*

Mark told me that Joan Gold had been with the firm for fifteen years and that she trains all the new recruits.

She beamed from ear to ear.

"So nice to meet you, Frank. Let me know if there is anything I can do to make this transition easier for you. There is only one thing I won't do, and that's get your coffee. I'm not your mother."

"That's fine, Joan. I know how to get my own coffee. Every morning I will stop at Starbucks on the way in to work."

We all started laughing.

Mark instructed me to follow him to the corporate offices, where I could get my coffee when I didn't want to stop at Starbucks. He also informed me that he'd left some briefs on my desk.

"I would like you to look them over because next week we will have a meeting with the rest of the attorneys and do some brainstorming on each individual case. You'll be asked your opinion on what you think the options are for our client's best defense. We do this because nine brains are better than one. Don't you agree?"

"Yes, I do."

Mark concluded, "Whoever's case it is makes the final decision."

I liked Mark. He seemed like an all right guy.

The corporate offices were closer to the reception area. Mark took me his office and then to Timothy's where he reintroduced me to his brother and partner. They were large rooms with views of the Hudson River. I was very impressed.

When Mark took me into the president's office, he remarked that nowadays his dad rarely comes into the office—no more than once or twice a week. After all, he was eighty-two, and although he was in good health, he did not have the stamina he once had. He said he tried to get him to retire and lead the good life.

"My dad told me the good life was this firm, and he wanted to come in until he died."

"That's dedication," I affirmed.

"Not like today's young people. No offense. I'm talking about my kids. They're spoiled and soft. I was raised differently. My brother and I had to work hard. We helped my father build this business. We had some tough times, but it paid off."

"You know, Mark, you remind me of my Uncle Frank. He always says the same thing. He's the most generous man I ever met and I don't know how much he has, but I know it's a considerable amount. But he has the same phi-losophy as you; only he expresses it differently. He never had the opportunity to go to college. His family was poor. He's a self-made man."

"Your uncle sounds like a good man. That's what I mean about the older generation. My father was also poor. He came to the United States with little money, worked his way through college and then law school. This firm is like his child. I sometimes think he had us just to keep it alive."

I thought that was a strange remark. Mark quickly changed the subject.

"Speaking of your uncle, he may want to consider using our firm for taxes, investments, or any other legal requirement. I'm sure there is something we could do for him."

"You know, Mark, that's his one fault. He doesn't trust anyone but him-self. But I'm expecting to get some referrals from him."

The presentation was over. We shook hands and Mark welcomed me aboard. He also reiterated that he had an open-door policy and to use it any time I needed.

I thanked him and told him I already liked my job. And I did.

I relished being in my office and looking over the briefs, one case at a time. I started to take notes on, in my opinion, what course of action I thought could be taken in the defense of the client. I wondered how far or how close I would come to my colleagues who were more experienced than I. Was I in the ball-park or far out in left field?

Before I knew it, it was after five and I'd skipped lunch. Joan peeked her head into my office and told me she was leaving and that I should do the same.

"Go home, Frank. It's OK to leave your room."

I looked up and saw her twinkling, mocking eyes and a big smile on her face. "You're right. I'm leaving right now. I'm starved. Good night, Joan. Have a good evening."

She waved her hand at me and left.

I had to get going anyway. My uncle called last night and asked me to meet him at Nate's Deli. He needed to go to the apartment to pick up some papers. He said he called to see if the coast was clear. I laughed to myself. Where did he ever get the idea that I was this great ladies' man? I guess it was flattering. But that was someone else—not me—at least not yet, but hopefully soon.

When I got to Nate's, Uncle Frank was already there, drinking a cup of coffee and reading a newspaper. He looked up just as I started walking toward his table. He waved me over, got up, and hugged me.

"Hey, kid, look at you. You're as sharp as a tack, haircut and all. You know, you're really not that bad looking. In fact, I think you look a lot like me."

I started to laugh.

"What's so funny, Frankie? You could look a lot worse than looking like me. You could look like your old man." He smiled.

"Tell me, how did your first day go? And before I forget, your father asked me to ask you how come they never see you anymore? And don't forget to call your mother."

"What is he talking about, they never see me? I'm there every Sunday for dinner."

He laughed.

"I know, kid, but it's already Monday and they miss you."

"I was surprised you asked me to meet you here, Uncle Frank. I didn't know you liked eating at delis that much."

"Are you kidding? That's why I married your aunt. That's the only thing she can cook. She microwaves the pastrami or corned beef and buys a loaf of Jewish rye. Then she microwaves the knishes and calls it dinner. But you know, Frankie, I relish whatever that women does for me. She excites me. But that's another story."

He asked me how my first day on the job went. He acted like I was back in school after being off for the summer.

I went into detail but left out the Darlene disaster.

Uncle Frank went on to say he needed to pick up some papers that were in the closet under the staircase.

"If you needed some papers, Uncle Frank, why didn't you just go in the apartment and get them? You don't need an appointment. It's your place."

"Well, kid, I don't like barging in. You're young and single. Besides you're paying me rent. It's yours for now. And I wanted to see how your first day went."

I said, "Speaking of the closet under the staircase, I hope you don't mind that I put some of my things in there because I noticed you were using it too."

"Sure, no problem. There's nothing in there that's of great importance. Just some files and IRS documents. If it were important, I would keep it in my safe. I don't like keeping the IRS documents in my office. I have people walking in and out all day. I also had a box of Pop's things he asked me to hold for him."

"I know. I saw albums and photographs in the box, so I looked at them. I didn't recognize anyone. The clothes they were wearing were so outdated, I figured they must have been Pop's and taken in Italy. What really surprised me were Pop's immigration papers. The last known address was from Sicily. He came here from Sicily? I thought Pop was from Naples."

My uncle looked surprised. "I also thought my father was from Naples. You know how it is, so many people coming in after the war. The authorities could have made a mistake during the processing of the immigrants when they arrived at Ellis Island. I don't know. I never even looked at that stuff."

"Another thing I don't understand, Uncle Frank, there's a German Lugar gun in the box."

"What? No, I don't recall Pop having a gun."

"A German Lugar is in the box. It's wrapped in a dirty rag."

"OK, kid, let's go up to the apartment. I want to see what the hell you're talking about."

Although I insisted he let me pay, he paid the tab. As soon as we got to the apartment, I went to the closet, unwrapped the rag, and showed him the gun.

"Frankie, are you sure this was in that box?"

"Yes, I'm positive. It was under the photo album."

"It must be a souvenir or something. Why would Pop have a gun? What's it wrapped in?"

"I don't know. It looks like a small shirt of some kind with a lot of dark stains on it. It looks like a kid's shirt."

"Why would he keep it in this rag? You know, kid, he's getting old. He probably forgot he even had it in that box. He asked me to hold a few things for him when he moved into his new apartment. I thought it was just pictures of our family. I never went through it."

"I guess I shouldn't have, either. I didn't mean to snoop around."

"Hey, that's OK. I never told you to stay out of that closet. But I'm telling you now. Just get what you need from there and stay out of the closet. Did you check to see if there were bullets in the clip?"

"Yes, there are two in the clip."

"Take them out, Frankie. I don't trust a loaded gun in the house with someone who can't shoot straight. Then put it back in the box where you found it."

Uncle Frank got what he needed and left.

I went to my room to watch some TV. I opened my mail, and there was my registration and application to take my bar exam. I started filling it out when I began thinking of Darlene. Darlene and I hadn't seen each other since this morning. I would really like to get to know her, maybe even ask her out for dinner, not that she would have accepted after I made such a fool of myself, not that I haven't already done so on other occasions. I'm sure I'll run into her soon, maybe tomorrow.

That was the last thing I remembered before falling asleep.

I was in the woods, crouching down, hiding from the enemy. I was dressed in an American camouflage uniform. Someone tapped me on the shoulder and said, "Hello, Frank." I turned and it was Tom. I didn't say anything. I just stared at him.

"Frank, I need your help."

I asked, "Help with what?" I could feel myself getting pissed. "Why don't you leave me the hell alone?"

"I can't, at least not at this time. You have to help me out."

I was agitated. "You dumb shit, you keep asking me to help you, but you don't tell me how."

"I'm telling you now. You have to find the murderer!"

"What the hell are you talking about? What murderer?"

He handed me a gun, a German Lugar. You have to find the man that owns this gun."

I opened my eyes. Sweat was pouring down my face. *Oh my God, it looked just like Pop's gun. This is getting out of hand. I need help.* The dream startled me so much that I immediately called Jessie without even thinking about the time.

She sounded like I had just woken her, and I was sure I did.

"Hello?" she said.

"I'm sorry, Jessie. I obviously woke you up."

"Frank, are you all right?"

"Yeah, I'm fine. I'm OK."

"You're fine? It's two o'clock in the morning. Who calls someone to chat at two o'clock? What's wrong?"

"I said I'm fine, Jessie. I'm sorry I woke you. I wasn't even thinking about the time. But I do need something. You said you knew of a good shrink in Montclair. Could you give me his name and number? I want to call him tomorrow."

"What's wrong, Frank? Is it the nightmares?"

"Yes, it's the nightmares. They're changing,"

"What do you mean, 'they're changing'?"

"Damn it, Jessie, they're just changing. They're becoming personal."

I was starting to get agitated and thought, *Why all these goddamn questions?*

I must have sounded angry when I said, "All I'm asking for is a name and phone number. Why the third degree?"

"OK, calm down. I'm just trying to understand and put this in perspective. No need to get pissy."

I asked her to please not use that word or tone. It sounded so juvenile.

She just laughed and repeated, "Pissy, pissy, pissy! OK, I'll get it for you. It's in my desk. Just a minute. Hold on."

"All right, I'll hold."

I only had to wait a minute or two before she was back.

"Here it is, Frank. His name is Dr. James Bass. He's at 2113 Main Street, Montclair, and his number is (973) 555-2762."

"Thanks, I got it."

"You know, Frank, you may not need a shrink. You may just need hypnosis. It might just be some childhood trauma."

"I know you mean well, Jessie, and thanks for the pop psychology, but you have known me how long? And you've known my family about the same amount of time. What the hell could have happened to cause this?"

"That's exactly my point! You don't know. Hypnosis could bring it out in the open. It doesn't have to be something your parents did. It could be something you saw, a movie, I don't know."

"That's right, you don't know and neither do I. That's why I'm going to a professional to find out what the hell is wrong with me, and to see if that Dr. Bass can get rid of whatever the hell it is."

"Good night, Frank. I would love to chat, but it's past my bedtime. Promise me you'll call and let me know if you get an appointment? I'll meet you afterwards. We could have lunch or dinner."

"I only hope he has Saturday or evening hours. I can't take any time off from work. I just started a new job."

"If that's the case, Frank, then why don't you go to a doctor in New York and save yourself a trip?"

"Because I don't want anyone to know I'm crazy."

"How would they find out if you don't put it in an insurance claim?"

"Think about it, Jessie. I work for a somewhat prestigious law firm. What if that particular shrink needed an attorney and came into my office, or worse yet, what if one of his patients sued him?"

"Good God, you are such a worrywart. What are the chances of that happening?"

"Good night, Jessie, and thanks."

I tried to reconcile in my mind the actual events of the dream and wondered why, after all these years, it was changing from entering the church to hiding in the woods. *How come we're having dialogue and who is Tom?* It was so weird, unlike a dream. It was more like an event that was currently taking place. And if I didn't wake up, I would think it was real.

What does this all mean? Maybe it has no meaning. Maybe it's what Jessie said, a memory of something I can't recall.

I'll call the doctor in the morning and see if I can set up an appointment. Let him try to figure out what's wrong with me. That's what I'll be paying him for.

Chapter 13

The next morning, I went to work feeling great. I was not only anxious to resume looking over the cases, I wanted to find Darlene's office and see if I could get her to go out with me. Her office had to be close to mine. After all, we shared the same secretary.

I started looking for her the minute I got to the office. I went to the office on the right of mine. No, that was Norman Shire's office. I went to the left. No, that was Bruce Thompson's. I felt stupid every time I went into someone's office. I used the excuse of wanting to get to know them better and "let's do lunch sometime."

On the other side of Bruce's office was Darlene's. She was sitting at her desk, diligently looking over the briefs and jotting down notes on her legal pad. When she looked up, she smiled.

"Hi, Frank. Come in and sit down. What can I do for you?"

"Here you are," I said. "I was looking all over for you. Nice office."

"Do you really think so, Frank? It's not as nice as yours. You have the corner office with two large windows and the view of the city. I only have one window and the view of the brick building next door."

"When did you see my office?"

"Well, it's no secret that from time to time I have to use the rest room and I pass your office on my way."

"Why didn't you stop in to say hello?"

"I guess because you had your head buried in the case files we're supposed to review."

Here was my opening.

"That brings me to my next question. Why don't we have dinner this evening and discuss those cases? You know, just some friendly competition between Yale and Harvard! Let's just see if there would be any differences in the way each of us would handle each individual case."

"Now, Frank, is this a real contest, or do you want to pick my brain so you can come up with all the right answers and look good when we have our meeting?"

I smiled. "You're a funny lady. I don't need your brain. I have one of my own, thank you."

We both started laughing.

"Well, to answer your question about going out to dinner, I don't think it's a good idea to get involved with anyone I work with. Being colleagues and all, you know what they say about getting involved in office relationships."

"Trust me; you've got me all wrong. Like you said, we're colleagues and if you were a guy, you wouldn't think twice about my offer. Two people working in the same office often go out for a drink or dinner. It seems to me you're gender-biased."

She smiled.

"So what you are saying is that this is just two colleagues going out for a drink?"

"Right, Darlene. We're just two colleagues that are new to the firm, going out for a drink."

"OK! Frank, meet me around 5:15 p.m. in the downstairs lobby. Let's go someplace close by. What about the Marriott Hotel that's right across the street?"

"That will work for me. See you later." I thought, *I can't believe I pulled that one off.*

I went to my office and waited for what I thought would be an appropriate time to call Dr. Bass's office to see if I could get an appointment. I almost talked myself into waiting but realized I had to resolve my situation if I wanted to lead a normal life. So I called and lucked out because of a last-minute cancellation. I got an appointment for this Saturday at 11:00 a.m.

The day just dragged. I couldn't wait to be with Darlene. Finally it was five o'clock. I ran out of my office so fast, I saw Joan's head spin around to watch me leave.

Darlene was also on time, but unfortunately it had started to rain. Luckily, we were just going across the street. Everyone in New York was looking for a cab. Neither one of us had an umbrella, so by the time we got to the hotel, we were drenched. We stood in the lobby, shaking ourselves off.

I finally spoke.

"You know, if you want we can get a room, dry ourselves off, and have room service, but that's just a suggestion."

She looked at me with eyes wide open and a smirk on her face.

"Now, Frank, are you trying to tell me that if I was Bruce or Norman, you would still make that same offer? After all, isn't this just a boy's night out thing?"

"You know, pretty lady, if they looked and smelled like you, I probably would."

We both started to laugh.

She affirmed, "You know, you're crazy, Frank. But you do have a certain charm about you."

I thought, *I might be crazier than she thinks.*

"I also noticed that about you, Darlene. You also have charm. I think we make the perfect couple."

Her eyes widened.

"I'm sorry I said that. Did I say couple? I mean, associate. What are you drinking? I'll buy this time. You can get me the next time we go out. Oh yes, we're going to be good buddies."

Again, we laughed.

Be still my heart and my dick, this lady turns me on.

That evening I couldn't get my mind off Darlene. I don't know if it was because I was so damned attracted to her or that I was afraid to fall asleep. I had such a good time being with her. She's smart, she has a great sense of humor, and for some reason I'm wildly attracted to her. And I think she feels the same about me. We just hit it off.

All of a sudden, I started thinking about my appointment with Dr. Bass. I wondered what my sessions would be like. I had never been in analysis before. *What should I tell him and how can he treat something that is as evasive as a dream? I hope he doesn't prescribe drugs. I don't know how effective that would be. I have to sleep. I have to sleep. I have to . . .* Before I knew it, I was out like a light.

The rest of the week was good. I was starting to get the hang of it, getting up early, going to the office, running into Darlene, and practicing what I've been interested in my whole life—the law.

Chapter 14

S aturday seemed to come in a flash and I was feeling great. Several times, the thought had occurred to me to cancel my appointment with Dr. Bass. But I knew the nightmares would return, so I arrived at the doctor's office ten minutes early. It turned out that I was the only patient in the waiting room. I figured he scheduled his appointments so his patients didn't run into each other. It was just as well. I knew a lot of people in Montclair. I just wanted to get this over with. I hoped he was on time. I was supposed to pick up Jessie for lunch at 12:30 p.m.

Finally, a door opened and out came a man with his hand stretched to shake mine.

He said, "Hello, I'm Dr. Bass. I assume you are Frank Scarpelli?"

I thought I would burst out laughing. I could hardly contain myself. He looked like all the pictures I had seen of Sigmund Freud. I stood up to shake his hand.

"Hello, Dr. Bass. Yes, I am Frank Scarpelli."

"Please, call me James. From the look on your face, you have noticed the resemblance between me and Sigmund Freud. Well, I can't help it. We're both Jewish. Thank God my mother never named me Sigmund. Sometimes I think I should shave off the beard, but it's kind of an icebreaker and my clients get a laugh out of it."

We both started laughing, and I was relieved to know he had a sense of humor.

I started thinking, *What if all this analysis is for nothing? What if I can't be cured and I have to go on like this for the rest of my life? I have to stop this negative thinking. I finally made the first step by coming here.*

His office was pretty much like you would expect a physiatrist's office to be: smartly furnished with a sofa on the far end of the wall and two comfortable chairs in front of his desk. On the wall behind his desk was a bookcase loaded with books.

He started to walk behind his desk. I asked him if he wanted me to lie down on the couch.

"No," he replied, "not unless you're tired and you need a nap. That's why I keep the couch in here. It's for when I need a nap. Frank, relax, I'm trying to alleviate some of the stress with my jokes, but I can see it's not working. Sorry about that."

"That's OK, Dr. Bass. I'm glad you have a sense of humor. It's just that I come from an Italian family and you're supposed to take care of your own problems and, mostly, you never let anyone know you have them. I don't feel hopeless or helpless. I just know this is something I need help with."

Dr. Bass stopped smiling.

"Frank, you did the right thing by coming here. Obviously, something is very upsetting to you, or you wouldn't be here."

He told me that he mainly used the couch for in-depth psychoanalysis or if hypnotherapy was required. He pointed to one of the chairs adjacent to his desk and asked me to take a seat.

I told him I would start from the beginning how I've had nightmares ever since I was about ten years old. Except for slight variations, it was always the same dream. It's like looking at the same play over and over again, but from time to time some dialogue or scenes were added. Except lately all of a sudden, everything was changing.

He interrupted, "What was the dream sequence like when you were a child?"

"I'm running through the woods. I'm with other people, but their faces are blurred. Their faces were like a photo that was out of focus. We're running as

124

fast as we can toward a church. I don't know where it is. The area and the church don't look familiar to me. The church doors are locked. The doors are huge and metal. We all start pounding on the door. 'Open the door; open the door.' And then it opens, and a priest says, 'Come in and close the door.' We rush in and stand there, the soldiers aim their guns at the priest. The guns are old. They look like World War II artillery Colt pistols. The priest ignores us, goes to the pulpit, and lights several candles. He never looks back at us. And then he asks, 'Why are you here?' And one of the men says, 'Revenge.' With that, this huge crucifix that's on the wall overlooking the pulpit crashes to the floor. That starts a chain reaction and the whole building starts to shake like an earthquake. And that's when I wake up, shaking, sweating, and with my heart pounding."

Dr. Bass asked me, "Why are you frightened?"

"Good question, Dr. Bass. I don't know why. Maybe it's the earthquake, but I think it's because I sense impending doom. It's like I know what the next sequence will be, and it scares me. I always wake up."

Dr. Bass made another observation, clarifying the problem. "Why are you afraid to follow it through? You really don't know for sure what the next sequence will actually be. What are you afraid of?"

Before thinking, I blurted out, "I'll die."

"Why will you die?" he asked.

"I don't know why. I just feel like if I see any more, I'll die."

"Are you in the dream?"

"Yes, and I'm with men I don't even know. I follow them and do exactly what they do."

"I see," he said. "I think what you're afraid of is that you won't wake up."

"I never thought of it that way, Dr. Bass. But you could be right."

"Frank, try to think. Do you will yourself to wake up? In other words, are you in control of waking yourself up, or are you so scared you wake up because it startles you?"

"I'm not sure. I really don't know."

"Frank, this is what I suggest you do: I want you to put a notebook and a pen next to your bed. Every time you have this dream, right down everything you remember, especially the changes. Try to focus on what causes you to wake up at that exact time. Did you wake yourself up because you don't want to follow through and learn the outcome? If so, you're in control of stopping the dream. Or is it the symptoms from the anxiety that wakes you up, such as the sweating and rapid heartbeat? You can either call me with that information or bring it with you the next time you come in."

"OK, Dr. Bass. I'll try to observe my reaction and write it down when I awake."

He went on. "You mentioned your dreams have changed. Do you remember when it started to change?"

"Yes, the day of graduation this past June. I fell asleep in the car on the way home. I noticed several changes, but for some reason it didn't scare me. But lately, there's been a big change. I'm interacting with the people in my dream and their faces are no longer blurred. Also, I'm not just observing. I'm asking questions."

"When did that start?" he asked.

"It started within the last couple of weeks."

"Think this over carefully before you answer, Frank. Did you ever notice whether there's a trigger that causes the dreams to change, a change in your personnel life, stress or an event?"

"No, I don't recall."

I knew I should have been honest with him, but I wasn't ready to tell him about Pop and the gun. Besides, Pop had nothing to do with my dreams. I've had them since I was a kid. I told myself that it was just a coincidence.

"I must say, Frank, this is very interesting. But don't worry. We'll get to the bottom of this."

All this time, he was taping our conversation.

"OK, now tell me all about Frank Scarpelli. Who is he? What does he like? What was his childhood like? You know what I mean. But you don't have to go into a lot of detail unless you think it has some bearing on your dreams."

After the session was over, I made an appointment for the following week. Dr. Bass thought that in order to get to the bottom of this, it might be best to go forward and not let too much time lapse between sessions. I'm sure he realized how uncomfortable I was and that I might decide to retreat and cope alone rather than go forward. I'd made up my mind during the session to go forward. He seemed very professional and easy to talk to. I felt we had already made some progress. It was a relief to be able to discuss my problem with someone. And who better than a professional? I vowed to go through with this, no matter what the outcome.

I stopped at Jessie's house to pick her up. When she answered the door, she ran into my arms, hugged me, and asked, "Did you go? What happened? Are you all right?"

"Yes to all your questions. I'm fine and I won't and can't tell you what happened. But I will tell you the doctor said it was not contagious or terminal."

"That's real funny, Frank. You scared the hell out of me the other night and now you're kidding around. Oh, please . . ."

I changed the subject.

"Now where do you want to have lunch because I only have ten bucks left? I've just been to the cleaners."

"No problem. I'll pay this time. You always pay."

"I was just kidding, Jessie. It was a joke. You can't pay. How do you think I'll feel when they bring over the check and I hand it to you? I'll look like a cheapskate. No way you're paying."

"You know, Frank, you are so behind the times. Where the hell have you been the last couple of years? Our age group does it all the time. It's called Dutch treat."

"Well, my friend, I guess I'm just 'square' or is that now called a 'nerd.' I like taking care of the little woman."

With that, she hit me on my arm. I knew that would get a rise out of her.

"You chauvinistic pig."

I couldn't help but laugh. "What? I thought I was being nice. But maybe you're right. It's the second time in the last week that someone accused me of being chauvinistic."

"Who?"

I wasn't ready to tell her about Darlene, so I told her it was one of the women I worked with.

"You better watch that, Frank. I'm sure you realize there are laws protecting women from chauvinistic harassment."

"No shit, Jessie. You must be kidding. I just spent six years in law school and I didn't even know there were harassment laws. Stupid me! I thought the laws were for harassment, not being chauvinistic."

"There is a fine line, mister . . ."

"Really, then I better watch it the next time I offer to pay for someone's lunch."

"You know what I meant. You know what, Frank Scarpelli? I'm ordering lobster. Screw you!"

Chapter 15

Today is Sunday, which means I go back to New Jersey to have dinner with the family. Although it's great being part of a family again, there are some Sundays that I would prefer not being there—even though it's hard to pass up my mother's cooking. Mom is a great cook.

She makes so much food that I have to cut down on my food intake for the rest of the week. Italian families don't just eat Sunday dinner, they feast. We start off with fruit cup or soup (depending on the weather) then the pasta with meatballs, sausage, salad, and Italian bread. Then comes the meal, a roast of some kind. It could be beef, pork, or lamb, with potatoes and vegetables. Then comes the coffee or espresso with anisette. Dessert is either Italian pastries, like cannoli or rum cake from Santo's Bakery, or a homemade chocolate mousse cake that happens to be my dad's favorite.

Al, Barbara, Julia, Willie, Katie, and me (now that I'm back in the area), we eat this meal in the dining room, and it takes at least two hours. That's because we can't move. We're expected to come every Sunday. It's a ritual. Pop comes every other week. He spends one Sunday with his son Al, and the other Sunday he goes to Uncle Frank's house.

On holidays and special occasions, we all get together at my uncle's place. His house is so much larger than my parents' place. Frank's house is six thousand square feet, with six bedrooms, five bathrooms, a large family room and a game room that has a standard blue felt slate Brunswick table, a poker table, and a bar that's stocked, and I mean stocked. I love Uncle Frank's house. You can sneak away and hide in one of the rooms.

After a while, the yakking and noise gets to be too much for me. Even as a kid, I needed to have my own space. So after a few hours of mingling with the family, I would go to one of the bedrooms by myself to watch television. After a while, someone would notice that I was missing and they'd start looking for me. They would eventually find me. In the meantime, though, I had peace and quiet.

I wonder if the doctor would consider that peculiar behavior. Here I go, analyzing everything I did.

This Sunday, Pop was at our house. I went there early and for some reason, I felt a little awkward when Pop walked in the door. I repressed that emotion, walked over, and gave him a hug, "Hi, Pop. How are you feeling?"

He smiled.

"Frankie, my boy, so good to see you. How is work? Do you like your job?"

I assured him I did and we made some small talk. Pop started telling us how he and his neighbor, a man who is also in his eighties, went to the senior center and met some fine ladies.

My father flipped. "At your age? You don't need any women."

My mother heard his remark from the kitchen and yelled back at him to leave Pop alone. What was wrong with him meeting a fine lady? He should be having a good time.

I thought, *How could I have mistrusted him?* I've known this man all of my life. He treated his grandchildren better than he treated his own sons. I felt guilty about my feelings of late, especially the awkwardness I felt when I walked in the room and saw him. This was my grandfather, and then I wondered, do I really know him? Or is this man a stranger?

A short time later, the rest of the family arrived. I noticed my sister-in-law was getting really big, and you know, what they say about pregnant women is true. She was glowing. And the other thing they say about pregnant women's emotional state is also true. She started to cry when my brother said my mother's meatballs were better than hers. I'm really not sure, maybe she would have cried even if she weren't pregnant.

It dawned on me that everyone was mated except Pop and me. And they all seemed very happy, even my sister. No one knew how she could be happy with Willie, but she was. I wondered what would happen if I had brought Darlene to dinner. How would my family handle the interracial thing? I've never known my family to be particularly prejudiced. There were never any slurs about other religions or racial preferences, but my mother made it be known she would prefer me to marry someone Italian or at least from the neighborhood, like my brother and sister did. The only person that Mom is prejudiced against is Uncle Frank. It was almost like my mother read my mind.

"Frankie, how come you never invite Jessie to Sunday dinner? You're still seeing her, aren't you?"

The question had all the earmarks of *"What's going on with you two?"*

"Yes, we sometimes talk on the phone and sometimes we go out. We're just good friends. Isn't that what you're really asking, Mom?"

Mom said, "You're so sensitive. Why don't I rephrase that? Why don't you invite Jessie over for dinner sometime? And why are you so secretive about your personnel life? We're all family."

Willie, my stupid brother-in-law put in his two cents.

"Yeah, Frank, tell us who you're banging these days."

I thought my mother was going to faint. She got pale and speechless. My sister elbowed him in the ribs, and my father got up and smacked him in the back of the head.

"What is wrong with you? Have you no respect for the women here, let alone your daughter?"

Willie put his hand to his head and started to rub it.

"I was kidding. Can't you people take a joke?"

All eyes gave him a look of disgust.

My mother announced dinner was ready. We all sat at our usual places, the same places since we were kids. Only now, we added a chair next to the person who had a partner. I decided to change the subject and get some straight answers from my grandfather.

"Pop, tell me what was it like in Italy. I was thinking of going there on my vacation, maybe seeing some of our relatives."

"I was from Naples, and we no longer have any relatives there."

My mother interjected, "You don't, but I still have family in Italy. You can visit my family in Rome. In fact, I'll go with you."

My grandfather sadly stated, "I don't like talking about the past, Frankie. It was a long time ago, and my memory is not too good."

I pushed on.

"Pop, did you come to the United States before or after the war?"

"Which war Frankie?"

"World War II."

He thought for a moment.

"I don't remember. I think it was before World War II.

My father shot me the evil eye, which meant shut up. I'd seen that look before, so I did.

After several hours, I said my good-byes and went home. I washed some clothes, mostly underwear and towels, everything else went to the cleaners. I watched TV and then went to bed after the eleven o'clock news. I started to feel myself going into my dream.

I was in the woods, crouching down, and I could hear the crickets and the sound of the brush rustling beneath my feet. And I woke up.

I immediately jotted down the event and followed up with, *I can control it.*

Chapter 16

As soon as I got to work, I checked to see if Darlene was in her office. She wasn't. I went to my desk and started reviewing my notes on the briefs I'd read. The meeting was this afternoon, and I wanted to be in good form when giving my opinion to the several cases we were reviewing. I would have to describe what legal method I would use in each client's defense. Junior would be there, reviewing all of our remarks.

I wasn't there long before Darlene came into my office with this beautiful smile on her face.

"Good morning, Frank."

"Good morning, Darlene. How was your weekend? From the look on your face, I'd say it went pretty well."

She gushed. "It went real well."

She then held out her left hand to show me a very large diamond engagement ring.

My enthusiasm waned. I tried desperately not to act like a jerk and say something stupid.

"Congratulations, I had no idea you were involved in a relationship."

She looked surprised at my remark. "You never asked. And we really haven't known each other long enough to discuss our personal lives."

"You're right, of course. It's a beautiful ring and I hope you'll be happy. Who's the lucky guy?"

She smiled. "His name is Bruce Cortland. We met at Yale when he was a sophomore and I was a freshman. The rest is history. We've been together ever since."

"What field is he in?"

"He's a doctor, living in Boston, but he's going to be doing his residency in New York. He's specializing in pediatrics."

"Great," I said "At what hospital?"

"He's not sure. He's had several offers, but he's not sure which one he'll choose."

"This guy's name is Bruce, Bruce Cortland? Is he related to the mega bucks Cortlands from Boston?"

At first she hesitated, "Yes, Bruce is the grandson of Thomas Cortland, the founder of the Cortland Hotel chains."

She excused herself and muttered, "I have to go to work. See you later, Frank."

"Right, Darlene, see you at the meeting." She glanced back at me as she was leaving and smiled.

What was that ache doing in my stomach? Thank God the windows don't open. Holy shit, I feel like crap. Darlene is everything I have ever wanted in a woman. Beauty, brains, a good sense of self, and something more, she has charisma and that perfume. I have to find out what the name of that perfume is. It drives me crazy.

I said to myself, "Get hold of yourself, Frank. The pain will pass and you will move on. It's not like I'd been in a relationship with her or that she dumped me for someone else. We just met. It's not that I'm in love with Darlene. You can't love someone you just met. I have to look at it for what it was, a strong attraction. Maybe it's lust—whatever.

If all I wanted was beauty and brains, I would be in love with Jessie, and I'm not. It would be a lot easier if I were. She knows my family and my friends. And we grew up in the same town. She also knows my problem and she's OK with that.

Besides, now is definitely not the time to get involved with women and all the more reason to explore all options in getting rid of the only thing in my life that has caused me some measure of stress and uncertainty. Another thing, I have to put a lot of time into my career. This firm has offered me a great opportunity, and I have to show them I'm worth it. This is actually a good thing. I need to keep my mind clear.

The meeting went well, and it was quite informative. The two trial attorneys were also present, in addition to Mark. Mark addressed the group.

"I'm sure everyone here was wondering why I brought in two more trial attorneys. The reason is we're expanding the firm to attract more high-profile criminal cases. I realize that will take some time, but it's a start. Frank and Darlene were hired for just that purpose. They both come from two of the best schools in the country, Harvard and Yale, with grades that show their high academic achievements. So let's move forward and put all our efforts into winning all of our cases to attract attention. Right now, we have a great team and that's what it takes—team effort."

Mark explained that he would assign two of the trial lawyers to specialize in criminal defense cases. In each case, that person would need an associate sitting second chair. That position would be open to whoever was available at the time. This way, all five trial attorneys would get the experience that was needed for criminal defense cases. He also confirmed that getting these particular cases would be difficult.

Mark affirmed, "This firm's main focus has been in libel, white-collar crime, real estate, accounting, corporate restructuring, bankruptcy, and so on. This firm had built its credibility in all of these areas. We now have the capital and manpower to expand into criminal defense. I don't have to tell you that that's where the big bucks are."

"I have also hired a public relations firm to get us publicity during and after each case to attract attention. When we get a high-profile case, we will all sit down, as we have in the past, to discuss all the information that's on the brief. After we have discussed the case, we will brainstorm on how it should be handled. The final decision will come from the attorney who is actually handling the case."

"My brother, Tim, will remain in charge of taxes, finance, and corporate reorganization. Any questions?"

Everyone shook his or her head.

We then continued having our weekly staff meetings and reviewing our cases.

After the meeting was over, Mark came into my office to tell me how impressed he was with my input and told me to keep up the good work. And as soon as a new case comes in, it would be mine.

I, of course, realized that until I passed the bar and have a hell of a lot more experience, I could only assist and do the legwork in helping to develop a defense strategy. I would need all the experience I could get until I passed the bar. Hopefully, by that time, I'd be ready to have my own caseload.

After the meeting, I felt inspired. I went to one of the best schools in the country, and now it was time to work on my career. Mark opened the door to a challenge: win all my cases, bring in more business, and last but not least, make more money. It sounded good to me.

I had run into Darlene on several occasions, and my feelings for her had not changed, but trying to manipulate after-hours time together did. To my regret, her engagement made her off limits, so I decided to keep our relationship strictly business. I wondered if I should tell Dr. Bass about her. I guess not. It didn't pertain to the reason I was seeing him. Besides, I shouldn't give up control of making my own decisions.

Before I knew it, it was Saturday and I was at the doctor's office. I was on time, as usual, and again there was no one in the office but me. Finally, at exactly ten o'clock, Dr. Bass came out of his office to greet me with a smile; he motioned for me to come into his office and asked me how my week went.

I told him that with the exception of last Sunday evening, the week was uneventful.

He asked, "Tell me about your dream that you had last Sunday. Did you write it all down?"

I explained how it started.

"I was in the woods crouched down, and I stopped it. I actually stopped it."

"I suspected you had the control, Frank. The only problem is you didn't complete the dream sequence. So you still don't know why you were there. I also have a feeling there is more to this than your willing to tell me. If you want me to help, I need to know everything. Are you holding anything back? Anything that might help me understand if these dreams are trying to tell you something? Or is it a suppressed memory? And to tell you the truth, I have all but ruled out that it's a memory of something you have seen or read."

I asked him why he ruled that out.

"You seem to have total recall of events and things that have happened in your lifetime. It seems likely that if you were trying to suppress an event that happened in your childhood, it would have to have been something so awful or so traumatic that you would try to suppress it by putting it into your subconscious mind. And your nightmares could be recalling that event. Or they are trying to give you a message."

"I don't understand, Dr. Bass. What kind of message?"

"At this point, it's all conjecture on my part. We haven't really spent enough time together. But my gut feeling tells me we would find out a lot sooner if you would follow through with the dream. You always stop it. Would you object to hypnosis?"

"I don't know. What are the risks?"

"Very minimal compared to the insight and direction the dreams are taking. It should reveal what your subconscious is suppressing."

"Suppressing? You think I'm suppressing? I've been looking for the truth or the cause of these nightmares for a long time."

"Frank, I understand. That's what you feel, but in reality you have stopped short of letting the dream take you to the end."

"That's right, Dr. Bass. You know why. I'm afraid I'll die."

"Frank, are you afraid you'll die or afraid you will have to face something you don't want to know about? Look at it this way: Did you ever dream you were falling?"

"Yes, doesn't everyone? I wake up before I hit the ground."

"My point exactly, you stop it, don't you?"

"Yes, but isn't that a knee-jerk reaction?"

"Yes," he continued, "you wake up startled from falling. But you don't have the same God-awful fear that causes your heart to palpitate. With your dreams, you don't know what to expect and you're still controlling the outcome. Why? You don't know where it will lead, but you're still so afraid of finding out, you wake up, frightened. It seems obvious your subconscious is trying to give you a message and it won't let go until your conscious mind understands and deals with it. Does this make any sense?"

"OK, Doc, let's try the hypnosis if you feel it will help."

"I really think it will. Is there anything that you're holding back, any information that might help me?"

"Nothing important."

"Let me be the judge of the importance, Frank. What is it? Does it have anything to do with the changes in your dreams?"

"I think it might, Doc, but I can't connect the dots."

"What is it, Frank?"

I told him about Pop, finding the gun, the pictures, and the inaccuracy in what my grandfather said about his past. I asked, "How come no one knew about the gun? And why is he lying about what part of Italy he came from?

138

Furthermore, the gun now winds up in my dreams. And what the hell does all of this have to do with the nightmares I've had since I was a kid?"

"Truthfully, I have no idea. All these things about your grandfather and his gun might have nothing to do with anything. You may have connected it to your dream because a gun is represented in military combat. Hypnosis could produce a deeper contact with your emotional life. It could result in understanding why you are repressing your fear of finding out what your dreams really mean. Frank, you will have free will and you will still be aware of what's going on. I will stop it anytime I think it will cause you more harm than good. Deep hypnosis is actually a relaxed mental state. You will feel uninhibited and relaxed. This way, I can access your subconscious mind. Did you want to schedule an appointment for next week or wait a few weeks to think it over? It's up to you."

"To be honest with you, Doc, this sounds a lot like weird shit."

"I know it does, Frank, but it's an option that should be considered. We have several options, and I know this is the best way to go. You don't need in-depth analysis. You're very intelligent and if you're telling me the truth—and I'm sure you are—you had a great childhood with loving and caring parents. You don't have a neurosis or psychosis. Everything about you is normal, and just because you have nightmares doesn't mean you're not. If you can live with this, I doubt it will kill you. But it will and does upset the quality of your life. Wouldn't it be better if it just stopped? Something is causing these dreams, and we have to find a way to open that door."

"OK, Doc, let's make it for next week."

"Frank, before you come in next week, look at the photos; look at the area, the people—anything that looks somewhat familiar."

"I don't understand. What could be familiar?"

"Well, Frank, that's what you're going to find out. And be sure to write everything down, even if you don't understand it."

I went back to my place in Manhattan. I walked around the city and got a corned beef sandwich at Nate's. Then I went to the lounge at the Marriott. Big mistake. The last time I was there was when I was with Darlene. It reminded me of her, and it put me in a lousy mood. So I had a few scotch and sodas and left.

When I got home, I had several more scotch and sodas and called Jessie. I asked her if she was free for dinner tomorrow. She said she was, so I invited her to my parent's house for Sunday dinner. She seemed happy about the prospect.

After I spoke to her, I started to get a twinge of a guilty conscience. Am I using her because I can't have Darlene? Did I invite her just to get my mother off my back? Or am I inviting her because she's a friend and I enjoy her company? I immediately took the latter. I had enough to worry about without having to analyze every move I made. She's my friend and I enjoy her company.

I decided not to follow Dr. Bass's instructions. I avoided looking at the pictures. I told myself that tonight was not the night I needed to focus on the negative. I'll do it tomorrow. I was already feeling lonely and dejected. I slept peacefully, though it could have been all that booze.

Everything went off without a hitch on Sunday. Jessie was perfect. She fit right in. She was happy. My family was happy. Frank had finally brought a date, and someone my mother approved of—which was no easy feat. Yes, Jessie would be perfect, if only we were in love.

Chapter 17

All I kept thinking about was working on my first case. Of course, I would only be assisting one of the senior staff members. I was no more than a paralegal, with six years of learning protocol and the law. Still, it was invaluable experience. Knowing the law is one thing, applying it is another.

In most cases, people's lives, their livelihoods, reputation, and their marriage could be at stake. They are entitled to the best defense their money could buy, and that takes experience—lots of experience—and manipulation in the interpretation of the law. And anyone who thinks otherwise is misinformed.

I was happy and quite surprised when Junior walked in and handed me a case file on Monday. I had no idea that I would be doing the legwork for Mark. I never thought that one of the senior partners would want my input.

He put the file on my desk and said, "Read this over and get me all the information you can to help build a defense for our client, Dr. Fischer. And next week, we will get together and determine what kind of defense and strategy would best suit his situation."

I asked, "What situation?"

He laughed. "Read the report and take notes. When you're done, ring up Millie, my assistant, and tell her you need to see me. Millie will set up a time when I'll be available. That's it, Frank. I don't have time to explain. I'm a busy man. That's why I hired you."

"That's right, Mark, you did. And you did the right thing."

I opened the Jerome Fischer file: Dr. Jerome Fischer, eighty-year-old retired physician, is accused of killing his eight-two-year-old wife by giving her a lethal dose of morphine, intravenously, while she slept. Mrs. Fischer had been ill with stomach cancer for a little over a year. Her treatment had little effect and the disease was now in its advanced stages. The doctor's prognosis was that the disease was terminal and she could die within the next couple of weeks or days.

Dr. Fischer is being charged with premeditated murder due to his confession at the time of her demise. Dr. Fischer stated that he killed her because he could no longer endure seeing his wife of fifty-one years racked with pain that would eventually lead to her death. The prosecutor stated he was a physician and had taken an oath to save lives. He waited for her nurse to leave before administering the morphine, and his confession alluded to that fact. Due to the circumstances and his age, the DA's office is willing to make a deal by offering him three to eight years for manslaughter.

Mark's note stated, *Due to his age, we are going to try and get him off. Get me enough evidence to prove it was a mercy killing. Hopefully, the jury will feel he did the right thing. Also, find a way to have his confession thrown out.*

It seems Dr. Fischer's daughter, Annabelle King, called Mark as soon as her father was arrested. Dr. Fischer had been a client of Mark Moran, Sr., and had been doing business with the firm since its conception.

At the arraignment, Junior convinced the judge to give Dr. Fischer bail by claiming he was a prominent New York City heart surgeon with ties to the community. And he was not a flight risk.

The judge agreed but asked that he surrender his passport. Although the prosecutor had asked that he be remanded, he didn't seem too upset that Dr. Fischer was awarded bail.

I started taking notes and planning my strategy. My first step was to get some information on Dr. Fischer's behavior during the time of the overdose, or perhaps "accidental" overdose. I will need to take depositions from, Dr. Fischer, his daughter, Mrs. Fischer's physician, and the nurse who cared for her.

Hopefully, they will all have similar stories. If it goes to court, we will need character witnesses. But the very first thing I have to do is brush up on the law to find some viable way to make this a mercy killing.

Soon after Mark left my office, Darlene came in with two cups of coffee. She handed me one and asked, "You take it black, don't you?"

"Yes, I like it black!"

We both started laughing. I don't know why. I guess we were both a little nervous. I know I was.

"This is quite a surprise, you bringing me coffee! What happened to wanting to be treated like one of the boys? My secretary won't even bring me coffee."

"You got me all wrong, Frank. I was going for coffee and, knowing how much you also like coffee, I thought it would be a nice gesture, and it also gave me an excuse to come in and talk to you and find out why Mark was here . . . and to tease you about being the teacher's pet."

"So what you're really looking for is a little dirt? First of all, I'm not the teacher's pet. Mark just recognizes talent when he sees it."

Darlene got this *yeah sure* smile on her face. I went on to tell her why Mark was in my office and explained the case.

Her expression changed. "What's wrong, Frank?"

"I don't know what you mean, Darlene. Nothing is wrong. Why?"

"We used to speak to each other and kid around with each other a lot more than we do now. I guess what I'm trying to say is, you seem to be avoiding me."

"Well," I replied, "you're engaged."

Darlene looked confused. "What does my engagement have to do with our friendship?"

Of course, she was right. I now realized just how immature I'd been acting. I was actually angry with her because she was in love with another man that she met before I came into the picture. After all, she has no idea how I feel about her. I guess Jessie was right. I do act like a spoiled child when I don't get my way.

"You're right. Your engagement should have nothing to do with our friendship. I don't know why I blurted out such a stupid remark. I've had some personal problems lately, and I guess between that and work I've just been preoccupied. I'm sorry. Let me make it up to you. What do you say we meet after work and I'll buy you a drink?"

"You're on. I'll meet you in the lobby."

We met in the lobby. As we walked across the street to the Marriott, I held her arm, as if to protect her from the oncoming traffic. I was a gentleman, protecting her from the crowds. The truth is I wanted to touch her, even if it was just her arm.

When we got to the lounge, it was so crowded, we couldn't even get a seat at the bar or at any of the cocktail tables, so we stood at the end of the bar waiting for a seat. In the meantime, the bartender who saw us standing there came over to take our order. I was about to speak when I felt a slap on my back. I turned around, thinking it was some kind of an impatient jerk. I was just about to say something or push the guy out of my space.

Darlene's eyes widened as if to say "Don't start anything" when I saw it was Uncle Frank. He slapped me on the back again and said, "You were about to take a swing at me, weren't you? Tell me the truth?"

"No, no swing. I'm with a lady. I was just going to give you a dirty look and tell you to keep your filthy hands to yourself."

He gave me a damn bear hug in front of Darlene and the rest of the place.

"I love you, Frankie. You have such composure. Me I would have been mad."

I turned to Darlene and introduced her to my uncle.

"Darlene, this is my Uncle Frank Scarpelli."

She held out her hand. "Hello, Frank. It's so nice to meet you."

Uncle Frank shook her hand and told her, "Any friend of Frankie's is a friend of mine."

"Frankie," she repeated, "I'll have to remember that."

I gave her a dirty look. She just smiled.

Uncle Frank asked, "What's the matter, kid, can't find a seat?

"You got it. This place is so damn crowded. What about you, Uncle Frank? What are you doing here at this time of night?"

"I'm meeting with some business associates. I usually conduct my business earlier, but tonight was an exception. You know how your aunt hates it when I don't come home for dinner. Why don't you and Darlene join us? Our table is right over there."

He pointed and waved at three men who looked and dressed very much like him.

I asked, "Who are they? They don't look familiar."

"That's because you wouldn't know them. Why can't you and your father understand that my business extends beyond Montclair? Why do you think I have an apartment in the city? You're just like your father. You don't listen."

"I don't think it's because we don't listen. It's that you never tell us anything about your business."

"There's nothing to tell. I'm a venture capitalist. I lend money to business-es. And I'm a real estate developer. Besides, this certainly isn't the time or the place to discuss my business."

He was right. This wasn't the time or the place to question him about his business. I never should have put him on the spot like that, especially in front of a stranger. Although, he didn't act like he was too upset.

"That reminds me, Frankie, why haven't I seen you in such a long time? Dottie keeps asking, 'How come we never see Frankie?' I told her you're busy. She said no one should be too busy for their family."

It had been quite a while since I went up to my uncle's place. I didn't know what to say. I'd been in Jersey for the last couple of weekends. On Saturdays, I'd been seeing Dr. Bass. And on Sundays, I had dinner at my parents' place.

I still haven't told anyone in my family that I'm seeing a psychiatrist. To tell the truth, I'm kind of ashamed that I can't handle my own problems.

As far as I know, not one member of my family has ever been to a shrink. Besides, years ago, I lied to them and told them that the nightmares had stopped. So now what do I tell them? I'm seeing a psychiatrist because all those many years ago, I lied.

"Uncle Frank, if you're not busy this Saturday, I'll stop in."

He slapped me on the back.

"We're not busy this Saturday. I'll tell your aunt and Robin you're coming over. Come for lunch."

He said he had to get back to his clients, so he said good-bye to Darlene, telling her now nice it was to meet her.

Before leaving, he said something to the bartender and handed him some money. I figured he was buying us a drink. Before I knew it, the waitress went over to one of the tables and put a *Reserved* sign on it. And the couple that was sitting there left.

She motioned for us to come over to the table and said, "Mr. Scarpelli said to put whatever you want on his tab."

Darlene looked at me and whispered, "I'm impressed. I'm really impressed."

I just grinned at her. As for me, I was more surprised than impressed. *How does he do it?*

Darlene declared, "I see good looks run in your family."

146

"What are you saying? I'm not the only good-looking one in the family?"

"No, you're not. Your uncle is a very handsome man."

"You really think so? I never thought about that."

"Yes, I certainly do. Not only that, he's so charming."

"You think he's handsome and charming? Well, don't get any ideas. He's a happily married man."

She just laughed.

I had such a great evening; I hated to have it end. There lies the problem with being just friends; she may not want more than friendship, but the more time I spend with her, the more I want more, lots more. We left the Marriott around eight o'clock. I called her a cab and gave her a friendly good-bye hug. I flagged down another cab for me and went home, alone as usual.

The week went so fast that before I knew it, it was Saturday and I was on my way to my appointment with Dr. Bass to start my first session of hypnotherapy.

Although I was reassured it was safe, I was hesitant. I wasn't sure I believed in it. I even did some of my own research. Supposedly, the subconscious is the storehouse for all your memories. While under hypnosis, I may be able to access past events that I had forgotten.

That's what scared me. Apparently, I didn't want to remember; that's why I controlled the dreams and never let them take me to the end. What lies at the end? I guess I'll soon find out in this session or sessions to come if I don't chicken out. *No, I thought, that's not even an option.*

I arrived on time, as usual, and as usual he came out of his office and greeted me in his usual manner.

"How are you doing, Frank?"

"Great. I'm doing just great."

If I were really great, I wouldn't be there and he knows that, so why does he ask me? I guess it's an icebreaker and helps to alleviate the stress of sitting and waiting.

Again, the doctor went into the method he would be using. It's called progressive relaxation and imagery. It is the method commonly used by psychiatrists. By speaking slowly to the subject in a soothing voice, Dr. Bass said he would gradually bring on total relaxation and focus, easing into full hypnosis. He said it usually takes anywhere from a few minutes to a half hour. He reiterated that it could take several sessions if I resist in giving full disclosures.

This time, I was led to the sofa. He thought that would be more relaxing and is the usual position I'm in when I have the reoccurring nightmares. Before we began, he told me he was going to tape our sessions and then asked if I had had any nightmares within the past week. I told him no and joked that maybe I was already cured.

"Wishful thinking, Frank. But you know better."

Laughing at myself calmed me down. What the hell? I had nothing to lose. If the dream continued after these sessions, I'd just have to learn to live with it.

Since my first meeting with Dr. Bass, I've had full confidence in his ability as a psychiatrist—probably because he make me feel relaxed and because he doesn't think I'm nuts.

"Frank, I'm going to take you back to your first set of dreams, the one you had before your most recent dreams, before you participated in the events."

After what seemed like a second, it began. Dr. Bass asked, "What are you doing, Frank?"

"I'm running through the woods."

"Why are you running?"

"We don't want to be seen, and we have to be there on time."

"Is someone chasing you?"

"No, I don't feel like anyone is chasing me."

"Stop and look around. Where are you?"

"I'm in another country. I'm in Italy."

"What makes you think that?"

"The people are speaking Italian."

"OK, Frank, now stop and look at yourself."

"I can't stop. I have to go to the church."

"Why is it so important to go to the church?"

"We'll be safe at the church. We have to meet the other partisans. Our orders were to rendezvous with this group and get back to the battalion with all the information."

"What information is that?"

"Maps, key striking locations, their headquarters, and where they keep their arsenal."

"Frank, are you in the service?"

"No, but the Americans are."

"What branch of the service are they in?"

"They're in the army. They're paratroopers."

"Frank, do you know what year it is?"

"It's 1943."

"Frank, look at your clothes. What are you wearing?"

"I'm wearing my clothes."

"What clothes are the Americans wearing?"

"They're wearing old-looking clothes."

"Why aren't they in uniform?"

"Mario said they'd look less conspicuous if they were spotted."

"The people you're with—are they talking?"

"Yes, but they're whispering."

"Frank, is someone coaching you on what to say?"

"Yes, TC is telling me what to say."

"Who is TC and what's he doing there?"

"He's Corporal Thomas Callahan, paratrooper for the United States Army."

"Last question. Who is the enemy?"

"The Germans and the Italians."

"OK, Frank, go on with the dream."

"We're running as fast as we can toward a church. The church doors are closed, and we start pounding on the door.

"Open the door! Open the door.

"And it starts to open. A priest says, 'Come in and close the door.'

"We rush in. We stand there with our guns raised. The priest ignores us and goes to the pulpit and lights the candles. He never looks back at us, but asks, 'Why are you here?'

"TC says, 'Revenge.' Then this huge crucifix that's hanging on the sidewall, overlooking the pulpit, crashes to the floor. That starts a chain reaction, and the whole building starts to shake like an earthquake."

"Frank, do not wake up like you usually do. The building will stop shaking. Did the building stop shaking?"

"Yes, it did."

"Frank, why does TC want revenge? What happened?"

"I don't want to talk about it! I don't want to talk about it!"

"OK, Frank, now calm down. This is not real. This is only a dream and it can't hurt you. I won't let it. I'm going to ask you again. Now remember, this is only a dream. It can't hurt you. Why do they want revenge?"

"They want me to punish Mario. They want me to kill him."

"Why? I thought he was helping you."

"He's a traitor. He lied to us. He massacred everyone in that church. He killed TC."

"Frank, it's time to wake up now. When I count to five, you will wake up and remember what has taken place. One, two, three, four, five, wake up."

When I came out of my altered state of consciousness, I was confused. I looked at Dr. Bass and asked him, "What the hell happened?"

He replied, "What happened is we finally made a breakthrough."

I asked, "What kind of a breakthrough? I'm more confused now than I was before."

"Frank, this is your first session, and believe me, it went exceptionally well. How about next week?"

"I don't know, Dr. Bass, I'm very uncomfortable with this kind of therapy."

"Some people are, Frank. It renders you a state of being out of control. But believe me, you're not." He also reminded me that we shouldn't stop now that we just starting making headway.

"OK, Doc, you win. I'll see you next week."

I wish I hadn't promised my uncle that I'd stop by, especially not for lunch. I was in no mood to see anyone nor did I feel like eating. But I know my life wouldn't be worth a plug nickel if I disappointed my aunt. My uncle is a great guy, but you don't ever want to upset his wife.

When I pulled up to the driveway of Uncle Frank's house, I noticed several new additions to the grounds: first there was this very high, large wrought-iron gate and a wrought-iron fence that surrounded the entire yard. My first reaction was, "What the hell is this? Did I drive up to the wrong house?" I looked again. It was the right house.

On each side of the gate was a brick post and the one on the left (the driver's side) had a telephone or intercom—whatever the hell it was.

I leaned out the car window and picked up the telephone. Before I could say anything, a voice said, "Hello, Frank, we've been expecting you."

The gate opened. I drove in and parked by one of the doors of the five-car garage. As I walked toward the front door, it opened. Aunt Dorothy was standing there, smiling and waving at me to come in. As I walked in, she hugged and kissed me.

"Frankie, I'm so glad you're here. It's been such a long time."

I asked, "What is going on here? This place looks like Fort Knox. When did you put up that fence and gate? And who was that on the phone?"

"Oh, please," she answered. "I hate all this. It's your uncle's idea. He claims it's for my protection."

"Protection from what?"

"Sweetheart, who knows what that man is thinking? He claims we need protection from terrorists. Believe me, Frank, I think your uncle is getting paranoid. He even hired a bodyguard."

"A bodyguard?"

"I know, your uncle's *meshuge*."

I looked at her.

"Crazy, sweetheart, it means crazy."

Pop must have heard me at the door and came walking as fast as he could with his arms open wide to greet me.

"Frankie, my boy! How are you?"

I walked into his arms and hugged him. He held me so tight, I could hardly breathe.

"Hi, Pop. How are you feeling?"

"You don't want to know and you wouldn't understand how it feels to be old."

"You're not that old, Pop."

"Yes, I am, and it's time for me to go."

That remark hit home and it made me feel lousy. I couldn't imagine our family without Pop.

152

Aunt Dorothy chimed in.

"Please, Dad, don't say that. You know how it upsets everyone. We all love you."

He put this big grin on his face.

"Now you see why I love my daughter-in-law. Isn't she sweet? Isn't she beautiful?"

"Yes, Pop, she is beautiful."

Aunt Dorothy was embarrassed.

"If you guys only knew how much I had to pay for this beauty."

Pop said, "Don't listen to her, Frankie. I knew her before Frank married her. She was always beautiful."

We both laughed!

For all that my aunt had in monetary value, there was never any pretentiousness or conceit. In fact, her affluence almost embarrassed her. I had the feeling that if it was all gone tomorrow and all she had left was her husband, her child, and her family, she would be just as happy as she is right now.

I asked if Uncle Frank was in.

"Of course, sweetheart, he's in his office. He's waiting for you. I'll call you soon. Lunch is almost ready."

I walked into the office. My uncle was at his desk with his head down, looking at some papers on his desk. I just stood looking at him. *And so Darlene thinks this middle-aged man is good looking. Well, I guess from a female point of view, he might be considered suave and debonair. But if you ask me, I think he looks very average.*

He felt my presence and looked up, got up from his chair, smiled, and gave me the bear hug my family was famous for.

"You look like hell. What's wrong?"

"Nothing is wrong."

"Come on, kid. What's wrong?"

I had to make up something. He's known me all of my life, and I guess my mood was on my face, so I lied. I was getting used to lying.

"Nothing much. A couple of days ago I had this twenty-four-hour virus thing. I'm better now, but I guess I still look lousy."

He looked at me and grinned. I don't think he bought it, but he dropped the subject.

I asked him, "What the hell is going on here? Why the gate and the bodyguard? I didn't know you were so important that some terrorist might come looking for you."

He motioned to me to shut the door.

I repeated, "What's up with that?"

"It's a precaution. I loan out a lot of money and sometimes I have problems collecting. Then I have to go to court. Sometimes, they can't take the heat and threaten me. I don't want some nut finding out where I live and putting my family in danger."

I didn't buy that story, but if he went to all that trouble of making it up, I would accept it. "Look, Uncle Frank, if you're in any legal trouble, let me handle it. I'm the lawyer in the family, and I might be able to help."

"No, it's nothing like that, kid. It's just a precaution."

"Then what's with the bodyguard?"

He laughed. "It's just a favor. John's father is an old friend of mine. John was a guard at AT&T. They were downsizing and they let him go. He's a big guy, so I'm helping him out until he finds another job. He just keeps an eye on the house and works the new security system I had installed."

There was a knock on the door. It was my aunt.

She whispered, "Lunch is ready."

Uncle Frank said, "Come on in, honey. We're through talking business."

She opened the door, and they smiled at each other like I wasn't even in the room. God, look at them, they're still hot for each other after all these years. Why can't I find that kind of love? I guess not too many people do.

Uncle Frank got up, and we went into the kitchen, which suited me just fine. I hate formal dining room affairs. On the table was a large platter of cold cuts, shrimp cocktail, potato salad, tossed salad, lox, cream cheese, bagels, rye bread, and apple pie.

"How many more people are you expecting?" I asked.

"Just us, sweetheart, just us."

"Aunt Dorothy, where's Robin? I wanted to see her. I got her a little something."

"Frankie, you didn't have to do that," she said. "Robin wanted to be here to see you, but her best friend, Sam, was having a sleepover birthday party."

"What? You let her go to some guy's house to sleep over?"

They both laughed.

"Are you kidding?" my uncle stated. "Sam's not a guy. Samantha lives a couple of houses down the street."

I brought out this little box I had in my pocket and asked my aunt to give it to her.

My aunt asked if she could open it.

"Sure, and if you don't think she'll like it, I can take it back and get something else."

My aunt opened the box and pulled out the locket I had bought for Robin. It was a gold heart with a small diamond in the middle.

"This is so beautiful. You shouldn't have!"

My uncle agreed. "Dottie is right. You should be saving your money."

"I just want to know if you think she'll like it."

My aunt told me she would love it. She then came over and kissed me on my cheek.

Pop had been very quiet but said, "That's very nice, Frankie."

My uncle announced, "Eat up, everyone. It's deli as usual. It's the specialty of the house."

My aunt leaned over and slapped my uncle's arm.

He pretended it hurt. "Ouch, you hurt me. You better be careful. I may sue you for abuse."

"Sue away. You deserved it. I'll get a good Jewish lawyer and take you for everything you've got. No offense, Frankie."

We all started to laugh.

"No offense taken, Aunt Dorothy."

My uncle asked when I was taking the bar exam and if I'd been studying. I told him I didn't have to take it until February and I haven't had time to study.

"You haven't had time? You spent six years in school and now you're going to blow it?"

"No, I won't blow it. I have plenty of time to study before the exam."

Uncle Frank changed the subject.

"Hey, Frankie, tell us about your girlfriend."

"I don't have a girlfriend."

"What about that beautiful girl you were with at the Marriott Hotel?"

Oh boy, that's all my aunt had to hear. She started in. "Who is this girl? What does she do? How old is she? What does she look like?"

I asked, "How come I cannot have a meal with any one of my family members without someone bringing up the fact that I'm not married. And how come I'm not in a relationship. Why does everyone think I'm missing out on something?"

My aunt replied, "Because we want to see you happy."

"I am happy. But I would be happier if my family would just stop playing matchmaker."

My aunt ignored what I had just said. "OK, Frankie, you made your point. Now tell me about her."

"First of all, she's not my girlfriend. She's my coworker. Darlene is an attorney, as soon as she passes the bar. She went to Yale. She's around twenty-five, engaged, and very beautiful."

"Well, if she's only engaged," my aunt stated. "You still have a chance."

I looked at her and shook my head. Everyone started to laugh. Even Pop came to life.

"You got a girlfriend, Frankie? I thought Jessie was your girlfriend. That's what your mother said."

"No, Pop, I don't have a girlfriend and Jessie is just a friend—not my girlfriend. I'll let everyone know the very day it happens to me."

Everyone laughed, including me.

My aunt concluded, "I'm sure when you're ready, you won't have any trouble finding someone. You are very handsome."

"Thank you, Aunt Dorothy. In fact, Darlene thought Uncle Frank was very handsome."

She looked amused. "Well, it seems Darlene has very good taste."

My uncle put his hand on hers, and they smiled at each other.

I asked them, "Do you want us to leave?"

My uncle laughed. "Watch your mouth, big shot. You're still not big enough to take me on."

"Oh, yeah? You could scare me when I was ten, but look at this." I made a muscle.

My aunt asked my uncle, "Frank, look at that big muscle. Aren't you scared?"

My uncle made a fist. "You will never get big enough for this. I broke a man's jaw with this fist."

We all started to laugh. It was fun being with them. I had forgotten how much. My parents were great, but they didn't kid around like Uncle Frank and Aunt Dorothy. I thought my parents took life a little too seriously.

My aunt asked my uncle if he had told me about the trip they were taking to Las Vegas next week.

"No, honey, I forgot. Thanks for reminding me." He began with, "I was wondering if you would let Pop stay at your place for a couple of days?"

"I would, but I have to work."

"I realize that. We can have him dropped off on Thursday and he can stay at your place until the weekend. Then you can take him to your father's place on Sunday."

"That would be great, except that I have an appointment on Saturday morning."

Uncle Frank asked, "Can't you cancel it?"

"I'm sorry, I can't. But can't I take him to my father's place on Saturday before going to my appointment?"

"Yeah, sure, that's OK."

Pop declared, "You know, Frankie, if you're busy, that's OK. I was just looking for a change of scenery."

"Pop, please don't think I don't want you to stay with me. I'd like having you around. But I'm a little afraid for you to be wandering around the streets of Manhattan while I'm at work. Uncle Frank, do you think it's wise for Pop to be wandering around New York all by himself?"

"Of course not. Are you crazy? Did you think I'd let my father wander the streets all by himself? I've got that covered. John will take care of Pop until you get home."

"John? Who's John?"

"John, my bodyguard. My security man and number one assistant. It's all settled. Dottie and me are going to Las Vegas. Robin will be going to Dottie's mother's house. And you're taking care of Pop."

After lunch was over, I asked Uncle Frank to show me his security system. He got up from the table and led the way. I don't know why I was surprised at his sophisticated system. I guess it was because I never knew anyone who went to that extreme to secure their home and property. But then I really never knew that many people who needed to have that much security. I'm sure people who have accumulated a lot of wealth need protection, and then there is my aunt's jewelry. I had no idea what that must be worth.

Uncle Frank had more than most of us realized. To us, he was just Uncle Frank. I wondered if my dad knew how much he was worth.

We went down the stairs to what used to be the recreation room. My aunt and uncle entertained in that room when they had a lot of guests. The room used to have a dance floor, a twenty-foot padded bar, refrigerator—you name it. It was bigger than most apartments.

Now it held John and all this surveillance equipment. I was a little surprised when I saw John. John looked like someone who could have been a contestant for the Mr. America title if he was a little more buff. He was very big. He looked to be in his early twenties. I would say he was about six foot four. He reminded me of Lou Ferrigno but not as muscular. John was clearly someone you wouldn't want to piss off.

He sat behind this huge desk. In front of him were eight TV monitors, surveying the front door, back door, the large entranceway, the bottom of the staircase, and the top of the staircase. There were also another two scanning the property, including the front gate.

"OK, now you're scaring me," I said.

"Come on, now, this is not that elaborate. Remember, I go out of town from time to time. I was always worried about Dottie and Robin. What's peace of mind worth?"

I agreed, "You're right, Uncle Frank. This is your home and your business."

We walked over to where John was sitting.

My uncle said, "Remember this face, John. This is my nephew, Frankie. I wouldn't want you to shoot him by mistake."

"Does he carry a gun?" I asked.

They thought that was funny and started howling.

"That's what bodyguards do," my uncle replied.

John come back with, "Don't worry, Frankie. It doesn't have a hair trigger. I'm in complete control."

"That's not much of a relief. I hate guns. They have a way of going off when least expected. You do realize that John can't take this gun out of state, assuming it's registered."

Mockingly, he replied, "You're not the only one who knows the law."

"So, John, I assume you know you're to take care of Pop while I'm at work?"

"He knows it now," my uncle replied.

He asked John if he could watch out for his father while I was at work and he was in Las Vegas with the missus. He also said that it was OK for Pop to walk around New York, that he needed the exercise, but not to let him get too tired.

He then reiterated, "Keep a close eye on Pop. No one is to lay a hand on my father."

John smiled a toothy grin. He had large white teeth with a small gap in his two front teeth.

"Whatever you want, boss," he said.

My uncle put his arm around John's shoulders and in a calm voice reminded him that he was told not to call him "boss," that Frank would be just fine.

John said, "I know you did, but to me *boss* is a sign of respect. My family and me, we owe you."

Before leaving, I shook John's hand. Mine was dwarfed in comparison. I told him how nice it was to meet him. He seemed like a decent enough guy. After we left, I asked Uncle Frank if John was from Montclair. He said he was from Newark, a tough street kid who needed a break.

I asked, "What did he mean when he said he owes you?"

He laughed and said, "You know, kid, you're such a lawyer. You ask so many questions. There are things I don't like to talk about."

"I just think it's odd that you have all this security and now a bodyguard. You're not doing anything illegal, are you, Uncle Frank?"

He stopped walking.

"No, kid, in spite of what your mother thinks, I'm a legitimate businessman who earns a lot of money. And like any other businessman, I have to be careful. *Madone!* You sound like a prosecutor, instead of a lawyer."

On the way home, I thought about Uncle Frank and his bodyguard, John. I knew my uncle helped a lot of people besides the family. I had heard stories about how he gave money to his friends, the church, and charities. Yet he never talked about his good deeds. To him, it was no big deal. I wondered, *What is the story behind John?*

I was beat when I got home. What a day!

I went to bed at twelve o'clock and before I knew it, I'm in the woods, crouched down. I'm looking and watching out for the German and Italian armies. The year is 1943, and I'm in a war zone in Italy during World War II. I'm beginning to get nervous. We're in a cramped area, and I'm afraid of what they'll do if they find us. There is a lot of underbrush and trees. There is so little room to spread out. Someone taps me on the shoulder. I turn. It's TC.

I ask, "What do you want from me?"

He replies, "What I want is what you're doing."

"What am I doing?"

"You're going to find the murderer, and justice will finally be served. And when you complete that mission, I'll be at peace—and so will you."

"Why me? Why did you pick me?"

"I didn't pick you." He smirks. "You were handed the gauntlet. All I know is you're here and I've been waiting for you to grow up. Why doesn't matter."

"It matters to me, TC."

TC starts to give us orders.

"Come on, guys, we have to go to the church."

"Wait," I whisper. "Why do we always have to go to the church?"

"Because we have to re-create the scene, you need see what happened so you will understand. That's where the murders took place."

"Someone was murdered in a church?"

"No, Frank, it wasn't just one murder; it was ten attempted murders, two were wounded and survived. It was a massacre. Frank, I have to go now. You're going to wake up. Find the owner of the gun and you'll find the murderer."

I started shouting, "That's not true. That can't be true."

I woke up, sweating like a pig and shaking all over. It can't be true. Pop couldn't have done such a horrendous thing. Oh, my God, what am I supposed to do? This will destroy the family, let alone what it would do to my grandfather if this ever got out. What does TC expect me to do—turn in my own grandfather for a crime that happened over sixty years ago?

It was impossible for me to get back to sleep. I felt angry and cursed. *Why is this happening to me?* I went down to the living room to clear my head. I thought, *If this doesn't stop, I might have to start smoking again. I wonder if I should stop the sessions with Dr. Bass. I don't want him or anyone else to know about Pop.*

Wait a minute. This is not real. I don't know that this is real. I could be making this up. This could all be just my imagination. Dr. Bass said it himself; hypnotherapy is not an exact science. It only brings your subconscious to the surface. The answer to how and why I developed this scenario still needs to be determined; I could be overreacting.

Even if it's true and this actually happened, a physician is bound by doctor-patient confidentiality. He can't tell anyone without my written consent.

I have to continue my sessions. I need his expertise in proving that this is a repetitious nightmare that has no validity. I think once I expose this as a fake, the nightmares will go away. Worst scenario: it's true and I was chosen, for God knows why, to right this terrible wrong. But what do I do about Pop? I'll have to protect him at any cost. He's old and what good would come out of exposing him now? He would have to go to jail. This is a war crime. He could be deported to Italy. My father and uncle will kill me. On the other hand, do I want to protect a murderer who committed this horrible crime, even if he is family?

I poured myself a large glass of scotch and went back to bed. Being awake was turning into as much of a nightmare as when I slept. *Thank God tomorrow is Sunday. I'm in no condition to go to work. I'll also give my mother a call and cancel dinner. Then I'll call Jessie and ask her if she wants to come over. I'm in no mood to be around my family.*

This time I waited for a more appropriate time to call everyone. I waited until 9:00 a.m. My mother was disappointed and tried to give me a guilt trip. When she realized it wasn't working, she put my dad on the phone. He was easy going and OK with me not coming for dinner. I then called Jessie.

She agreed to come over. In fact, she seemed happy that I invited her. She expressed her need for some R & R. She asked me how the hypnosis went. I told her I didn't want to go into detail, but that didn't stop her. She still went on with the third degree.

"Come on, Frank, tell me what happened."

"Look, Jessie, I'm tired of thinking and talking about it. Let's just have a good time today and not talk or think about anything negative."

"All right, Frank, you're on. I'll see you around eleven."

I was glad she stopped questioning me. Because of our close friendship, I tend to spill my guts and then resent her advice. I'm starting to sound like a whiner. I hate that in men. I don't want to sound like a wimp. Women should do the whining and the men the comforting. We're supposed to be the stronger sex.

It's hard to believe that in this day and age, I still think that way. Maybe it's the New Jersey male thing. You're supposed to take care of the little woman. She's not supposed to take care of you. It's amazing with all that education I'm still a chauvinistic bastard. I'm going to have to work on that. Jessie would have my head if she knew how I really felt.

I made a pot of coffee and straightened up the place. I took a shower and before I knew it, there was a knock on the door. I unlocked the door. Jessie walked in and we hugged. She whispered in my ear, "I've missed you. It's been a week since we've seen each other."

I went to pull away, but she pulled me back and kissed me.

I said, "Jessie."

"Be quiet, Frank, I know what I'm doing."

We kissed again and this time our tongues met. All that touching and caressing filled us with passion and the desire for more, much more. She wasn't wearing a bra and the touch of her erect nipples made me hot.

"Jessie, stop! I don't have a rubber down here. I'll have to go upstairs."

164

"You worry too much, Frank. I'm on the pill."

My mouth was so dry, I could hardly speak. My body was pulsating. We dropped to the floor, not wanting to break the spell. We couldn't get our clothes off fast enough. She was moaning, while I was thrusting. Before I knew it, it was over. We were both out of breath, content, and quiet. We wanted to savor the experience for as long as we could.

"You planned this, didn't you, Jessie? You seduced me, didn't you?"

She laughed. "Yes, I did. Now you just try telling that to the judge."

"I will. I'm very persuasive. But in the meantime, are you hungry?"

"I wasn't hungry when I got here, but after that workout, I'm famished."

"Well, Jessie, what do you say we take a shower and then go to brunch?"

I French kissed her again.

"You're the type of woman who knows and goes after exactly what she wants. Aren't you?"

She kissed me back.

"Yes, but in the end it backfires because I never seem to get what I want."

Chapter 18

I obviously felt a lot better on Monday morning. I had a good night's sleep, and I was ready to go over my one and only case with Junior. Although it was actually a pseudo case, I felt sure that I was the one in control. I was doing all of the footwork and research. Hopefully, Mark would go along with my recommendation on my defense strategy. This was a small case, but it was still going to be a challenge in trying to get our client off without any time. After all, any kind of hands-on experience was important when you're a greenhorn.

No sooner was I at my desk than Millie, Mark's secretary, called and announced that Mark wanted to see me and to bring my notes on the Dr. Fischer case. When I opened the door to his office, Mark was sitting at his desk. He looked up when he saw me standing in front of him.

"Have a seat, Frank. I'll be with you in a minute. I just have to finish signing some contracts."

I sat down in the soft leather chair that was in front of his desk. His office was really cool. All of the woodwork was done in a dark walnut finish. The ceilings were high. The top three quarters of the walls were dark green. The other portion was dark walnut paneling.

His desk and all the furniture matched. There was one wall with just windows overlooking the Hudson River. Next to the windows were a round table and four overstuffed chairs that matched the carpet. A brown leather sectional sofa was across from the windows, and the chairs in front of his desk were cream-colored tuft leather.

The carpet was a green, beige, black, and cream in an oriental style—very plush. No curtains on the windows, just wide blinds that must have been on a remote control device. They were so large. There were the usual paintings, licenses, and copies of his diplomas. Junior had great credentials. He graduated from Princeton University, just like I heard his dad did.

The one thing that struck me odd was the painting of his father, himself, and his brother. Again, it crossed my mind that they did not even resemble each other. Mark's father had more prominent features, and his coloring was much darker. The boys' complexions, on the other hand, were much lighter. I figured they must resemble their mother. Or maybe they were adopted, whatever. I began reading my notes.

Within a few minutes, Mark put down his pen and asked, "How was your weekend?"

"It was good, Mark," I said, although it really sucked. "How was yours?"

"I had to work all weekend. I'm sure you've heard the expression. 'Having your own business is not what it's cracked up to be.' Have you given much thought to the strategy we should use in the Fischer case?"

"Yes, I have."

"OK, Frank, let me hear it."

I handed him a copy of my notes.

"First, let me hear your thoughts before I go over the brief."

I told him I was confident that we could get him off.

"If we forget that he signed a confession," Mark said.

"No. I still think we may be able to have it thrown out. I say we go for the defense of temporary insanity."

"That's a great defense, Frank, but can we prove it? You do realize that very few cases have ever been won by using that strategy."

"I'm confident that that's the way to go, Mark. There were a lot of extenuating circumstances. And I think it would be harder trying to prove assisted suicide, for which he could still serve time. Plus, his confession stating that he killed his wife."

Mark reminded me that in the confession, Dr. Fischer stated that his wife begged him to end her suffering.

"That's true, Mark, but unless we have a witness, it's just hearsay. If we don't take the manslaughter plea, it will go to trial. The DA will say he's a physician, and being a physician, he knew exactly what he was doing. He knew that much morphine would kill her. Then they'll bring in the officer who arrested him as well as the two officers who interrogated him and got him to sign the confession. And then they will bring in a psychiatrist to say he was in his right mind when he did it."

"OK, Frank, you made an excellent case. Now tell me how we can prove he was insane at the time of the murder. How are we going to dispute the characterization you just described?"

"OK, let me lay out some of my evidence, and you tell me if we have a case. After all, you're the one with the experience. For one thing, there is motive. What's his motive? He's eighty, he's a physician, and he knew she would probably have died within the next few days or weeks. Even if he hated her, he had only a few more weeks to wait for her demise.

"Another thing, I have a copy of his confession. This document does not even resemble a man who knew what he was saying, let alone what he was doing."

Mark asked, "What do you mean?"

"His confession shows he was incoherent, spouting sentences."

"Of course, he must have been terribly upset."

"It's not just that, he wrote it like he was spaced out, out of touch with reality. They took his confession, word for word. The grammar was inconsistent for a man of his education, and his signature doesn't even look like his. Although I'm sure it is his, it's scribbled."

"Spell it out, Frank. What have you got?"

"The taped confession confirms that his words were slurred and his voice, incoherent. He was more than upset. He was on drugs."

"How do you know this? Do you have proof? And why didn't they test him for drugs when he was at the precinct?"

"I don't know why he wasn't tested. But nothing I have here indicates that he was. That's something we'll have to find out. It could be because he kept saying he killed his wife and they wanted to get his statement as quickly as possible."

"What kind of drug or drugs was he on?" Mark asked.

"Amphetamines. I can get his doctor to state that amphetamines are a stimulant drug that act on the nervous system, the brain, and the spinal cord. Large doses of amphetamines could cause psychosis and substance-related mental disorders. Add that to major depression and grief, and you have a man who was insane when he killed his wife.

"Last Tuesday, I went to visit Annabelle King, Dr. Fischer's daughter. And this is the statement she gave me." I opened the file on Mark's desk and handed him the testimonial.

Mother started to get sick about a year ago. My father took her to the best doctors in New York who diagnosed her with stomach cancer. My father would not accept that prognosis, so he took her to the best doctors in the United States. They all said the same thing. She was too old for the evasive drugs they would have to give her. And she would probably die anyway. They all recommended that he take her home and make her as comfortable as possible.

My father heard of this clinic in Mexico that could give her experimental medication that was illegal in this country. Nothing worked. They told him they were sorry, but there was nothing else they could do for her. When I picked them up at the airport, my father looked worse than my mother. He started grieving before her death.

When we arrived at the house, we put my mother to bed. My father refused to leave her bedside. He just sat and held her hand until she fell asleep, and then he started to cry. I told my father that my mother knew he did everything he could to help her. She was now in God's hands. He blamed himself. He stated that he killed her! I tried to reason with him. Everyone knew that he did everything humanly possible to save her life.

He got angry with me. He said he was a physician and he should have seen the signs. I reminded him that he was a cardiologist and that my mother had been seeing her own physician. And no one saw it coming until it was too late.

"Annabelle is willing to sign an affidavit or go to court if it comes to that. She will state that he told her he killed his wife before she even passed away. I called Mrs. Fischer's doctor, Dr. Roberts, and asked for an appointment to interview him about his patient Mrs. Fischer. He agreed and I went there last Wednesday. I got some very pertinent information that could also help Dr. Fischer's case."

"Go on, Frank, you're doing quite well."

I went on to say, "It seems their nurse came in during the day. She worked from eight o'clock in the morning till six in the evening. She left right after she gave Mrs. Fischer her dinner and medication, although most of her nutrients were administered intravenously.

"A couple of weeks ago, Dr. Fischer asked him for a prescription for stimulants so he could stay awake during the evening to attend to his wife's needs. Dr. Roberts said he didn't like the idea and suggested getting an evening nurse. Dr. Fischer said that wasn't necessary, that most of her care was administered during the day and she slept most of the night. Dr. Fischer just wanted to stay awake a few hours longer in case she needed him. Dr. Roberts gave him a prescription and told him he should take just one a day around midafternoon. This should have kept Dr. Fischer alert for a couple of hours longer than usual. He gave him a two-month supply."

"When he was called in to sign Mrs. Fischer's death certificate, he saw an empty bottle of the prescription he'd given Dr. Fischer sitting on the night table. He will also sign an affidavit and will appear in court, if necessary, stating that if Dr. Fischer took that many tablets in that short a time, he may not have known right from wrong when he administered the morphine to his wife. And in his condition, it could have been an accident."

"This is good work, Frank. I'll bring in a psychiatrist to examine him. Also, speak to the nurse and some of his friends. I'm sure there are other people who must have seen a big change in his behavior leading up to the death of Mrs. Fischer. Let's see what the shrink says and if he agrees that Dr. Fischer is mentally incompetent. I would think the district attorney would likely dismiss the case rather than lose if we go to trial. Although, if they find him insane at the time of the murder, he will have to go to a clinic for treatment for severe depression and drug dependency, which is still a lot better than jail. Now I just hope we can get Dr. Fischer to go along with our defense."

I left Mark's office feeling pretty good about this case, but I still had to call Barbara Tate, the nurse, and get her story. I worked all morning, finalizing the Fischer case, and I still had the afternoon to visit Barbara Tate if she was available. I telephoned her to see if she would see me.

Barbara Tate indicated that she really didn't have much to tell me, but she was in between jobs right now and I could come over sometime in the afternoon. We made an appointment for two o'clock.

She lived downtown, so I took a cab to her apartment. Although she might have thought she had nothing to offer, I had a feeling her statement would either help our case or even hinder it.

When I arrived, I asked her if she minded that I taped our conversation. She said she didn't mind.

My first question was, "Had you noticed a difference in Dr. Fischer's behavior within the last couple of weeks?"

Barbara stated that she had noticed a big difference in Dr. Fischer the week before his wife died. She noticed considerable weight loss and even spoke to him about it. She told him he needed to eat if he wanted to keep up his strength to help his wife get through this. He said he had trouble keeping food down and wasn't really hungry.

She said he looked disheveled. He'd stopped shaving and combing his hair. And his clothes looked like he slept in them. "When I was hired to take care of Mrs. Fischer, Dr. Fischer's appearance was that of a man who had pride in his appearance, but for the past few weeks, he didn't even look like the same person."

I asked her about his manner.

"He was depressed. He seemed down like anyone would be under the circumstances."

My next question was, "Did he act like any normal man would under these circumstances?"

"No, he was different."

"In what way?"

"Well, like I had told the detectives, his appearance for one. And he appeared to be exceptionally nervous. His hands would shake. He even had outbursts."

"What kind of outbursts?"

"Mumbling and crying."

"Did you ever hear Mrs. Fisher ask Dr. Fischer to help her die?"

She hesitated.

"Yes, I did once. It was two weeks ago. I was just about to walk into the room when I heard her say in a very low voice, 'If you loved me, you would help me die. Don't worry, my dearest, I will see you on the other side.'"

"What did he say?"

"Nothing. He said nothing. I pretended not to hear and went on with my duties."

"If you noticed these changes in Dr. Fischer, why didn't you tell his doctor?"

"I was about to when Dr. Roberts called me to tell me that Mrs. Fischer had died."

I asked Barbara if she would sign a statement to the effect of what she had just told me.

"Yes, if you like, I will."

I shut off the tape recorder and asked Barbara, "Off the record, Barbara, how do you personally feel about assisted suicide?"

"I'm a religious person, Mr. Scarpelli. I couldn't or wouldn't do it to myself or anyone else. But then, no one knows what they would do if they were in the amount of pain and suffering that Mrs. Fischer was. We had to increase the dose of morphine on a daily basis. It could have been an accident."

She'd done it. She'd admitted that it could have been an accident.

I thanked Barbara Tate and left feeling very sorry for a man who had been put in Dr. Fischer's position. I wondered if I'd get used to hearing these sad stories.

When I got home, I started thinking about TC and all those people who were killed in the church. If it was true, that was premeditated murder. I had to talk to someone. I needed some advice. *I should call Dr. Bass and tell him about the last sequence of my dream.* I was in such deep thought that when my cell phone rang, it startled me.

It was Jessie. She was her usual cheerful self.

"Hi, Frank. I just called to see how your week was going so far. I'm going on a field trip to the Museum of the City of New York, and I wondered if you would meet me there and help me keep an eye on the kids."

"Are you out of your fuckin' mind?"

She laughed. "Got you! I knew that would be your reaction." She kept on laughing.

"You know what, Jessie? I'm going to hang up now. Right now, I'm not in the mood for this."

Her voice got really quiet. "What's the matter, Frank, you sound terrible. What's wrong?"

"Nothing you could fix, so let me hang up."

"Frank, I'm coming over. I've never heard you like this. What happened? Is it your job?"

"No, it's not my job. In fact, right now that's the only normal thing in my life. Please, Jessie, don't be offended, but I'm going to hang up now."

Her last words were, "I'm coming over."

Forty-five minutes later, Jessie was knocking at my door.

I opened it.

"Do you want a beer?"

"You scared the shit out of me, and all you can say is, 'You want a beer?'"

"I asked you not to come here."

"I know, but I'm here anyway. You would do the same for me; at least I hope you would."

I just looked at her and laughed. I couldn't help it. She was wearing a jogging outfit that was two sizes too big, and she hadn't bothered to put makeup on. She looked funny but cute.

She took the beer I handed her, and we sat on the couch. I started telling her about my sessions with Dr. Bass and the dream I had the other night, the gun in the closet, and my grandfather's refusal to admit that he was from Sicily and not Naples.

After I finished, she reminded me that I was assuming that TC was a real person.

"What proof do you have that this massacre actually took place? You said it's a dream."

"I know what I said, but don't forget about the hypnosis."

"That's not concrete proof, Frank. You're assuming your dreams are real."

I reminded her that it seemed that Dr. Bass might also agree with that assumption.

"God, Frank, you're an attorney. You should know the difference."

"Thanks for reminding me of my shortcomings, Jessie, as if I don't feel crappy enough."

"Well," she stated, "If you really want to know the truth, find out. Either go online or hire a private investigator."

"I know, I could have investigated this all along. Don't you understand the implication of this? You're obviously not getting the full picture here. What if it's true, and what if my grandfather actually did this horrible thing? What do I do, turn him in to the authorities? I can't do that. And I'm sure my feelings for him will change. That alone will hurt him. Sure, I think about the families of the victims. They have a right to have justice done, but either way, it will destroy my whole family if I pursue this. I've come too far, and now I don't know how to stop it."

She leaned over, put her arms around me, and held me close.

"Frank, you are the most just and fair-minded person I know. I also know that when the time comes, you will do the right thing."

As gentlemanly as possible, I said, "Are you trying to coerce me into having sex with you?"

"You conceited bastard!" she yelled.

I laughed so hard at the expression on her face, I could hardly catch my breath.

She handed me her empty beer bottle.

"I'll have another. Thank you."

184

Jessie stayed a couple of hours, and I was really glad she showed up. It was good to get it off my chest. Before she left, we had decided she would help me with the research. She had a couple of days off from school, some kind of teachers' convention, so she had the time. She promised to get back to me with whatever she found out, even if she thought it would upset me. We also discussed hiring a private investigator, but Jessie was sure she could go online and get all the information she needed. At the door, she kissed me on the cheek. And then she French kissed me.

I went to bed soon after she left and had a great night's sleep. Pop would be coming here on Thursday, and I had to get my shit together.

Chapter 19

It's Thursday morning. Pop and John should have arrived at my place. The previous night, I did some grocery shopping. I tried to remember all of Pop's favorite foods. Fresh fruit was one thing I knew he liked, as well as eggs and bacon—although, with his heart problems, that wasn't the best thing for him. Cheese—all kinds of cheese—crackers, cold cuts, and he also liked tomato juice. I bought a couple of bottles of *vino*. He loved Chianti. I figured we would eat our dinners out.

I never thought about John. I wondered if he planned on staying overnight. It was a two-bedroom condo. *Where the hell would he sleep?* The only bed big enough for him was mine. *Shit!*

When I got home, Pop and John were watching the news. John was drinking a beer, and Pop was drinking his Chianti in a drinking glass. He always drank his wine in just a regular drinking glass.

I said, "Hello," to John and shook his hand. Pop stood so he could give me a hug. I felt so damn guilty. I was sorry I ever started this mess. What was this going to do to our relationship?

I asked Pop how his day was and where he had gone. He seemed happy and excited when he told me he had gone to the Metropolitan Museum. But he also confessed it was hard for him to walk around too long. So John took him back to my place to take a nap.

He told John he could leave if he had other things to do. But John wouldn't leave until I got home.

At that point, I realized that John had not said a word since I walked in the door.

"Well, John, I'm here now. It's OK for you to leave. And I want to thank you for taking such good care of my grandfather."

"I'm not leaving," John finally said in that deep voice of his.

"It's OK. You can go now. Come back tomorrow morning around eight o'clock."

Again, John said, "I'm not leaving. The boss said I should stay with Mr. Scarpelli, so I'm staying here until you take your grandfather to Albert's house on Saturday."

I knew by the tone of his voice there was no getting rid of him.

"OK. What do you both want for dinner?"

Pop said, "Pasta. I want pasta."

"Is that OK with you, John?"

He nodded.

"All right, there's a great Italian restaurant just a couple of doors down the street. We can walk to it, but first I'd like to change clothes."

The elevator ride from my apartment to the vestibule was quite embarrassing. It's quite obvious I look Italian. It's also quite obvious the three of us look Italian. You would think, no big deal. But at this time of night, everyone in the building was coming home from work or going somewhere, and the elevator was more crowded than usual. Here I was with this big galoot who not only looked like a bodyguard, he stood like a bodyguard.

He seemed to scrutinize everyone who came in and then out of the elevator. And to make matters worse, he stood in front of me and Pop, as if to protect us from anyone getting too close. Talk about profiling; I got some very strange looks. I'm sure they must have thought we were either gangsters or we were in the witness protection program.

As soon as we entered the restaurant, we were immediately seated. One look at John and they didn't want any trouble. This was really good for my image. *I'm going to kill my uncle. Tomorrow night, we'll order takeout.*

It was no surprise that John wound up in my room, Pop in his, and me on the couch. With John there, I didn't even have the time to talk to my grandfather about his immigration papers or the people in the album. I'm not even sure he could remember anyway. It was such a long time ago. Maybe it was for the best. He's not well and there was no point in upsetting him.

Saturday finally arrived and in spite of my doubts, I really enjoyed their company. After Pop went to bed, John and I drank, watched the sports channel, and played poker. He won two hundred bucks from me. If he didn't leave soon, I would be speaking just like him. It took me six years to get rid of my Jersey accent.

As it turned out, I was able to complete my part of the Fischer case, and the file was left on Junior's desk to be reviewed on Monday.

When we were all getting ready to leave, I hugged Pop and told him how much I enjoyed having him stay with me. He had tears in his eyes and thanked me for having him. He kissed me on both cheeks.

I offered John three hundred dollars for taking care of Pop, but he refused to take it. He told me the boss had already taken care of him. And he liked being with the old guy.

John encouraged me to go to my appointment and that he would drive my grandfather to my parents' place. I thanked him and shook his hand. He was a good guy. Without him, watching over Pop and working would have been difficult. I would have been ill at ease, knowing that he was walking around this big city all alone.

Once we got over to the Jersey side, we all decided to stop for breakfast. Pop drove with me until we got to the diner. I kept looking over at him. He was in such a good mood, smiling and making conversation. He told me how much he enjoyed these past few days with me. It made me think how much I dreaded my appointment with Dr. Bass. *I think I'll tell him to drop this whole mess.*

We stopped at a diner in Clifton, and I've got to say, I was getting used to being seated immediately and getting served quickly. *I ought to bring John with me the next time I go to the Marriott.*

While driving to the doctor's office in Montclair, I got a call from Jessie. She wanted to know the time I'd be leaving the doctor's office. I told her it would probably around twelve o'clock.

"Why?" I asked her.

She asked me to stop at her house after my session, that it was important that we talk.

"I want to show you something, Frank."

"What? Tell me now."

"No, not now. I'll see you later."

"Great."

Talk about opening a can of worms.

I was ten minutes late in getting to the office. This time, Dr. Bass was waiting for me in the waiting room.

"Hi, Frank. I was beginning to think that you weren't going to show."

"Sorry I'm late, Doc. To tell you the truth, I was hesitant about coming in. I had decided I no longer wanted to participate in hypnotherapy."

"Frank, come on in the office so we can discuss the progress you've made so far."

We walked in and I took the chair in front of his desk.

"What progress?" I asked.

His response was that the use of hypnosis opened a lot of doors and may have gotten us closer to the truth.

"But they're not facts. And it still has to be authenticated. We still need to know whether those episodes are true or a figment of your imagination."

My response to his analysis was, "All I know is I not only still have the nightmares, I'm also experiencing daytime anxiety."

"Think about it, Frank. Isn't that why you came here? Wasn't it to get to the truth? And now that we're getting close to making headway into your subconscious, your fears are starting to surface. Let's talk about what you're afraid of: First, you thought you would die if you let the dream take you to the end. But now you know it's not death you're afraid of. It's the truth."

I became defensive. "Forgive me, Dr. Bass, but what the hell are you talking about?"

"You tell me, Frank. You're the one that's holding back a kind of hypothesis that you're afraid to confront. Isn't that right?"

I started to deny his accusation but decided that there was no point in lying. Dr. Bass was trying to help me. *Isn't that what I'm paying him for? Besides, it might eventually come out anyway.*

I told him what TC had said in my last dream.

"I asked TC what he wanted from me. He said I was doing exactly what he wanted. I asked him in what way was I helping him. He said I was going to find the murderer and justice will be served. And when that was done, we will all be at peace, including me. I asked him why he picked me. He said he didn't pick me. He said some crap like I was handed the gauntlet. He claims they have been waiting for me to grow up. I also asked TC why we always go to the church. His answer was, to re-create the scene because that's where the murders took place. I asked him, What murders? He said there were ten attempted murders, but two were wounded. It was a massacre. And his last words were, 'Find the owner of the gun, and you'll find the murderer.'"

Dr. Bass look stunned.

"Did you check to see if a massacre took place in Italy in 1943?" he asked.

"No, I haven't had time. I've confided in a friend, and she's helping me with the research."

"To tell you the truth, Frank, this is uncanny. I now see why you're hesitant in going through with this. You're afraid for your grandfather and the fallout from your family."

"You've got it right. My grandfather is in his mid-eighties and he's ill. What do I do? Turn him into the authorities?"

"So you have already convicted him. Just because he lied about where he was born and he owns a German Lugar?"

"Yes, to me, the evidence is overwhelming."

"Really! Why? Has he ever shown any sign of violence? Does he fly off the handle easily? Did he beat his children?"

"No to all your questions. Pop was so distraught when his wife died that he never remarried. As far as I know, he never even looked at another woman. I assume it was because he loved her. Of course, he had to work hard; he raised his two children by himself. He never had any family support. I assume they stayed in Italy."

"Frank, does he meet the profile of a mass murderer?"

"I'm not sure, Doc. Lately, I haven't been sure of anything. I only know that the evidence is leading up to him and it's tearing me apart."

"Let's play devil's advocate. Even if it's true, you need to know, or you will never be free of your nightmares. Can you live with that?"

"But what if it's true? What do I do? Turn in my own grandfather?"

"What about the victims' families, Frank? Don't their families need closure?"

"I know! But what has all this got to do with me? Why has this been tormenting me since I was a kid?"

He walked over to me and put his hand on my shoulder.

"Frank, those are the questions you're unwilling to find the answers to. One thing I do know: if this is not resolved, the guilt could destroy you. You may have to confront your grandfather."

"I can't do that. He's an old man with a bad heart. I don't take only him down; my whole family goes with him—including my own career. My father and uncle are respected businessmen. If this gets out, it could destroy their businesses. Tell me, Doc, will I feel any better knowing the truth? Just dealing with what I know now is killing me."

"Frank, you're upset and understandably so. I'm just trying to encourage you not to jump to conclusions until you know all the facts. Dealing with the what-ifs is harder than dealing with reality. I don't think we should go on with the hypnotherapy today. I suggest you check into TC's account of what happened to see if it's true. And then we can go from there. Don't forget to let me know if any changes take place. And I shouldn't have to tell an attorney, you're innocent until proven guilty. I'm here for you, Frank. We can see this through together."

I felt somewhat relieved. At least I had someone to talk to.

On my way to Jessie's house, I thought about what Dr. Bass had said.

"You're innocent until proven guilty."

I, of all people, should adhere to that doctrine. I studied the law, for God's sakes. I'm allowing my dreams and relevant evidence to cloud my objectiveness because it's personal. And I'm scared of what the outcome could be.

As soon as I pulled up to Jessie's house, I experienced that feeling of fight or flight. I wanted to flee but didn't. I walked up to the door, but before I could knock, it opened and a somber Jessie asked me to come in.

I got a sinking feeling in the pit of my stomach like I knew what she was about to say.

She motioned for me to sit on the couch and handed me some printouts that were on the coffee table.

"It's all here in black and white, Frank. TC was right. There was a massacre in 1943 in a church named Cathedral Monreale—Sicily, Italy. It seems the United States and England launched a campaign called *HUSKY* to try and take control of the Mediterranean Passageway. By the time they got to Sicily, the Germans were already there. There's a lot of information about the campaign. It's all in the documents I'll be giving you. Also, online, I obtained a list of the men and women in the service who died in combat. A Thomas Callahan from Philadelphia was listed as being killed in Sicily during that *HUSKY* campaign. Frank, I hate telling you this, but your dreams are true. This is all so weird. What are you going to do?"

I tried composing myself. "I don't know what I'm going to do. All I know is I have to prove Pop's innocence."

"How are you going to prove that? It happened sixty-four years ago. What about the gun?"

"I don't know how, Jessie, but I have to. TC said the murderer is the person who owned the gun. We don't know if Pop owned the gun. He could have bought the gun or maybe someone gave him the gun to hold for him or her. Or maybe he found the gun."

"Well, Frank, we're either jumping to conclusions, or you're grasping for straws. There is only one way you're going to get straight answers. You're going to have to speak to your grandfather."

"I don't have to get any answers. I can drop the whole thing."

"You can't do that, Frank!"

"Yes, I can. Who's going to stop me?"

Jessie stared at me with disgust in her eyes. "You can't do that. It was a massacre. Eight people are dead and two innocent people were wounded. Don't you understand that you will never be at peace if you do nothing? And you will live to regret it for the rest of your life."

I was starting to get pissed and lashed out at her. "I will live to regret it if I do. Can't you understand he's my grandfather? You know him. Can you see him doing this horrible thing?"

"No, I can't. That's why we have to find out who really did it."

"Jessie, give me one good reason why this can't wait until he dies? He's a sick man. He can go at any time."

"Frank, listen to yourself. Did it ever cross your mind that your grandfather may want to repent? He is Catholic. Or maybe he knows who did this."

"I know who did this, Jessie."

"You do? Who is it?"

"Mario Moretti killed those people."

"Well then, Frank, what's the problem? Let's look for Mario Moretti."

"The problem is, whoever did this must have another identity. I'm sure there is still a warrant out for his arrest."

"That's true, but it's not that easy to hide. We now have computers and access to all kinds of information, and don't forget DNA and fingerprints."

I said, "Do you think that after sixty-four years and countless people holding the gun, including me, they will find any evidence of fingerprints?"

"Frank, if you knew the name of the person who did this, why didn't you tell me that before?"

"It just came to me when I was under hypnosis. TC revealed the name of the murderer."

"Frank, why don't we see if we can find him?"

"I wouldn't know where to start. Let's use that strategy first, before going to my grandfather for some answers."

"You know, Frank, you can always go to TC for more information."

"I realize that, but that's an option. I want to waive that until I have no other choice."

Jessie came over to the couch, sat down, and put her head on my shoulder. She asked in a soft and gentle voice, "Do you want to go to lunch, or do you want to eat here? I can make us something to eat in no time."

"Thanks for the offer, but if you don't mind, I just want to head home. I have to absorb all of this and see where I'm going to go from here. I also have to read over the information you gave me and do some investigating on my own."

I got up and walked out.

When I got home, I was emotionally exhausted. I had to think, but for now I had to run and clear my head. I put on my running gear and headed for the park. I ran like I had never run before.

After, I stopped at Nate's, picked up a couple of hot dogs, and went home. Instead of trying to sort things out, I decided not to think about it for the rest of the evening. I watched TV and downed four scotch and sodas.

I also tried studying but couldn't concentrate. So I went to bed after the eleven o'clock news and prayed that I wouldn't have to deal with my dreams tonight. I finally fell asleep and slept peacefully all evening.

Chapter 20

I dressed carefully on Monday morning. I was sure Junior would be call-ing me into his office to discuss the Fischer case.

I stopped at Starbucks on my way to the office and even picked up a latte for Darlene. I walked into her office with a smile on my face, but she was looking out the window of her office. Not wanting to startle her, I cleared my throat. She turned, so I reached out and handed her the coffee.

"I thought you might be needing this."

She forced a smile.

"Thanks, Frank, I certainly do. How did you know?"

"Intuition. And it's Monday. Darlene, are you OK? Do you want to talk?"

"About what?"

"It's obvious something is bothering you."

"It's nothing, Frank. I'm just out of sorts today."

"OK, but if you change your mind, you know where to find me."

Darlene forced another smile.

"Thanks for the offer and the latte."

I sat at my desk and noticed a pile of briefs in my in basket with a Post-it note saying: *Frank, you have to review these briefs by tomorrow. The meeting will start at 10:30 a.m. Mark Junior, will be in attendance. Joan.*

I thought, *Thank you, Joan, for giving me fair warning that Mark would be at that meeting.* I had just started to read the first case when Darlene walked in my office and closed the door.

She sat across from my desk and said, "I think I owe you an explanation."

I asked, "Are you OK? Are you sick? Was there a death in the family? What's going on?"

"I broke off my engagement to Bruce."

I tried not to sound too ecstatic.

"Why? What happened?"

"I'm not sure, Frank. It was a few things, little things."

She broke off her engagement for "little things"? It didn't compute.

"OK, like what?"

"He decided he wanted to get married sooner than we planned."

"How much sooner?"

"Next month. And that he decided to do his residency in California and not New York like we had planned. He also wanted me to put my career on hold and have a baby."

"What? Give up your career? Boy, that's a hell of a lot of nerve."

She smiled. "And that's exactly what I told him when I handed him his ring."

"Have you really thought about this, Darlene? Are you sure you won't regret this in a couple of weeks or even months?"

She looked somber but not really upset.

"No, I don't think so. I was starting to have reservations."

"About what? Can you be more specific?"

"Oh, I don't know, Frank. I guess I was questioning as to whether I was really in love with Bruce or if I just loved him."

I asked, "Is there a difference?"

She smiled. "You know what, Frank, you think about it. I have to go back to work now."

She opened the door and left. And there I sat in a state of confusion. *Women!*

As soon as I got home, I changed into my jeans, made a very large ham sandwich, got a beer, and went into my office to do some research on my computer. It was time to get down to business and to start looking for Mario Moretti.

I checked the State Department Web site, the office of war crimes. The Coalition for International Justice and the International Criminal Tribunal were looking for twenty-one fugitives. And none were from WWII. I then checked the WWII site and found the *HUSKY* campaign but no information that pertained to civilians. I wondered if the Pentagon had a file that was open to the public, like the Freedom of Information Act.

I was about to start looking when the phone rang. To my surprise, it was Darlene.

"Frank, I'll come to the point. I've been walking around for an hour. I'm just too tired to walk around anymore. Can I come up to your place? I don't want to go home yet. I just want some company."

"Sure, Darlene. You could stay the night if you want."

"For heaven's sakes, how can you hit on me at a time like this? Grow up. And if you think this is more than what it is, forget it."

"I'm sorry, Darlene. That was a very bad joke and a very insensitive remark. Why don't I pick you up? Where are you?"

"No, thanks. I'll just catch a cab."

I gave Darlene my address and called down to Harvey, the doorman, to let her in when she arrived.

I was starting to get excited at the prospect of seeing her. I had to remind myself what she needed was a friend. It was the only reason she was coming over. I knew how she felt. I would rather confide in a friend than tell my family anything that was bothering me. It's not that they're not supportive. It's that they don't just listen. They give advice and then they get upset when you don't take it. I hate when they treat me like a kid.

I don't think it took me more than six seconds to answer the doorbell. When I opened the door, she looked like she had been crying.

I gave her a friendly hug.

"Come in. Have a seat. Would you like a glass of wine or some sherry?"

"Wine would be nice, Frank, thanks."

She walked into the living room. "This is some place you have here. I had no idea that you had this kind of money."

"I'm not. I'm leasing it from a friend. Unfortunately, it's just temporary."

"I didn't think you bought this on your salary. And if you did, I'm not getting paid nearly as much as you are.

"I hope I'm not intruding, Frank. It was nice of you to see me."

I was starting to feel sorry for her. I just didn't know what I could say that would make her feel better. Historically, I got nervous when I saw her and I usually put my big foot in my mouth.

"You're not disturbing me, Darlene. I enjoy the company. Can I get you something to eat? Do you want a ham sandwich? Do you want to just talk?"

She laughed. "No, thanks! I'll just finish my wine and let you get on with whatever you've been doing."

"You don't have to leave. I was just on my computer, doing some research and searching the Web."

"What were you looking for? Maybe I can help."

"I doubt it!"

"You never know, Frank. I'm pretty smart."

"I'm not exactly surprised. I knew that from the moment I met you."

"Oh, right, that's why you asked me if I was hired to be your secretary?"

"See, you're not only smart, you also have a great memory. I knew you weren't hired to be my secretary. I was trying to make conversation."

"You know what, Frank?"

I leaned in just a little closer.

She leaned in even closer to me and whispered, "You are so full of shit!"

192

The remark came at the exact moment that I'd taken a mouthful of beer. It was so unexpected I started choking.

Darlene asked, "Are you all right?"

She started pounding me on my back. I stood up to catch my breath, and she stood up to slap me on my back. I turned and faced her. I looked into those beautiful brown eyes and thought, *She is going to hate me for this.* I put my arms around her and kissed her beautiful lips. Surprisingly, she responded and then pulled back.

"I'm sorry, Darlene. I know you're going to hate me, but I couldn't help it. I'm very fond of you."

"It's OK, Frank. I wanted you to kiss me."

I held her in my arms and kissed her again. This time, she didn't pull away. She responded.

A thought came to me, and I opened my big mouth again. "Am I playing second fiddle here?"

"What?"

I asked, "Are you on the rebound?"

She laughed so hard that she was doubled over.

I asked her, "What's so damn funny?"

"Frank, you jerk, you're the reason for my breakup with Bruce."

"What did I do to break you up?"

"I was having reservations about marrying Bruce because of the way I was feeling about you. And to tell you the truth, I'm not sure what this feeling is. I'm not even sure if you feel the same about me. That's the real reason I'm here."

She started to cry. First she was laughing, and then she was crying.

I didn't know what to do.

"Darlene, sweetheart, please don't cry. I haven't had a lot of experience with women, and you're freaking me out. I don't know what to do. I don't even know what to say."

She stopped crying, walked into my arms, and kissed me.

I whispered, "All I know is I liked this scene a hell of a lot."

"Frank we have to take this slow to see where it's going."

"How slow?" I asked.

"We have to get to know each other on a personal level."

"What's to know, Darlene? I know you. You know me."

"I don't know anything about you, Frank. And you don't know anything about me or my family. We don't have to do this now."

I asked her, "What do you want to do now?" And then I suggested we sit on the couch and make out.

"No. I don't think so. Just let me help you find what you're looking for on the Internet."

"Damn," I said, "wrong answer. OK, you can help me, but that may be difficult."

"Just try me, Mr. Scarpelli. I'm a computer whiz."

"OK, here goes: A friend of mine came from Italy. Actually, it was Sicily in the town of Palermo. He had a relative that was murdered. He knows the name of the person who killed him, but he doesn't know where to find him; he's been missing for sixty-four years. He now wants to find him and bring him in."

"Frank, this sounds like something the authorities should be investigating."

"Yes, except that it happened in 1943."

"That was during World War II."

"Now do you see my dilemma?"

"Was he an Italian soldier?"

"No. He was supposed to be a partisan. But it turns out he was actually a spy for the Germans. He killed five American soldiers and several of his patriots."

"Who is your friend?"

"Just someone from my hometown in New Jersey."

"I may be able to help, Frank."

"I don't know, Darlene. I've already checked the State Department Web site, the Office of War Crimes, the Coalition for International Justice, and the International Criminal Tribunal. I was just going to check the Pentagon to see if I could find that person's name."

She asked me the name of the person I was looking for.

"His name is Mario Moretti."

As she was writing, she repeated the name.

I asked her where she thought she could find it.

"That's too much trouble, Frank. I'll ask my father."

"Who's your daddy?"

She gave half of a smile. "Is that supposed to be funny?"

"I don't know, Darlene, I thought it was."

She started laughing. "Frank, you're a trip. But to answer your question, my 'daddy' is Matthew Walker Banks. I'm sure you've heard of him."

"I don't believe this. You're four-star General Banks's daughter?"

"Apparently so. He might be able to find this under the Freedom of Information Act. But I can't make any promises; after all, Mario was an Italian civilian. Frank, did you check to see if he came to the United States? Look under Ellis Island to see if he's listed."

"Great idea, sweetheart. I'm glad you showed up to help."

She smiled. "I'm glad I could be of some help. My problem seems infinitesimal compared to the real problems in the world. You helped me put things in perspective. Thank you! You know, I'm starting to get hungry. I think I'll take that ham sandwich now—with mustard and hold the mayo. And if you have any coffee, I like it black."

"You see, Darlene. We do have something in common. That's exactly the way I take my ham and coffee."

When I awoke the next morning, I was in a great mood. Before Darlene left, we checked the listing of immigrants coming into the country from 1943 to 1950. Although, it was quite obvious if he came into this country, he would have changed his name and used forged documents. I doubted that someone as devious as Mario would have had any problem in obtaining them.

Darlene was going to see if she could find out if he tried to enter Canada. It was a kick working with her and having her so near. I hated to see her leave. I suggested she stay the night, but she felt we didn't know each other well enough. I hoped getting to know each other wasn't going to take too long.

There was something about the way she smelled. I don't know what it was, but it was potent. I wondered if that was what they called pheromones. Or she just had the greatest perfume in the world. All I know is I wanted to see a lot more of her.

I also wondered if I should come clean with her about why I was looking for Mario. On second thought, I'd have to know her a lot better before I could trust her, like I did Jessie.

Oh boy, come to think about it, what about Jessie? I can't get into all this now. I have to go to work.

As soon as I entered my office, there was a note and a Starbucks coffee on my desk. The note was simple: *Thanks for last night.*

I called her office and she answered.

"Thanks for the coffee and last night. It was great but not as eventful as I would have liked."

She started laughing. "Listen, Mr. Future Attorney. Watch what you say in an office. It could be misconstrued as sexual harassment."

"Come on, now. Did I say anything about sex? You're the one with the dirty mind."

And then I hung up.

The staff meeting was in a few of hours, so it gave me time to review the briefs and my notes. I was so engrossed in my work that I hadn't noticed that Mark had entered my office.

"I thought I would find you hard at work and not at the water cooler," he said. "That is my feeble attempt at a joke. How are you, Frank?"

"I'm good, Mark. Did you get my notes and testimonials on the Fischer case?"

"Yes, that's why I'm here. I'm going to go with your recommendation for the insanity plea. Annabelle King will be arriving at our office this afternoon, accompany her will be her father and a Dr. Morris Baker. Dr. Baker is the founder of the Baker Clinic in upstate New York. If they can get Dr. Fischer to go along with the plea, I'll setup an appointment to meet with the district attorney to see if we can do some plea-bargaining.

"I would like you to attend both these meetings. How is your schedule?"

"I'm open and I'll be glad to attend. Thanks for the opportunity."

"You earned it, Frank. That was good work. You convinced me he was out of his mind. Now let's see if you can convince the DA. I'll have Millie give you a call as soon as they arrive. They're due here around one o'clock this afternoon."

I was a little disappointed that I would have to skip lunch. I thought I would take that time to do some investigating on Mario Moretti.

It was about ten after one when Millie called to tell me that Annabelle King, Dr. Fischer, and Dr. Baker had arrived and they were waiting for me.

After the introductions, Dr. Baker gave us his statement: Annabelle had contacted him, knowing that he has had great success in treating mental disorders and addictions. She informed me that her father's attorney had requested that her father, Dr. Fischer, be given a complete physical and psychological evaluation. Although he had read about the case in the newspaper, he had never met Dr. Fischer until last week.

"I agreed to see him only if Annabelle would bring him to the clinic for testing, that he and his associate would have to base their evaluation on the results of the tests."

Dr. Baker also told us that Dr. Fisher stayed at the clinic for three days. Within that time, he and his associate Dr. Evan Smith gave him a complete physical and the usual standard tests to evaluate his competency, sanity, and the degree for which he was responsible, or not responsible, for his actions.

"Dr. Smith and I both agree and could say for certain that Dr. Fischer was not in his right mind when he gave his wife the lethal overdose of morphine or, for that matter, when he signed a confession stating that he deliberately killed her."

He pulled a file out of his briefcase that he said were the test results. If it went to trial, both he and Dr. Smith would testify on Dr. Fischer's behalf.

Dr. Baker presented Mark with a testimonial, alluding to his findings for the district attorney.

Mark thanked Dr. Baker and took his analysis and deposition. He told him we would contact him, should it go to trial. On the other hand, we would try to get the DA's office to drop the charges of manslaughter. If he did, I was sure he would want some kind of assurance that Dr. Fischer would go into a treatment program and that he would be confined to the Baker Clinic until he was well enough to leave.

During this whole time, Dr. Fischer sat quietly, never saying a word. It was quite obvious that he was deeply depressed and he couldn't have cared less about what his fate would be. When his wife died, his world ceased to exist. It was very odd for a physician who had seen death so many times before.

Before we went to the DA's office, Mark wanted to be reassured that Dr. Fischer would go along with the insanity plea.

"Dr. Fischer?"

He did not consent nor did he reply. Realizing that her father was ignoring the proceedings and would not reply to any questions, Dr. Fisher's daughter leaned in toward her father and spoke to him in a very low voice.

"Dad, you have to agree to the plea. Do you understand what's at stake here?"

He just nodded his head yes.

"OK, everyone," Mark declared. "Let's get going. We have to be in Michael's office in twenty minutes."

Mark called Millie and asked her to have the chauffeur bring his car around to the front of the building. We had no time to lose.

We arrived at the DA's office just a few minutes late and were escorted into Michael Bonito's office. We all introduced ourselves. It was the first time I had met Michael Bonito, and I was a little surprised by his appearance. He looked to be in his early forties, balding, short, portly, and casually dressed—actually a little sloppy, no tie and a couple of stains on his shirt.

We went over all the statements of the people we interviewed, as well as the evaluation of Dr. Fischer's competency at the time of his wife's death and at the time he signed the confession.

Michael was very thorough and looked over every bit of the information we brought to the table.

He said, "OK, I'll plea it down to second- or third-degree manslaughter—three to seven years. With good behavior, he'll be out in three years."

Mark stated, "That's unacceptable. For God's sakes, Michael, Dr. Fischer is in his eighties."

I decided to put in my two cents' worth.

"What we have here, Michael, is an old man, a reputable heart surgeon. If we take this to court, chances are you'll lose. Besides the cost of the trial, think of the publicity. The DA's office is going after an eighty-year-old respected cardiologist without a blemish on his record who was so distraught over his wife's suffering that he started taking amphetamines so he could stay awake all night long to take care of her. Which, in part, brought on his psychosis. Here, read the nurse's statement again. 'She was in so much pain, they had to increase the dose of morphine on a daily basis. It was an accident.' And what about Dr. Baker's evaluation? Do you really want to go to court with all we have?"

Then Mark asked Michael, "Why wasn't he tested for drugs when they picked him up? The detectives had to see he was incoherent. And why didn't they call me, his attorney?"

Michael told us that the officer in charge said he didn't ask for an attorney.

Mark replied, "Come on, Michael. In the condition he was in, he should have been sent to a hospital. Look at the copy of his confession."

Michael looked at the confession and then at Dr. Fischer and his daughter.

"OK, but there are conditions. And if they are not met, there will be consequences and a trial date set. I will put him on two years' probation, starting after he gets out of the clinic. Before we release him into his daughter's custody, I want reassurance that he will leave here and go straight to the clinic where he will be treated for substance-related mental illness. He will stay there until considered cured by the attending physician. Upon his release, you are to notify my office to start the probation. Is that clear to everyone here?"

We all nodded our heads except Dr. Fischer. Annabelle smiled at the DA and said, "Bless you!"

"Thanks, but to tell you the truth," he said, "I could have lost this one. And I figured I would save the city of New York a lot of money on a trial."

After we left the office, Annabelle thanked us and told us how wonderful she thought we both were. And then she started to cry.

Dr. Fisher finally broke his silence. "Don't cry, my darling. Don't cry."

After we got back to the office, Mark admitted he was very pleased with the way things worked out.

"Good work, Frank. You did a great job. I'm glad we went with your recommendations. You did all the footwork, and you deserve the credit. I like your style. You keep quiet, you listen, and then you make your move. You're going to make a hell of a lawyer."

I thanked him and told him I was just following his lead. And I was impressed at how he allowed me to interject my opinions into the conversation with the DA. He could have been annoyed that I stated my view as I saw it, but that was a risk I was willing to take. Mark hit him from one end and I from the other, and this time it worked out.

During our morning meeting, Mark told everyone about the case we were working on. The minute I got back from the DA's office, Norman, Bruce, Darlene, and Joan came into my office asking how it went. I told them we won. They all shook my hand and congratulated me. My secretary leaned over and kissed me on the cheek.

"I knew you could do it," she whispered.

Chapter 21

After I returned home, I checked the calls on my cell phone. Dr. Bass reaffirmed my appointment. He rescheduled another patient so he could see me this Saturday at 10:00 a.m., as I had requested. Jessie called to ask if I was up for doing something on Saturday night. She wanted to come into the city.

Jessie—what am I going to tell her about Darlene? I had already made plans with Darlene to go out to dinner on Saturday night. I had made reservations at The Tavern on the Green.

I also wondered if I should tell my family and friends about her. I thought better of it. It's too soon to call. She just got out of a long-term relationship. It's too soon for her to make any decisions about us. Like she said, we have to take it slow. As far as I was concerned, I would just as soon go faster, a lot faster. *I also have to call Uncle Frank to see if he could meet me at the apartment on Sunday morning, it's time we had a talk.*

And again, I'll have to call my parents and cancel Sunday dinner. That should go over really well.

First, I called Uncle Frank on his cell phone. He said he would come if it were important. But he didn't know what could be so damn important that he had to drive all the way into the city alone on a Sunday. He agreed anyway. He also said that Pop was so happy to have spent that time with me but that he didn't need John to babysit him. He could take care of himself.

I asked him what his reply to Pop was.

"I told him John had nothing to do while I was in Las Vegas. And if he doesn't work, he doesn't get paid. He bought it. What time do you want me there on Sunday?"

"How about ten o'clock in the morning?"

"Good, I'll be get back in time to have Sunday dinner with the family. I think we're having deli, but I not sure."

I then called my father on his cell phone, the coward that I am. I told him I wouldn't be there for dinner on Sunday. He told me my mother was going to have a fit and asked why I couldn't make it.

"I met this girl," I told him.

"Say no more. That ought to keep her happy. You finally have a date."

Sarcastically, I remarked, "Thanks a lot, Dad."

"I'm sorry, Frankie, but your mother and I were wondering if you were queer."

"What!" I started to laugh.

"Why are you laughing? You're not, are you?"

I couldn't stop. That's how absurd the statement was.

"Frankie, stop that confounded laughing. It's only natural we think that. What are you, twenty-five already and you're not even married?"

"I'm sorry, Dad, but it's funny that you would presume that just because I'm still single, at the ripe old age of twenty-five, I must be gay. And the term is *gay* not *queer*. Rest assured, I'm not. But tell me, Dad. What if I was? Would you love me any less?"

There was a pause.

"Dad, did you hear me?"

"I heard you. No, Son, I wouldn't love you any less. I couldn't."

"I love you too, Dad. And, Dad, I won't be twenty-five until next month."

I called Jessie and told her I was busy on Saturday but I was free on Sunday if she was available and didn't mind meeting at around noon. She said she was free and the reason for coming into New York was to go shopping for some clothes and maybe some Christmas gifts. It was now late October, and she was getting into the holiday spirit.

204

I told her I would still go and we could have lunch at Noodles when we were through.

She agreed and asked if she could park her car in my garage space and meet me at my apartment.

"Sure, no problem."

I had a very full weekend. That's great. It gave me no time to think. I didn't need to think right now.

I was kind of worried about my uncle's reaction to my meddling in my grandfather's affairs. I was also going to have to confide in him that my nightmares had not subsided, but had been ongoing and in fact have gotten worse. I started to rehearse.

"The dreams were upsetting my way of life, and this was the only thing Dr. Bass and I could think of to stop them once and for all."

I certainly couldn't tell my father. He gets too emotional. Uncle Frank is cool and introspective. He's more of a thinker than a hothead.

The more I thought about it, the more I realized I shouldn't have told Darlene about Mario Moretti. I appreciated her offer to help me find Mario, but she didn't know the whole story. And I don't want her to. The less people knew, the better. It was a family matter. I decided to take a closer look at Pop's immigration papers. At least they should have the town he came from and the date he immigrated. *Why didn't I think of this before?*

I pulled out Pop's stuff and found the immigration papers for Angelo Michael Scarpelli of Palermo, Sicily. Born: August 27, 1923. Height: five feet nine inches. Weight: 165 pounds. The description fit, but the rest of the document could have been forged before entering this country. *How would I know if he did? How would anyone know?* One question still remained. Was our last name really Scarpelli or Moretti? I can't do this anymore. I put everything back in the box and went to bed.

Chapter 22

I t was finally Friday and I was looking forward to the weekend in more ways than one.

As far as my career went, I know I have made the right decision in choosing law. I found that working on a case or just discussing cases with my associates energized and excited me. It was like putting together a puzzle. You had to try and make all the pieces fit because you wanted to win. It was imperative you win; your reputation is everything.

This weekend would prove to be full of apprehension and excitement. This was my first real date with Darlene, and I hoped I wouldn't blow it. I think I finally got what Darlene was trying to say about her relationship with Bruce. She loved him, but she was not in love with him.

I love Jessie, but I'm not in love with her. I don't feel the same intensity and excitement that I feel when I'm with Darlene. I'm sure Jessie knows that we're just friends, but then again, you don't screw your friends. We can't do that anymore. Although it's fun, it's also unethical.

I went right home after work, deciding not to go out with Norman and Bruce to the Marriott for a couple of drinks. I just wanted to relax, have a couple of beers, and watch a basketball game or maybe a couple of movies. I also decided not to go to the closet and look at all the "evidence." I also didn't want to trigger an episode. I wanted to wait until tomorrow when I was under hypnosis and Dr. Bass could stop it.

I awoke the next morning to a usual fall day. It was windy, cold, and raining. I was surprised that I felt calm and in control, not the least bit nervous or apprehensive about my meeting with Dr. Bass.

What I find out today could possibly be the worst thing that has ever happened to our family. But if Pop did this, we should all have a say on how to handle the situation. Like it or not, the fallout will affect the whole family. I also have to downplay this whole thing about my grandfather with Jessie. I shouldn't have told her. She has a big mouth.

There was no traffic on the way to the doctor's office, so I had time to stop at the diner to have breakfast. I decided to go to Uncle Frank's place. Vito saw me and came over.

"Hi, Frankie. What are doing here so early on a Saturday morning?"

I told him I had an appointment in Montclair and had some time, so I stopped in for some breakfast.

"You're a lawyer, aren't you kid?"

I told him I hoped to be and that I was taking the bar exam in February.

He said, "Your Uncle Frank talks about you all the time."

"He does?"

"Yeah, he's a great family man, your uncle, and a great friend. Do you have any idea how many people he's helped out from the neighborhood?"

"No, my uncle doesn't talk to me about his work and relationships."

"Yeah, that's OK because sometimes it's better not to know."

I asked, "Why shouldn't I know?"

"Because your uncle always kids around and says, "What you don't know, you can't testify to."

"Why? Is he doing anything illegal?"

"Calm down, kid. I've got a big mouth. Don't listen to me."

"No, Vito. Tell me what you meant by that remark."

"It's like this: your uncle is a very successful businessman. And he's highly respected, especially in Jersey. When you're in business and you're very successful, you can make enemies. That's all I'm saying. Some people like to lie about successful people, and sometimes they have to go to court to clear their name. It's tough. I need to get back to work now. Let me know what you want for breakfast, and I'll get it for you."

"I already know what I want, Vito. You can get me a Taylor ham sandwich with mustard on a hard roll, tomato juice, and black coffee."

"Coming right up, kid. Oh and, Frankie, don't tell your uncle we had this conversation."

I was just starting to find out things about family members I never knew. Maybe Uncle Frank was right. Maybe it was better not to know. I guess every family has some skeletons in the closet.

I walked into Dr. Bass's office, hoping this would be my last visit, although I knew it probably wouldn't be. After waiting for only five minutes, the doctor came out to greet me.

We shook hands and he asked, "What's up? You sounded like this visit was urgent."

"It is to me, Doc. I appreciate you seeing me on such short notice."

He opened the door to his office, and I went straight for the couch.

"Are you now ready to resume the hypnotherapy?" he asked.

"Yes, I'm ready. I want to get this over with." I asked him if it was possible for him to direct me to the church at the time of the shooting.

"I can if you're receptive, Frank. Remember what I told you about free will? You have been avoiding this scene for most of your life."

"That's true, but you said I would know when I was ready. I think I'm ready now."

I lay there, listening to Dr. Bass's voice and then the command.

"Frank, you're in the Cathedral Monreale. Are you in the church, Frank?"

"Yes, I'm in the church."

"Is anyone with you?"

"Yes, I'm standing next to TC."

TC looked at me and smiled. This time, I smiled back.

"We're standing just behind the altar, under this huge mosaic icon of Jesus Christ. In front of us and behind us are large stained-glass windows."

"What else can you see? Who else is in the church?"

"Right in front of us is a priest. He's lighting the candles that are on the altar. And he's speaking in Italian."

"What is TC doing?"

"He's just standing there with four other soldiers and some civilians, a few men and a couple of women."

"What are they doing?"

"Nothing. They're just looking at the bronze front doors of the church. It's like they're waiting for something or someone."

"Do they have their guns with them?"

"Yes, everyone is carrying guns."

"Frank, are you carrying a gun? Are they all Americans?"

"No."

"How do you know that, Frank?"

"TC and four other guys are speaking English and have American weapons. The other people are speaking Italian and carrying different weapons. One of the men at the door is holding a machine gun. I think it's Italian, but I'm not sure."

"Are the Americans wearing their uniforms?"

"No, not now. Now they're dressed in civilian clothes."

"What's happening now, Frank?"

"Mario's coming over to the front doors. He's locking the front doors of the church. TC asked him what the hell he was doing. He yelled at Mario, 'We thought the rest of your men were coming with the information. Where the fuck are they, Mario?' Mario told him not to worry, that he's just being cautious. He's just standing there in front of the doors with the guy who has the machine gun."

210

"Frank, how do you know what Mario is saying?"

"Mario speaks English."

"What's going on now, Frank?"

"TC is saying, 'I don't like this. Let's get out of here, guys. Stand away from the doors, Mario.' Mario is pointing his gun at TC. It's a German Lugar. Oh, my God. He's going to shoot."

"What's happening now?"

"Mario just gave the order to the guy with the machine gun to shoot. The others all started shouting. Everyone is panicking. Oh, my God, bullets are everywhere. Everyone is falling down. They're all wounded and bleeding. It's so awful. That monster! Oh God, how could you let this happen? This is horrible. It's a massacre."

"Frank, are you all right?"

"I can't breathe. I feel sick."

"Frank, I'm going to wake you up."

"No, I have to see his face up close. I have to see Mario's face. Wait, there is someone banging on the front doors. They want to come in. They're shouting in Italian, 'Let me in. Open the door.' Mario looks scared. Mario just shot his friend, the guy with the machine gun. Now he's running away. He's running down the basement stairs. No, he's coming back up. I hear gunfire and someone is coming up the stairs. It's a man. His shoulder is bleeding. He's yelling in Italian. Mario is escaping. He's running out the front door. He's getting away. Oh, my God, this is awful. This is awful. There's blood everywhere! He even shot the priest. I can't breathe! I can't breathe!"

"Frank, when I count to five, you will wake up: One, two, three, four, and five."

"I can't breathe, Dr. Bass. I think I'm going to die."

Dr. Bass ran over to his desk drawer and pulled out a paper bag.

"You're just hyperventilating, Frank. Breathe into this paper bag."

I was breathing heavily at first, then slowly. It was a few seconds before my breathing was back to normal and my hands stopped shaking.

I stood up and told Dr. Bass, "This was, without a doubt, the worst experience of my life!"

"Let me give you something to calm you down, Frank."

"No thanks, Doc. I have to drive home."

"It's OK, Frank. This won't impair your driving."

I took the pill and a glass of water, but I couldn't get that vision out of my head. It was a horrible experience. I witnessed a massacre and thought I was going to die just like they all died, right in that church.

"Rest, Frank, just rest and let the medication take effect. You've had a very bad experience. Did you see Mario's face?"

"Yes, but I couldn't recognize him. All of these people, except the priest, are all in their late teens or early twenties. Now they would all be in their eighties. There is no way I could recognize them."

"Frank, do you understand Italian?"

"Some Italian. I picked up some Italian from my grandparents."

Dr. Bass suggested I go home and look at my grandfather's old pictures and see if I could recognize anyone from my hypnotic state.

"I could, Dr. Bass, but I don't know who the people in the pictures are."

"Ask him, Frank. Ask your grandfather."

I finally had the nerve to address my situation. "Tell me, Dr. Bass, do you know what's wrong with me?"

He hesitated at first and then tried to explain. "Well, Frank, I have to be honest with you. I have never had a patient who has had this kind of experience before. But I have heard of it and, our profession hates to admit it exists. You're experiencing what is called a psychic phenomenon."

"What does that mean, Dr. Bass? This is crazy, especially coming from a professional such as yourself."

"I'll boil it down for you. It's something that can't be explained."

"Does this mean I'm psychic?"

"You could say that. Another explanation would be that in fact what you call dreams may not be dreams at all, but a spirit who has found a way to cross over into what some parapsychologists believe to be a parallel universe, and he's been communicating with you. In essence, you're communicating with a dead man. For some reason, you were chosen to know about a terrible event that took place sixty-three years ago. Why? I don't know. It may be to expose the criminals. What did TC tell you? You were handed the gauntlet? What I'm trying to tell you is I don't have the answers, and I'm as puzzled as you are. Do you believe in God, Frank?"

"Yes, I do. And I think he's punishing me for some reason and I don't know why."

"Have you thought about the religious implication of your dreams? The crime took place in a sanctuary, a house of worship. Could God have chosen you as a vehicle to expose the person who tried to kill . . . how many people?"

"Ten people."

Dr. Bass went on. "'Vengeance is mine, saith the Lord.' That's a quote taken from all of the bibles."

"I find this so hard to believe. If anyone else told me this crap, I would say that they were crazy. If all this is true, and quite frankly I'm still not sure, I believe I was chosen. Why me?"

"I'm sorry, Frank, but I don't have an answer to that question. But I think you will—once you know the truth about what really happened in Sicily in 1943."

Dr. Bass asked if I would give him permission to document my case. He promised not to use my real name.

"I'm sorry, Doc. I can't let you release my records until I know to what degree my grandfather is implicated."

"You're right, of course. What if he is Mario? What are you going to do?"

"I don't know. If this gets out, it could not only destroy the integrity of my family in the community, but our careers as well. This decision will have to be decided by the whole family. What happened in that church was horrific, and believe me, I know. I've seen it. It's what nightmares are made of. I only hope you're right, Dr. Bass, that if Mario is exposed, my job will be finished and so will my torment. Doc, do you know how successful being regressed while under hypnosis is? Say before they were born?"

"Yes, I have read text on that subject. You're referring to reincarnation. It's not a science and highly suspect. Why, Frank? Do you think you were reincarnated?"

"Lately, it has occurred to me."

"Are you thinking you're TC?"

"I'm not sure, but I was wondering about that possibility."

"No, Frank, that's not the case here. And frankly, I don't believe in it, but then I didn't believe in the supernatural. While under hypnosis, you confronted him. He said you were an observer. In all of your meetings with TC, you responded as if you were observing. You use words like *they,* or *TC said.* You never said *I.* Plus, you don't know locations or the names of the people involved. If you were TC, you would have known the names of the people and the places. In other words, you would be TC, telling your story, not observing it."

He went on. "I know this is strange to you. It sounds strange to me. Psychiatry is a science, and I believe in science, not voodoo. I can't even give you a scientific explanation. But if you ask me, my analysis would be that TC is a spirit and he's here on a mission. This may be more about your grandfather than you. Your grandfather is very close to you. I think you may have bonded so closely with him, perhaps right after you were born and during your childhood, that you intuitively picked up on his fears. Or maybe his regrets."

"You could be right, Doc. When I think about it, a lot of my nightmares occur after I had been in the presence my grandfather. I never thought about that. I'd never made the connection. Your analysis could be right."

"Well, Frank, it certainly seems we're on the right track. I'm just sorry I couldn't have been of more help."

"Are you kidding? You gave me the courage to follow through. You have helped me a lot. Before I started coming to you, I thought I was going *meshuge.*"

"Tell me, Frank, how does a nice Catholic boy like you know the word *meshuge?*"

I laughed. "It helps if you have a Jewish aunt."

We shook hands before I left his office with the knowledge that he was as bewildered as I was. I went home feeling like I had been in a war and, in essence, I was. I was now going home to peace and quiet until it was time to pick up Darlene. I couldn't wait to see her. I needed a diversion.

She smiled when she greeted me at the door. I got that stupid schoolboy feeling like some goddess just recognized my existence. She looked that great. I wasn't really surprised when I entered her apartment. The furniture was composed of period pieces, maybe antiques, with a big striped gold and white overstuffed couch and loveseat. If I were a connoisseur of good taste I would say her place was what you might call elegant.

I brought her yellow roses. She thanked me and immediately put them in a vase. I told her I liked what she did with the place and then we left.

On the way to the restaurant, Darlene did most of the talking, which was OK with me. With all the crap on my mind, I was not in the mood for small talk. Besides, I liked listening to her. She didn't ramble like Jessie. And she talked about interesting things, mostly lawyer stuff, cases, new laws, current events, and everything that I considered interesting conversation.

When we arrived at Tavern on the Green, it was packed. Thankfully, I had made reservations for seven in the Terrace Room. It was a little smaller than the other rooms, with the overhead lights dimmed. I thought it would be romantic.

It wasn't too long into our dinner that Darlene remarked; "I forgot to tell you my dad did some checking for you and came up with some information on Mario Moretti."

I was stunned. "He did what?"

She repeated, "You know, Frank, the information on Mario Moretti? I have the report in my purse."

She handed me a printout of the report. Although stunned, I tried acting nonchalant, like it was no big deal.

"Please thank your father for me. I'll give it to my friend. I'm sure he'll appreciate the effort."

I thought, *I spent the good part of my morning with Mario Moretti, just enough time to get to hate his guts.* I took the folded piece of paper and put it inside my jacket pocket. I wanted to act cool, so she didn't think it was that important or that it was of my concern.

It did make me anxious to see what was in the report. I almost left the table with the excuse of needing the restroom. But I thought better of it. I wasn't going to let Mario ruin my evening. He had already ruined my whole day.

After dinner, we went to the Marriott to listen to some music. We had a couple of drinks and danced. I'm not very good. But I had already warned her that I wasn't Fred Astaire. Darlene was such a lady. She never said a word when the music was rock and roll and I looked like such a jerk trying to find a beat. Thankfully, there were enough slow dances and romantic music to find our timing.

I was having a great time with her. We both had the same caustic sense of humor, and we laughed a lot. This lady was not boring. I just hoped she felt the same about me.

We danced until two. The last song of the evening was an old one called "At Last." I felt like they were playing it just for us.

I brought her home and kissed her good night outside her door but not before asking her if I could come in. She didn't think that would be a good idea. I asked her if her husband was due home. She laughed.

"No. I told you I wanted to take it slow. And why put temptation in the way of our good sense?"

"Well, at least it's nice to know you find the possibility of us making love tempting. OK, you're running the show for now."

She arched her eyebrow with that remark, as I knew she would. Then I kissed her. She kissed me back.

I whispered in her ear, "Do you want me to walk out of here looking like this?" And I looked down at the bulge in my pants.

She didn't get it at first and looked down. She laughed and slapped me on my arm.

"Yes, Frank, as tempting as that is, the answer is still no."

"You're a heartless woman, Darlene Banks."

She kissed me again, and this time, she put her tongue in my mouth. She whispered, "I know, darling, but I'm worth waiting for."

It was difficult leaving her. It was not just the sex; I wanted to spend the night holding her.

The minute I got home, I took the folded report from my pocket and opened it. It was a two-page computer printout. There was a picture of Mario looking just like he did when I saw him at the church. My hands started to shake, while my mind went to that awful place in time. I will never forget it.

* * *

Vengeance Is Mine

The Office of War Crimes

Washington, D.C.

At large is Mario Moretti. Publicly indicted for war crimes in Sicily.

On July 9, 1943, Mario Moretti, working underground for the German Army, betrayed his comrades and the American Military by killing five American soldiers, three Italian civilians, and wounding two in a church in Palermo, Sicily, during the World War II invasion of Sicily. The United States and the Italian governments have issued an indictment for this individual for Crimes against Humanity. These murders were committed without provocation. The U.S. government calls on all citizens to help apprehend Mario Moretti and bring him to justice for the killing of the following American soldiers: Lieutenant Harvey Bradshaw, Corporal Thomas Callahan, Private Jerry Stein, Private Ralph Watson, and Private Leon Jones. If you have any information that might lead to the capture of Mario Moretti, call the U.S. Department of State (202) 555-1227 or your local law enforcement office. The Italian government is expected to seek extradition. Proceed with caution; he is known to be very dangerous. Mario Moretti was born in 1921 and is thought to be living in the United States or Canada. There is a $100,000 reward for information leading to his arrest.

There were pictures of the American soldiers and the Italian partisans. The pictures of Mario were of a man in his early twenties. *How would anyone be able to recognize him as he looks today? I'm surprised that they are still looking for him.*

How strange is the fact that I can recognize them? They were all in my dreams during the hypnosis sessions. I saw it all as it was happening. It was a terrible experience. If anyone told me they had dreams or visions of a murder that took place sixty-three years ago, I would have thought they were nuts. I have absolutely no connection to TC. We're not even related. He's Irish. I'm

218

Italian. He's from Philly. I'm from New Jersey. So why has he dominated my life?

I finally went to bed after downing three scotch and sodas.

Chapter 23

The next morning, I got up with a hangover. I took a shower, downed some aspirin and waited for my uncle to show up. When the doorbell rang, I knew it had to be him. He used a signal: rap, rap, rap, pause, rap, rap. He'd been doing that for as long as I could remember. I opened the door, and he came in, but not without giving me a bear hug.

As he walked in, he said, "It's good the way you keep this place. It's clean. I like that."

"I made coffee, Uncle Frank, and I picked up some Danish."

"Just coffee. I'm trying to cut down on the sugar." He patted his stomach. "It's going all here."

"Are you kidding? You look good for a man of your age."

"A man of my age? I don't know if that's a compliment or an insult."

"I assure you, Uncle Frank, it's a compliment."

"What's up, Frankie? You look like shit this morning, and you've got me worried. Are you in any trouble?"

"I'm not in trouble, but I have a problem that I need to talk to you about."

"What could I do for you, kid?"

"This is hard to say because you're going to be pissed at me. But regardless of the consequences, I have to do this."

"Do what?"

I started to hem and haw. To tell the truth, I was a little afraid of how he would react.

"Just get to it, kid. I can't be here all day."

I started with, "Do you remember when I was a kid, how I had those terrible nightmares?"

"Sure, I remember, but they went away."

"They didn't go away, Uncle Frank. They never went away. I told everyone they did because I didn't want to worry them and I didn't want to see a psychiatrist. After I graduated from college, the nightmares started to get worse, and it was starting to affect my life and my job. I couldn't be up all night and do well the next morning. So I went to see a psychiatrist in New Jersey."

"What's the shrink's name?"

"His name is Dr. James Bass. He was a referral from a friend. I didn't want to go to anyone in New York. Although it's a big city, it's too close to where I work."

"What did the doctor say?"

"He said there was something in my subconscious that I couldn't deal with."

"What things, Frankie? That's a load of crap. You have a good family and great parents."

"It's not like that, Uncle Frank. It has nothing to do with my parents, or my childhood."

"Then what's the problem?"

"I know this is going to sound weird. I keep dreaming about this place in Sicily in 1943 during WWII. A massacre that was committed in a church called Monreale Cathedral in Palermo."

"I don't understand. What does any of this have to do with you? You could be dreaming this whole thing up."

"That's exactly what I thought until I went through hypnotherapy. It seemed so real that I checked it out. It seems the United States and Great Britain went there to invade Sicily in 1943 during a campaign they called *HUSKY*. The Americans sent paratroopers to meet with a group of Italian partisans who were supposed to help them. One was a traitor and a murderer. He killed eight

222

people and wounded two in the Monreale Cathedral. Five were American soldiers, and the others were civilians. They were his comrades and friends."

"OK, kid, now why are you telling me this?"

"Because when I was in hypnosis, I witnessed it."

"Frankie, this can't be real."

"Uncle Frank, I know how this sounds, but it's true. I checked out the story. It happened. I was told by one of the soldiers that if I found the German Lugar, I would find the murderer."

"What are you saying? It's Pop's gun? The one in the closet?"

"I'm afraid so. Pop said he was from Naples, but his immigration papers said he was from Sicily and that's where the murders took place."

"Listen to yourself. You know this man. I know this man. He could never do anything like this. He goes to church every Sunday. It would be impossible for him to commit such a sin. How many people have you confided in?"

"My doctor knows."

"Drop this, Frankie. You will destroy my father and our whole family. I mean it. Drop it."

"I can't, Uncle Frank. I have to know. The doctor said my dreams would never go away until I know the truth. I can't live like this."

He moved closer to me and put his arm around my shoulder. He saw how upset I was.

"OK, kid, now what do you want me to do?"

"I just want you to ask Pop about the gun. I swear I won't go to the authorities, Uncle Frank, and my doctor cannot divulge anything I say to him. It's privileged information."

He said in a very low voice, "Do you realize how much this could upset him? Are you willing to live with the consequences?"

"No, I love my grandfather. I wouldn't do anything to hurt him or the family. If you tell me to drop this, I will. I had to tell someone, and who else but you?"

"You know, kid, I think this is weird shit. And I don't understand this at all, but I believe you and I trust your judgment. I'll ask my father. Then I'm going to do some investigating on my own. I'll get back to you. Don't sweat this and don't get upset. I'm going to try and help you. But this is just between you and me."

"OK. From now on, it's just you and me."

He slapped me lightly on the face, looked in my eyes, and smiled. "You're a good-looking kid. You know that? You look a lot like me."

Before he left, he went to the closet and took out the gun and the rag it was wrapped in, as well as all of the pictures that Pop had given him. He asked me for a bag to put it in.

I asked him if he wanted paper or plastic.

"Are you working part time in a grocery store? What the hell do I care if it's paper or plastic? Just give me a bag, *madone*." He started to laugh. "You know, kid, sometimes I worry about you."

He put everything in the bag, including the printout that Darlene's father had given me, and then he left.

No sooner did my uncle leave than, I got a call from my brother, Al. He wanted to know how come they never see me anymore. I reminded him that I missed two Sundays out of how many? He reminded me I had missed a lot of Sundays in the six years I was away at school.

He also heard that I had a girlfriend and he wanted to know what she was like and when the family could meet her.

I told him I was busy at work and would try to make it sometime soon.

He reminded me that the baby was due at any time, and that everyone was expected to show up at St. Barnabas Hospital for the arrival. I told him there was no way I would miss the birth of my brother's first child and that he could count on me being there.

He said, "Good," and hung up.

My sister had already called at nine o'clock that morning.

"Frankie, Mom is really upset."

"Why?" I asked as if I didn't know.

"You know why. The only time she gets to see you is on Sundays, and this is the second week you're not showing up."

"I'm sorry, Julia. It can't be helped. I'll be there next Sunday."

She went on and on about when was she going to meet my girlfriend.

"What's her name?"

"Her name is Darlene. She's one of the attorneys in my office."

"What about Jessie, Frank? Have you thought about her feelings?"

"Jessie and I are just friends. And I don't really have time to talk about this right now."

"Really, Frankie, is that all she is to you? Are you sure? Don't hurt her. She doesn't deserve it. First, her husband walks out on her and now you?"

I started to feel guilty, so I went on the defensive. "Why don't you mind your own damn business? You have an enough to worry about with that idiot husband of yours."

"That's a cheap shot, even from you."

I was too pissed to apologize. "I'll see you next Sunday, Julia.

Before hanging up, she said, "I love you, little brother."

She was right. I was going to have to tell Jessie about Darlene. I was going to tell her today.

When Norman, the concierge, called me to tell me Jessie was here, I asked him, "Have her wait in the lobby. I'm on my way down."

I didn't want her to come up to my apartment—not that I didn't trust myself. Who was I kidding? I was afraid to trust myself. I certainly didn't want to wind up in a romantic interlude. Now that I had a chance with Darlene, I didn't want to screw up my chances by jeopardizing Darlene's and my relationship with lies. I just hoped Jessie and I could still stay friends. I would hate to lose her friendship.

When I got downstairs, Jessie was waiting for me on a big overstuffed chair. She looked so small in that large chair. She was wearing a suede jacket with a heavy sheared lining.

I asked her, "Where are you going—to the North Pole?"

"It's cold out there and you're not dressed warm enough. You better go up and change."

I had on a heavy wool sweater and jeans.

"Thanks for the advice, Mom, but I'm fine. Let's go."

"You must be desperate for company, Frank. I never thought I could get you to go shopping for clothes with me."

"Under normal circumstances, you would be right, but I also need clothes. I was in school a long time. I have no idea what the best-dressed attorney is wearing these days."

"Oh, please. I think I'm going to puke."

We both laughed. She hated when I acted full of myself. She always put me in my place. I only said it to piss her off.

First, we went to Bloomingdale's and then Macy's. She pulled stuff off the rack and I shook my head. Then I pulled out stuff and showed it to her, and she said no. We finally wound up at Nordstrom's; there we found a few outfits we both agreed on.

With our packages in hand, we headed to Fifth Avenue. On a side street across from the Dakota is a restaurant called Noodles. Jessie and I both enjoyed going there. It was really cold out, but if I were frozen stiff, I wouldn't have let her know. We both ordered a brandy to warm up.

"By the way," she said. "Did you do any more research on that Mario guy?"

I lied and said, "No. I haven't had the time. I've been too busy at work. I'm going to drop it for a while."

"Drop it? Are you kidding?"

"Not for good. I just need to drop it for now."

"Jessie, I have something to tell you."

"Uh-oh, you look serious. What is it?"

"It's nothing bad, and I'm sure you will be happy for me."

She got serious.

"What is it, Frank? Did you meet someone?"

"Well, I didn't just meet her. She works in my office and we started dating."

"It's just like I told you years ago, Frank. Someday you will find and fall in love with your own kind."

"Don't do this, Jessie. It's not that she's my kind. There is no kind. You were my kind. It has everything to do with how I feel when I'm with her—like you must have felt when you met and married Parker."

Her eyes welled up like she was going to cry. I felt like a bastard.

"Jessie, this isn't payback for dumping me. We have never really been in love. We're just good friends. That's why you were able to fall in love with someone other than me. As for me, it's taken me a long time to find someone. And I'm not even sure where it's going."

Her whole attitude suddenly changed to anger and resentment. "You lousy son of a bitch! Did you tell her about me and that you've been screwing me?"

"Wait just a minute. And keep your voice down before everyone in this place hears your big mouth. You were the one who made most of the advances."

"You're some gentleman, Frank Scarpelli. I didn't hear you say no."

"Well, Jessie, who the hell in their right mind would? You're a beautiful and desirable woman. I would have to be nuts not to want to make love to you."

Tears were streaming down her face, and I felt like the biggest asshole on Earth. She asked me if I had a hankie. I pulled one out of my back pocket and gave it to her. She blew her nose and wiped her tears.

"Does this mean we can't see each other anymore?" she asked.

I reached over and held both her hands. "No, you're still and always will be my best friend. And I love you very much."

She smiled and asked what her name was.

"Darlene Banks."

"Is she any relation to General Matthew Banks?"

I quietly responded, "Yes, she's his daughter."

Her eyes opened wide, and she had that shit-eating grin on her face.

"Jessie, I'm buying, what do you want for lunch?"

When I got home from shopping, I called Darlene. I wanted to tell her what a great time I had Saturday night. She seemed happy to hear from me, but her voice was a little down. I asked her if she was OK. She said she was "just fine" and that she also had a wonderful time last night.

I started to get a little worried. "You sound a little down, Darlene. Are you missing Bruce?"

She laughed. "No, Frank. I'm not missing Bruce. I'm missing you."

I felt relieved. "Well, that can be rectified. I can be over in five minutes, or you could come here."

She laughed. "No, thanks. I'll see you tomorrow at work."

"All right. If I can't convince you to see me tonight, I'll see you tomorrow. Remember, it's your turn to pick up the coffee. I don't want to spoil you completely. I like it black and hot."

She laughed again. "Do you know that sometimes you're just like a little boy?"

"You're probably right. And do you know that men never really grow up."

Chapter 24

I was quite surprised when I arrived at work and there was a Starbucks coffee sitting on my desk. Darlene was more the activist type. You didn't tell her what to do.

I went to her office to thank her. Her perfume permeated the room. I walked up close to her face and said, "Thank you for the coffee. Tomorrow, it'll be my turn."

She smiled and looked at the door to see if anyone was coming. Then she kissed me on the cheek. "You're welcome."

"I thought you knew that teasing is unfair. The ground rules are: You have to play fair."

She said in a low, teasing voice, "Now is not a game, Mr. Scarpelli. It's the office and we have to conduct ourselves accordingly."

"What can I say? You're right!"

I walked back into my office.

I started looking at briefs that had been placed on my desk. One in particular had a Post-it note on it that read: *Frank, see me on this, it's priority. Mark.*

I started reading. It was a case where our client killed her abusive husband with a frying pan while he was trying to strangle her.

I was surprised that Mark wanted my input on this case. The man who was killed was Judge Herbert Smith. I wondered why he asked me to help him with such a high-profile case. With the exception of Darlene, who is busy assisting Norman with his cases, everyone in the office has had much more experience than I. Maybe it's because I had never come up against the honorable judge, therefore I had no prejudices? I was just getting into Mrs. Smith's statement when I heard a commotion in the reception area. Someone was obviously upset and excited. I was surprised but not at all interested in finding out who they were or why they were here.

All of a sudden, Joan came running into my office and announced, "Someone is here to see you, Frank. He doesn't have an appointment and he refuses to leave the premises. He said he's your grandfather. He's with this huge guy who looks kind of scary."

"What? My grandfather is here?"

I got up and walked into the reception area, passing everyone who was looking to see what the commotion was. I was stunned. It was Pop, and he was with John.

I asked John, "What's up? What's Pop doing here?"

He responded in his usually soft, calm manner. "He wanted to see you, so the boss told me to bring him here."

"Why didn't you warn me? Why did you bring him here? Why didn't you go to the apartment? I could have met you there. You should have known better."

"Why shouldn't I bring him here, Frankie? Are you ashamed of him?"

I didn't answer. I went over to my grandfather. "Pop, what's wrong? Why are you so upset? If you wanted to speak to me, why didn't you call? Now sit down. Calm down and catch your breath."

He looked as white as a ghost. I was starting to worry about his health and wondered if I should call 911. People were walking in and out of the office. It was also very embarrassing.

"Pop, are you sure you're all right? What did you want to see me about?"

"No, I'm not all right, Frankie. I have to speak to you alone. I can't talk with everyone here."

"OK. Come into my office. We'll be alone there. John, you stay here!"

"Can't do it, Frankie. Your uncle told me to watch him, and I can't watch him from here."

"Jesus Christ, John, it's OK. He's with me. You don't have to take my uncle so literally."

"Sorry, Frankie. I have to go with Mr. Scarpelli."

"OK, then both of you come into my office. We're creating a scene."

Just then, Mark came out of his office and asked if everything was all right. I apologized for the commotion and introduced Mark to my grandfather. Mark shook his hand.

"It's a pleasure meeting you, Mr. Scarpelli. Frank, why don't you take your grandfather into one of the conference rooms? He's obviously is upset and he needs to speak to you."

Sandra, the receptionist, heard Mark and told him that Conference Room 2 was free.

I led my grandfather and John into the room.

I closed the door and asked, "What is this about, Pop? What was so urgent that you had to see me right now? If you called, I could have come to you."

He looked awful and I was getting very worried.

"Pop, I think maybe we should take you to the hospital. You're not looking well."

"I'm OK, Frankie. I just need a glass of water."

John went into the reception area and asked Sandra for a cup of water.

While he was gone, Pop said, "I am so surprised at you! How could you? How could you think I could do such a horrible thing?"

I asked, "What horrible thing?" as if I didn't know what he was talking about. Just in case he wasn't talking about the murders, I played dumb.

"You know, the massacre at Cathedral Monreale. How could you ever think that I was a murderer, a criminal, and a traitor?"

He started to cry.

"Oh, my God. Pop, I'm sorry. I didn't mean it. I found the gun in the closet—" John came back into the room with the water and handed it to my grandfather.

"John, I think we should take my grandfather to the hospital."

"Do you think? I better call the boss."

"Yes, John, I think."

My grandfather was adamant. "I'm not going to a hospital right now."

I started to speak, but Pop cut me off.

"Tell me, Frankie, how long have you been looking for Mario?"

"About a month."

"A month? I have been looking for him for sixty-three years. And here he is—right in your office. *Grazie a Dio, grazie a Dio.*"

"What are you talking about? Have you gone mad?"

John was starting to furrow his brow, giving me a dirty look.

I lowered my tone.

"Pop, please explain to me what you're talking about?"

"I'm talking about the pictures outside the elevator doors." His voice was becoming labored.

"John, call 911."

John not only called 911 on his cell phone, he called my uncle and told him what had happened and that he'd let him know where the paramedics would be taking him.

Pop's breathing was getting worse, but he continued to speak.

"The pictures in your office are of Mario Moretti. *Grazie a Dio!* I finally found the bastard."

After that, he passed out.

Before we knew it, the paramedics were there. They said he was alive, but he was in bad shape. He had had a severe heart attack. They gave him oxygen and a shot and took him to the hospital.

The office staff was in the reception area, including Darlene and Mark. Mark told me to go with my grandfather and stay with him for as long as he needed me.

John and I went to the lobby to catch the elevator. While waiting for the elevator, I looked at the pictures. So that's what got my grandfather all riled up. It was the portrait of Mark Moran, Sr. *How could that be? No, he couldn't be Mario Moretti.*

But to tell the truth, right here and now, I didn't give a shit about Mario, TC, or myself. I only cared about my grandfather. God, please don't let him die. This is all my fault.

John and I followed behind the ambulance to Bellevue Hospital. From my office, it was the closest hospital. The paramedics wheeled him into the intensive care unit. He was hooked up to every monitor known to medical science. They refused to let me in his room, so John and I waited in the waiting room that was close by.

It was only a half hour before my uncle and my father showed. They were visibly shaken and upset. I was sure some of that was directed at me. I asked where Al was, and my dad said he'd told him to stay in Montclair.

"Barbara is due to have the baby any time now, and she can't leave town." My father asked, "What did the doctor say? Is he going to live or what?"

"I don't know, Dad. The doctor has not come out of the room."

He glared at me. "What the hell happened?"

"Pop showed up at my office to see me. Hanging on the wall of our office is a picture of the owner and founder of the firm, Mark Moran. He got very upset after seeing the picture and said he knew him—that he was Mario Moretti. That's all I know."

Uncle Frank stated, "You've got to be kidding. Pop said he had been looking for Mario for sixty-three years."

My father started to get all excited.

"What the hell did you do, Frankie? What is all this crap you conjured up? Frank told me all about it on the way over here. Why did you have to get your grandfather involved?"

My uncle came to my defense. "Stop it, Al. He had no choice. In a way, it was my fault. I shouldn't have had John drive Pop to his office. He said if John or I didn't take him, he would go anyway. He would have taken the bus. I couldn't have him do that."

"Stay out of this, Frank. This is between my son and me."

He looked at me with such disgust. I had never seen him look at me like that.

"I'm sorry, Dad. I had no choice."

"What do you mean, you had no choice? I could kick your ass for what you've done to my father and this family."

I was starting to get hot. "Watch it, Dad. I'm not a kid. You can't intimidate me anymore."

Then he really got mad. "Tell me what you're going to do if I walk over there and beat the crap out of you."

"You'll force me to defend myself. Keep in mind, I'm younger and I'm in much better shape than you."

He went to take a step toward me. Uncle Frank stepped in between us.

"You know, Al, you're acting like a jerk. I know you feel bad, but you don't have to take it out on the kid. I was just as much to blame as he was. Last night I confronted Pop about the gun, his papers, and I also asked him about the pictures he had. I showed him the printout that showed the massacre that took place at the church. And then I asked him if he knew anything about it. And why did he lie to us about where he was from? He told me the whole story. Before he did, I was also concerned that he might have been involved. He wanted to see Frankie and explain to him what really happened. He didn't want his grandson to think he was that murdering bastard, Mario."

Uncle Frank turned to me.

"Frankie, you said he saw a picture of Mr. Moran and thought he was Mario?"

"Yes, Uncle Frank. It was the strangest thing. How would he know what Mario looked like? He hadn't seen him since he was nineteen or twenty years old. And the picture is a man in his forties who is not supposed to be Italian. He doesn't even have an Italian accent."

My father started to calm down, some, although he was starting to get impatient. He hated the conversation, and he was also mad at the doctor. "Where's that freaking doctor? I don't trust him. I want them to bring in a specialist. In fact, we should take him back to Jersey."

John, who had been silent through this whole conversation, asked, "Who wants coffee? I'll go get it."

In unison, we all said, "Me."

Uncle Frank said, "Let me tell you the story Pop told me about what happened that night in Sicily: It seems Pop had a twin sister named Angelina. They both belonged to the Italian resistance, along with Angelina's husband, Peter Sorrento, and some of his friends from Palermo—including the priest, Father Ferranti. Mario, it seems, was the self-appointed leader. He had been schooled in London and spoke English fluently."

I asked, "How come he was schooled in England?"

"Pop said it was because he was always getting into trouble—stealing, fighting, and just a big pain in the ass. So his uncle who lived in London said he would take him back with him and put him in a boarding school close to his home, before he wound up in jail.

"Anyway, Mario lived in London for about five years. When the war broke out, his uncle thought he would be safer in Italy, so he sent him back to Sicily.

Pop said they had started the resistance before Mario came back, but once they realized how well Mario spoke English, they let him take charge.

"It seems his uncle knew some English diplomats and informed them of the resistance. He told them he thought his nephew could be of some help because he spoke fluent English. That's how the Americans and the British were able to contact him before they started to invade Sicily.

"Pop, Angelina and Peter, and a few of the others in the group were with Mario the night the paratroopers landed. They all stayed together until the next evening. While they were hiding in the basement of the church, Pop and Peter went to meet with another group who had all the information the Americans needed—where the Germans and Italians hid their arsenal, the location of their headquarters, outposts, and a detailed map of the area. They tried to get any information they thought would help.

"At least, that was what Mario had promised them. When Pop got back to the church with the rest of the group, they heard shooting and yelling. They tried to open the front door of the church, but it was locked. Pop said they banged on the door for a while. And again, they heard more gunfire. They ran to the cellar door and up the stairs, expecting to see the German or Italian army.

"Peter was the first to enter the sanctuary when they heard another shot. Peter started to fall back down the stairs. He'd also been shot. He caught his balance and kept on going with the rest of the band close behind. When they all managed to get into the sanctuary, there was Mario with a German Lugar in his hand. When Mario saw them all pile in, he dropped his gun and ran out the front door.

"Pop said he couldn't believe what had just happened. Everyone in that church had been shot and there was his sister, Angelina, lying next to an American in a pool of blood. He took off his shirt and he tried to stop the bleeding.

She started to whisper something. He had to get closer to hear her. He leaned closer and that's how he got her blood all over him.

"'Traitors,' she murmured, 'Mario and Antonio are traitors. Kill him, Angelo, kill him for me.' And then she died. They checked to see if anyone was alive. Father Ferranti was badly wounded and so was Antonio Pasco. Pop picked up Mario's gun and swore in God's house he would seek vengeance. Pop has been searching for Mario for sixty-three years."

Uncle Frank shook his head. "What your dad and I didn't know, Frankie, is that many a night when he didn't come home until late in the evening, he was searching for Mario. Sometimes, he would get a lead. He had heard that Mario had moved to Princeton, New Jersey, but the leads never amounted to anything.

"But you knew all about this, didn't you, kid?"

"I know he was in Princeton."

"Did you dream that too?" my father asked.

"No, I saw it on the wall of his office. He got his law degree from Princeton."

"What is this bullshit, and how come you never told your mother and me about all this nonsense?"

"Why do you think, Dad? It's because of the reaction I'm getting now. I knew you wouldn't believe me."

"You should have just kept your mouth shut," he said.

All of sudden, my mother, sister, and Aunt Dorothy came into the waiting room. My mother and sister were visibly upset, while Aunt Dorothy was crying her eyes out.

My uncle got up to comfort her. "Don't cry, sweetheart. Pop's going to make it. He has to. He's waited a long time for this day. Now it's time for Mario Moretti to get what's coming to him."

My mother asked if it was a heart attack.

We all nodded.

My dad finally noticed that my mother was in the room. "Terry, how did you get here so fast?"

"John came and picked us all up."

We looked up to see John carrying a box filled with hot coffee for all of us.

"Good kid, that John," my uncle remarked.

"You got that right, Uncle Frank."

We mostly sat in silence while drinking our coffee and waiting. We sat for a half hour before the doctor came in and asked if we were all waiting for Mr. Scarpelli.

My uncle and dad got up.

"Well," the doctor said, "Thanks to the paramedics, he survived this attack. But he's going to have to take it easy for a while, with as little stress as possible. He has got to take his medication. He told me he forgot to take his medicine today. That could have helped bring on the attack."

My uncle stated, "Don't worry, Doc. Pretty soon all of his worries will be over. When can we take him home?"

"If he remains stable, in about three days. I want to keep him here for observation."

My father asked if the family could see him.

The doctor was specific. "Yes, you can all go in and see him. But keep in mind, he went through a terrible ordeal and he's been sedated. He needs rest, so just stay for a few minutes. But first, he said he wanted to see his grandson, Frankie, alone."

I was a little surprised but glad. I needed to set things right with him. I needed to apologize.

When I walked into the room and saw how frail and vulnerable he looked, I could hardly contain my emotions. But I did. I smiled and went as close to him as I could. He was hooked up to several monitors.

240

I asked him, "How are you feeling, Pop? You gave us a scare."

His voice was low and hoarse. "Don't worry. I'm OK. I want you to know that my heart attack was not your fault. It had nothing to do with you. I forgot to take my medicine this morning. And I know I shouldn't let myself get upset. But when I saw Mario's picture on the wall in your office, I was upset and relieved at the same time."

"I don't want you to think about that now. The doctor said you shouldn't get upset."

"I'm not upset now. I'm glad that I'm going to live to see that devil punished. I can now die in peace, knowing that it was me who found him. Frankie, you have to promise me he will pay. You have to make him pay. Ruin his life the way he ruined mine. You're a lawyer. You know what to do."

"I do, Pop, and I will."

He smiled at me. "Good boy! I can now die a happy man."

"Don't say that. The family is not ready to let you go."

He smiled again. "It's nice you all love me and I love all of you, especially you, Frankie. Did you know from the time you were born, you were my favorite?"

"No, Pop, I never thought about it. You were always good and kind to all of us."

"Don't tell the others, Frankie. That's our secret."

I could hear my voice quiver as I assured him that I wouldn't tell anyone.

"It's up to God. He will take me when it's time. I'm just grateful he let me live long enough to find the devil."

He was getting tired, so I went to get the rest of the family. I went into the waiting room and told everyone that they could go in now, including John. Everyone went in, except my father. He came over to me and hugged me.

"I'm sorry, Frankie. I don't know what got into me."

I reassured him that I understood and I did. But I also realized that this was a wake-up call for my father. His children we're now grown and we were not going to be bullied.

Together, we walked into Pop's room and stood around his bed with the rest of the family.

Pop said, "I'm OK, everyone. Not to worry."

My Aunt Dorothy started to cry, and my uncle put his arm around her.

Pop said, "Don't cry; no one cry. I'm a happy man, thanks to my grandson, Frankie."

My dad looked at him then back at me and asked, "How could he be happy when he's just had a heart attack?"

Pop was tired and closed his eyes. We all started to panic and called the nurse. She checked the monitor and assured us that he was just sleeping.

On the way to the parking lot, I asked my uncle if I should I quit my job.

"That would not be the smartest thing to do right now. We need someone on the inside. Besides, Pop is old. He could have been mistaken. The last time he saw Mario was when he was nineteen or twenty years old. I have friends. I'm going to check up on Mark Moran."

"I did notice some odd things about Mark Senior. He has very dark brown eyes and a very stern manner. His sons are nothing like him. They have blue eyes and they appear to be easy going."

He slapped me on the back of the head. "You're an attorney and you call that evidence? It's probably the dumbest thing I have ever heard you say."

I laughed. "That's not the dumbest thing I have ever said. Trust me!"

When I got back to the office, I asked Millie to let me know when Mark Junior was available. I had to speak to him about the Maude Smith case. She agreed and inquired about my grandfather. In fact, everyone I passed on the way to my office asked about Pop. I felt no awkwardness for the morning's disruption. I vowed never to be embarrassed by Pop or, for that matter, any

242

member of my family again. One by one, my group came into my office to inquire about Pop, Norman, Bruce, Joan, and Darlene. After they all left, Darlene asked me to call her in the evening. I told her I would, but only after I got back from the hospital.

I started to think of what the implications would be if Mark Senior were Mario Moretti. The publicity would ruin the firm's credibility. Everyone working here would eventually be out of a job. And what about Mark Junior and Tim? They seemed like decent guys. What about their families? No matter how you looked at it, it was a bad situation. I knew how I felt when I thought it could be my grandfather. I was sure they'd be just as shocked to find out their father was a mass murderer.

I promised my grandfather I would ruin Mario and I will do everything in my power to do it. If Mark is Mario, he will wish he never ran into the Scarpellis. This is what we Italians call a "vendetta." But we have no intention of killing Mario or harming any of his family. We will see that he's punished to the full extent of the law.

In this country premeditated murder brings the death penalty. And if Sicily tries to get him extradited him, we'll try to fight it. He murdered five American soldiers and there is still a warrant out for his arrest. There is no statute of limitations on murder in this country. We will have to be very careful. If Mario has a clue that we're on to him, he'll leave the country and go somewhere where he could possibly have immunity from extradition. *But I'm getting ahead of myself. This is all circumstantial evidence. It's hearsay. Mark Senior may not even be Mario.*

After work, I went to the hospital to visit Pop. Although he continued to profess he felt fine and wanted to go home, he still looked awful. Aunt Dorothy and John came in a few minutes after I got there. I asked where my uncle was. She said he would come later on. He was bringing Robin with him.

It occurred to me, for all the squawking I'd done about John, I now realized what a valuable asset he was to the family. I had such peace of mind knowing a member of my family was in his hands. *It's funny how you tend to misjudge people.*

Aunt Dorothy started fussing over Pop, fixing his pillow, straightening out his bedsheets and his blanket. You would have thought he'd hate being fussed over. I would have. But then again, I'm a pain in the ass. He just let her do her thing without so much as a grimace on his face. He looked like he enjoyed the attention.

"Now, Pop, isn't that better?" she said.

He smiled and nodded.

Just then, my uncle walked in with Robin who immediately ran up to Pop and kissed his cheek.

"I love you, Grandpa."

She then placed this huge bouquet of flowers on his nightstand. His face lit up at the sight of Robin. She was an unspoiled and loving child who had to babysit for extra spending money. I'm sure it was because her father told her, "There are no free lunches."

Uncle Frank came over to me. "Let's go outside. I want to talk to you."

We both went into the waiting room.

"I just want you to know, Frankie, I hired a private investigator to do a background check on Mark Moran, Sr. I expect it will take several days for all the information to be accumulated. And if there is no paper trail, we will have to find another way to prove his identity."

"There has to be something, Uncle Frank. He went to a university. He got his license to practice law from Princeton University."

"That's true, but if he entered this country as Mark Moran and his English is impeccable, there would be no reason to question him."

244

"Uncle Frank, what if his papers were from England? What if he went to England first and then came to the United States?"

"You may have something. Why don't we check out Immigration to see if he immigrated from England and Canada and see if he's listed under Mark Moran."

I thought about it. "What about the gun? It could still have Mario's prints on it. I know my prints are on it and whoever else touched it, but there is a slight chance it could still have Mario's prints on it. If it does, we could match the gun prints to Mark's prints to confirm his identity."

My uncle asked, "How could we get his prints? You said he rarely comes in to the office."

"That's true, but his office is full of his prints. I can try to lift them off his telephone or his desk. Anything. I have the key to the office."

He was emphatic. "No, it's too risky. If you got caught, you could kiss your career good-bye. No, I won't let you do this. I'll take care of it."

I asked him, "How?"

"How many times do I have to say this? Some things you don't need to know."

"Right, then I can't testify."

"Frankie, you got it. The genius finally got it."

Pop was very quiet during our visit. I was starting to worry that even if we did find Mario, he might not live long enough to see him punished.

After I got home, I called Darlene and told her the details of my grandfather's illness and his prognosis, that he would probably be going to my uncle's within the next couple of days. We also made plans for Friday night on the condition my grandfather did not take a turn for the worse.

I called Jessie and told her about Pop's heart attack. She felt terrible but kept questioning me as to why he was at my office. I don't know why she can never get the message that there are things you sometimes don't want to talk about. Why can't she just drop it? She just goes on and on with question upon question. I realized I was the one who invited her in by telling her about my dreams. But now I'm backing off. And she should respect my privacy.

"Calm down, Jessie. I do not want to discuss this with you right now. I'll call you later."

"Fine, Frank, you do that."

She slammed down the phone.

I thought about calling Dr. Bass and bringing him up to speed but decided my uncle was right. The less people knew about our plans, the better.

The phone rang at 1:30 in the morning. I was scared to death. I thought it might be the hospital, calling about my grandfather. It was my uncle.

"What's up? You scared the hell out of me."

"It's done. Frankie."

"What are you talking about?"

"We got the fingerprints."

"You burglarized my office?"

"Of course not. They took nothing. No one will ever know."

"How did you know what to do?"

"I didn't. This guy I know went in and he took a friend with him. He's a forensic expert."

"Uncle Frank, is there anyone you don't know?"

He laughed.

"This is not the time for this conversation. I just wanted you to know that we will know in twenty-four hours."

"And what if the prints match, Uncle Frank? We can't go to the DA's office. They'll ask how we got Mark Moran's prints."

"Let me worry about that, kid. Our first step is making sure that Mark is really Mario before we go through all the trouble of looking for further evidence."

I asked my uncle if my dad knew what he was up to. He asked me if I was kidding. He couldn't tell my father because he would tell my mother. And she would have had him arrested for aiding and abetting. He advised me to go back to sleep. He said he only called me because he was afraid I would do something foolish, like snooping around and being obvious.

I told him I had been working on a plan of sorts. He told me to forget about it, that he would take care of everything. And then he hung up.

I was a little apprehensive about going in to work the next morning. Although there was nothing to suspect, I didn't know what to expect. Nothing had been taken from the office except fingerprints. I was sure my uncle only hired professionals. And he was right. I didn't want to know.

When I arrived at work the next morning, it was the same as always. I said my usual good mornings and went to my office. I was starting to get nervous and anxious. Millie came into my office and said Mark wanted to see me. I was a little apprehensive before knocking on his door.

He told me to, "Come in." He immediately asked about my grandfather and then asked me to take a seat. He expressed concern for Pop and asked me how he was doing; if I knew what got him so upset. I told him that Pop has a heart condition and he had forgotten to take his medication. What got him upset was that he thought because he still has a thick Italian accent, Sandra didn't understand who he was looking for.

His next question was, "Who is that big guy with him?"

I told him that John is a very close family friend, and he offered to drive my grandfather in to New York. I also told him that my grandfather came to New York to visit friends and that he was planning to spend the evening at my place. But he needed the key to my apartment. That's why he showed up at the office.

"You're lucky, Frank. I never knew my grandfather on my father's side. He passed away before I was born."

"I'm sorry to hear that, Mark. Was your father born in the United States?"

"No, he was born in England. I think it was London. He came to the United States in 1946 after World War II. My mother is American. They met here in the United States and they married. Like they say, the rest is history. I really admire and respect my father. He had nothing when he came to this country. He worked his way through law school, and look at all he's accomplished."

"I'm impressed, Mark. That's a real Horatio Alger story. No wonder you're proud."

I thought I was going to choke on my words.

"Well," Mark said, "let's get down to business. I asked you to see me because I need your help in the Maude Smith case. But I wondered if you thought your grandfather's illness would interfere with the time needed to come up with a defense strategy. If so, I could have someone else assist me."

"No, Mark. My grandfather's illness should not have any bearing on my job or the time it will take to prepare an outline for self-defense. I assume you're going for a self-defense strategy?"

"You're right, Frank. Self-defense is an affirmative defense to use. The problem will be proving it. That's where you come in. So why don't you get started?"

That was my cue to leave. The meeting was over.

I went to lunch at a nearby coffee shop and called my uncle to give him the information I had just received from Junior about his father's past. I thought this information might be helpful. As soon as he answered, I told him I had some information that might interest him.

"I have some information for you too. The prints match. Mark Moran is Mario Moretti."

I can't say I was surprised. I was surprised that they were able to get the prints off the gun after such a long period of time.

"OK, I told you mine, kid, now you tell me yours."

I told him what Junior had told me, that his father was born in England and he came to this country in 1946.

He said, "That doesn't make any sense. We know he's Italian and that he was born in Sicily, but then, it's doubtful that he told his kids the truth about anything. He's been covering his tracks since he hightailed it out of Italy, although it's a start. Good work, Frankie. Now keep your ears open and your mouth shut. We don't want you to do anything that might tip our hand."

I assured him that I was smarter than what he gave me credit for. He laughed so hard I hung up on him. *When will they stop acting like I'm a wet-nosed kid?*

I no sooner hung up from talking to Uncle Frank when my brother Al called. "I'm on my way to the hospital. It's time."

I asked him, "Time for what?"

"Don't screw around, Frankie. I'm in no mood for jokes."

"OK. Now take it easy and calm down. Why don't you ask Dad to drive Barbara to the hospital?"

"No, I'm fine. I can drive. I'll see you later. Come as soon as you can."

I assured him I would. *Who had time to work?*

At three o'clock, I called my father and asked if there was any news about the baby. He told me that the first one usually takes a long time. I also asked him if he knew when Pop would be getting out of the hospital. He told me that when my aunt and uncle went to visit him this morning, the doctor told them that he would be able to leave tomorrow if his vital signs were as normal as they were today.

"Dad, isn't that too soon to leave?"

"I thought the same thing, but what do I know? I'm not a doctor. He's going to be living with Frank and Dottie. Frank insisted. He doesn't want Pop to live alone anymore. They're looking into hiring a nurse for just a couple of weeks or until he's OK."

"That sounds like a good plan. I guess I'll see you at St. Barnabas in a couple of hours."

I returned to reading Maude Smith's statement and started taking notes. Before I knew it, it was getting late. I had to drive in all that traffic to get to a hospital that was in Livingston, New Jersey. But I knew if I didn't show, my life wouldn't be worth a plug nickel.

By the time I got to the hospital, my sister and niece had arrived. Al was a wreck. First, he would go into Barbara's room and stay with her for a few minutes. Then he would come out and tell us it wasn't time.

My mother said, "He's going nuts. He's been doing that same routine for five hours."

I sat down, picked up a magazine, and for the life of me I couldn't keep my mind on anything I was reading. But I kept flipping through the pages anyway. I thought if it looked like I was engrossed in something, the family would leave me alone and I wouldn't have to talk to anyone or answer any questions.

I was into my magazine when I heard everyone laughing. I looked up to get in on the joke, and they were all looking at me. I checked my socks. They matched. No stains on my suit and tie. I asked them, "What?" They kept laughing their heads off.

My dad finally divulged the reason they were laughing. "We didn't know you liked reading *Oprah*."

I looked at the cover and saw I had picked up the Oprah magazine. I didn't want them to know that I didn't know what I was reading, so I admitted, "I know what I'm reading and it's a damn good magazine. It's time I got in touch with my feminine side. Right, Dad?"

My wise-ass sister smiled. "I'm glad you like it. Maybe now we'll finally have something to talk about."

Again everyone started laughing.

Al came out of Barbara's room all upset. "Can you all just quiet down?" he said and then ran back into the room to be with his wife.

My mother got serious and shrugged her shoulders as if to say, "What's up with him?" We all got hysterical again. I guess we were all tired. First, there was the anguish with Pop. Now there was a new baby on the way. It had been one hell of a week.

I was starting to get hungry.

"I don't know about you all, but I'm starved. I'm going down to the cafeteria to get something to eat."

One by one, they all got up and followed me to the elevator. The only people who didn't go were Barbara's parents. They decided to wait it out.

We were there about a half hour when Al came down and walked over to our table. "Where did everyone go? What's with you people? Doesn't anyone in this family care about this baby?"

His behavior was so out of character for him.

My father said, "We were hungry, Al."

My mother chimed in, "Eat, Al. You should eat."

"I don't have the time to eat. We had the baby. We had a baby boy, and no one was there."

We all jumped up, hugged him, left the rest of our food on our plates, and ran to the elevator.

Al was so excited when he described what the baby looked like. "He's beautiful, eight pounds and two ounces. And he's twenty-two inches long."

Once out of the elevator, we ran into Barbara's room. There she was, holding their beautiful baby boy. We took turns kissing Barbara for a job well done. She looked exhausted.

Al told us, "His name is Michael. Michael William Scarpelli."

I thought, *Thank God. Now I can go home.*

On the way home, I started thinking about how much had happened since I graduated. Prior to that time, my six years at school were routine. I would go to school, go home for the holidays, and work in my father's office for the summer months. Come September, I'd go back to school. It was the same schedule for six years. But since this past June, it was like all hell broke loose. Now my life has more responsibility, but it's much more exciting.

Chapter 25

Seeing Dr. Bass was the best thing I could have done. Since my last visit to his office, I had not heard from TC. It was like he was waiting for something—I guessed, for justice. *Isn't that what this whole thing was about?* I wondered if I would ever see him again and hoped against hope that I wouldn't.

I started to think about what our next step should be now that the fingerprints matched. It was still going to be tough, trying to prove he murdered all those people, even though we had Pop as a witness and even though he still had a price on his head. That was a long time ago, and he'd lived an exemplary life and was well known in the annals of justice. If Mario could get the gun thrown out, it would be just be my grandfather's word against his.

Wait a minute! Pop said his brother-in-law, Peter Sorrento, survived. I wondered if he was still alive. He could be. He would be around the same age as Pop and Mario. I'm going to check that out. If he is still alive, we could bring him here to corroborate Pop's testimony.

With two witnesses and the fingerprints, the government had an excellent case for identification. We might also be able to bring in an expert on photo enhancement. Pop said he recognized Mario from the painting because Mario in the painting looked just like his father had in Italy. Although, Pop claimed he would remember Mario's face anywhere. And he would have recognized him if he had ever found him.

I had been so busy, I shut my cell phone off. It wasn't until I got home that I checked my messages. Two messages: one from Uncle Frank and the other from Jessie. I was beat so I decided not to call them back until tomorrow. A salami sandwich, a beer, the football game, and bed sounded much more inviting.

I was in a sound sleep when the phone rang. I picked up.

My uncle asked, "Is it a boy or a girl?"

"Are you out of your mind? It's two in the morning and you needed to know now?"

He started laughing. "You know, Frankie, this is really funny. Rarely have I ever seen you pissed off. You're usually so reserved. But now I see you do have the Scarpelli temper."

"You're damn right I do. And you'll see it again if you keep pushing all the wrong buttons."

He kept laughing. "What a tough guy. You really scare me."

I was ready to hang up when my thoughts of a witness came back to me, so I mentioned it to him.

"We need someone to corroborate Pop's account of the murders, and I was wondering if Peter Sorrento is still alive."

He said, "I'm way ahead of you, kid. Peter is alive and he's willing to testify. And look at that—I never even finished high school."

I said, "Swell," and hung up.

After I got to work, I walked into Darlene's office and handed her a latte. She claimed she hadn't seen or heard from me in quite a while. She was wondering if we were still on for Friday night.

It dawned on me that I hadn't even called her.

"I'm sorry, Darlene. I've been so damn busy with family matters; I haven't had a chance to call. First, my grandfather's heart attack, then last night I had to rush to St. Barnabas Hospital in New Jersey because my brother's wife was having a baby. By the way, it was a boy and they named him Michael."

Darlene smiled. "You have been busy."

"Yes, but everything will soon be under control. My grandfather is moving in with my aunt and uncle, and today the baby comes home from the hospital. I miss you, Darlene. Why do we have to wait until Friday? Why can't we go out for dinner tonight?"

"You're on, Frank. Our usual place?"

"Sure, that's fine with me. I can't wait to spend some time with you."

On the way back to my office, my cell phone rang. It was my uncle. I went into my office and closed the door. He said he got the report back from the investigator.

"It seems Mario changed his name to Mark Moran when he landed in London, England, in 1943. Probably close to the same time he left Sicily. He enrolled at City University in London, where he met Alice Crenshaw, an American who was married to an English soldier. They started out as friends and then Alice received the news that her husband was killed in action. She decided to stay at the University to get her degree.

"That's when their friendship turned into a relationship. They got married nine months later. They both graduated and soon after, Mr. and Mrs. Moran came to the United States. Being he was the husband of an American citizen, he did not have to go through the usual channels to get a visa. They applied and he received a visa through the American Consulate and soon after received his citizenship.

"They moved to the town of Princeton, New Jersey. He was accepted at Princeton University, where he earned his law degree. They later moved to New York City, where he worked for the firm of Johnson, Johnson, and Mayhew for five years. He later started his own business. Mark and Alice adopted two male children who they named Mark and Timothy. They had the adoption papers sealed.

"Apparently, the boys were never told. Mark is known as a proficient and ruthless attorney who specialized in winning fraud, divorce, and what is known as white-color crime cases for his wealthy clients. The one thing that is not known is how he got off the island of Sicily."

He came up for air.

"It's a good thing, Frankie. At least we have a paper trail for Mark Moran." He said if we didn't have this information, the fingerprints, and witnesses, we might not have had a strong case. "John and I are coming over tonight to discuss how this is going to go down."

"I can't do it tonight. I have a dinner date with Darlene."

"Then break it. This is too important."

"I can't. I won't be late. It's just for a couple of hours after work. Can't we do this later on at the apartment?"

"How about I buy you both dinner at the Marriott?"

"Thanks, but no thanks. I want to be alone with her."

He laughed. "You're right, kid. I forgot. At your age the hormones are really kicking in."

"Me? What about you and Aunt Dorothy? You're married fifteen years and you both still make goggle eyes at each other. And what about those sly innuendos you think no one can catch? Plus, you still go out for romantic dinners and weekend getaways. What's that all about?"

"You're right, Frankie. When you're right, you're right. That woman is the light of my life. Without her, I'm nothing. John and I will wait for you at the apartment. What time will you be finished?"

"I'll call you before I leave the restaurant."

This time was different when we walked over to the Marriott. It was the first time we went as a couple, and not associates. I put my arm around her as we walked across the street. The weather was brisk and I could feel her shiver.

For some reason, we had little trouble getting a table. Maybe it was because this time we went into the dining room so we could have a private conversation.

She started to look around.

"Are you meeting someone else here?"

"No, I'm looking around for your Uncle Frank."

I asked, "Why, do you have a thing for him? If so, you better get over it. He's a happily married man. And the one thing you have to know about me, I don't play second fiddle to anyone."

"No, silly. I don't have a thing for him. I enjoy his company. He's different. He kind of reminds me of Humphrey Bogart in a way. He can be tough with the men, but he's a gentleman around women. He also gives the impression that he's strong and in control. Women like to feel protected and safe. When you're with him, you feel safe. But actually, I have a thing for his namesake, who is very much like the man I described."

"I'm glad you clarified that, Darlene, because his namesake has a thing for you."

It took all I had not to lean over and kiss her passionately. Instead, I controlled my emotions. All I could do was look into those beautiful dark brown eyes and wish we were in my bedroom.

No sooner had the waiter come over to take our order than it dawned on me. What if this thing goes down with Mario? Being seen with me might put her in jeopardy. Mario Moretti is a ruthless killer. No telling what he might do to stop my grandfather and Peter from testifying.

I guess I didn't want to think about it until now. The firm was right across the street. I had to tell her what was going on. And after tonight, I wouldn't be able to see her until Mario was taken into custody.

This is the woman I'm in love with. My God, the *love* word actually crossed my mind.

"Darlene, I have something to tell you, and you can't tell anyone about our conversation."

She got serious. "What is it, Frank? It sounds ominous."

"I don't know how to put this, but there's going to be a shake-up at the firm. And it might be wise if you started looking for another job. In fact, you should leave the firm as soon as possible."

"What are you talking about? Why would I do that? What kind of a shake-up? I'm sorry, Frank, you're going to have to be a lot more specific and give me some kind of explanation."

"I can't go into it right now. In all probability the firm as we know it may no longer exist."

"Do you mean that the firm is in financial trouble?"

"No, it's not that. My family and I are going to bring it down like a house of cards."

She looked very angry. "Why? Why would you do such a thing?"

"You know that information you gave me on the fugitive named Mario Moretti? Well, we have evidence that proves that Mark Moran, Sr., is actually Mario Moretti."

"Come on, Frank. That is too much of a coincidence. You're teasing me, aren't you?"

"I know it sounds crazy, but Mark has been identified by two credible witnesses. They will sign a deposition and swear to it in court that Mark Moran is Mario Moretti."

"God, Frank, shouldn't you tell my father?"

"No, Darlene, I don't want anyone to know until my uncle and I decide how we're going to initiate his arrest. There are many factors to consider. After I leave here, I'm going back to my place, where I'm to meet with my uncle and John. We're going to discuss how we're going to have Mark apprehended and by whose authority. This is not a war crime. He was not in the Italian army."

"Maybe so, but he killed five servicemen and three Italian civilians."

"I know that, Darlene, but this is also a family matter. I recently found out that my Aunt Angelina, my grandfather's twin sister, was one of the people killed. Uncle Peter, my aunt's husband, who still lives in Palermo, Sicily, was contacted. He's flying in to New York to testify, along with my grandfather."

"Frank, what are the legal ramifications? That crime was committed in Italy."

"I know that, but Pop and his brother-in-law witnessed the murders."

"Oh, my God, Frank. How horrible."

"We're thinking of going to see district attorney, Michael Bonito, to see if he's willing to press charges against Mario for killing those five Americans before Italy has him extradited. And then again, we might be able to turn him over to the military so they can try him for the murder of those five soldiers."

"You know, Frank, a man like that could be very dangerous. You had better be careful and watch your back. I think it would be safer if you stayed at my place."

"You would do that for me?"

She leaned in really close and said, "Yes, I would do that for you."

"Thanks, sweetheart, but I won't put you in that kind of jeopardy. In fact, after we decide what action we're taking, I won't be seeing you for a while."

"Don't be so sure, Mr. Scarpelli."

I didn't like the way she said that, and I certainly didn't need to be worrying about her. Right now I had enough on my plate.

After dinner, I drove Darlene home and walked her to her door. We kissed, and the excitement was again overwhelming. I would have liked being inside her door instead of outside. But before we could begin, I had an old score to settle.

I got home at nine o'clock. My uncle and John were watching a football game, drinking beer, and eating pretzels. Uncle Frank looked up when I entered the room.

"Hi, kid, you're just in time to watch the end of this game."

"Come on, guys, you know I had a date with my girl tonight and cut it short to meet with you. Why don't we get started? I'll get a beer and we'll hash out a plan."

There was a knock on my door. I wondered who the hell it could be.

"Uncle Frank, did you ask my dad to join us?"

"Are you kidding?"

John took a gun out of his holster and aimed it at the door.

I asked, "Are you out of your mind? Put that damn thing away. Holy shit, when did you get so suspicious?"

My uncle agreed and told John to put the gun away.

I opened the door and it was Darlene.

"Didn't I just drive you home?"

"Yes, but I figured two good attorneys are better than one."

"How did you get past the doorman?"

"I told Willie that I was your surprise birthday present and it would be a shame to spoil the surprise."

My uncle shouted, "Let her in, kid. She's one smart lady."

They both got up and greeted her.

She smiled and sat down. "Hi, Frank. Hi, John. Don't worry about me. I'm bound by client confidentiality not to repeat anything I hear in this room. Little Frank is now my client."

"Hey, I don't like that 'little Frank' thing."

"Well, how am I going to distinguish to whom I'm speaking? You're both named Frank."

"I see your point. You can call me 'young Frank.'"

260

My uncle groaned, "I don't think so. Young Frank as opposed to Old Frank. I'm not ready to be called Old Frank. Why can't Darlene call you what the family calls you when we get together? Frankie."

They all looked in my direction. "OK. Frankie. But only when my uncle is around."

"As I see it, gentlemen, this is a very complicated case and I wish you would let my father help," Darlene said.

"Darlene, I told you I wanted to keep you out of this. What kind of respect will your father have for me if I drag his daughter into this mess?"

"He's been a military man for most of his life. He could advise you on how to conduct this investigation and what your legal government options are. This is not a civilian matter. This happened during a war, so technically it's a war crime. The Department of State should probably be the branch to handle this case."

I interjected, "I know the United Nations Security Council established the International Criminal Tribunal for Yugoslavia, but I don't think it applies in these circumstances."

My uncle intervened. "I don't understand a word you two are talking about. As far as I'm concerned, Mario Moretti killed eight innocent people. And one was my aunt. Now I realize we can't prosecute him for the crimes he committed in Italy unless he goes back to Italy, but as a civilian, he also mur-dered five Americans in cold blood."

Darlene reiterated, "That's my point, Frank. They were not American civil-ians. They were American soldiers, invading Sicily during wartime. Please, let me ask my father for his help."

I emphatically said, "No!"

"You are so stubborn, Frankie. I had no idea you were so pig-headed."

She looked so cute when she was mad. I started to laugh. Then she started to laugh. I realized in a lot of ways, she was a lot like me: quiet, a quick sense of humor, not very emotional, always in control, and stubborn as hell.

"I've made a decision," my uncle announced. "What we'll do is go down to Michael, the district attorney, and put our cards on the table. Let him advise us as to who has the jurisdiction. In the meantime, he can have him arrested on murder charges and hold him without bail. This way he can't flee."

We all agreed.

Darlene asked, "Does anyone want coffee?

We all said yes.

Even though we had a tentative agreement, we were up all night hashing this all out.

After everyone left, Darlene helped clean the coffee table and put the cups in the dishwasher. I followed her into the kitchen. I stood behind her while she was loading it. I put my arms around her waist.

"You were marvelous. You don't let me get away with a thing. I like gutsy women. Or did you just come here to see my uncle?"

She turned around and faced me. She put her arms around my neck and then her fingers through the back of my hair. She said, "All kidding aside, Frank, I want to help."

"No, Darlene. I'm adamant about this one thing. It's out of the question, and I don't want to discuss it. You could be in danger, and I won't allow that."

"I realize that and I'll be careful. At least let me help you make some of the legal decisions, as long as you're not going to take my father's advice."

"OK, that's a promise. This could go down in a couple of days or weeks. We're not sure and we still have to wait for Peter to get here from Italy. Once he gets here, we will let the DA decide the course of action. Now you said you had a birthday present for me?"

"Come on, now. You know that was just a way to get the doorman to let me in."

"Are you a person that offers a gift and then takes it back?"

"Not usually, but in this instance—"

I started by unbuttoning her blouse and unhooking her bra. We started kissing, then my hands started to caress her body, first her breasts, then her nipples, and then I moved my hand down to her panties.

I whispered, "Please stay the night."

She pulled away and started for the hallway. I thought, *Shit, I blew it and now she's going for her coat.*

When I walked in, she was walking up the stairs toward my bedroom.

She said, "Come on, slowpoke."

I ran to catch up to her. We were laughing all the way up the stairs and landed on the bed, exhausted. It started out to be one hell of a day, but what a great night. I was a little nervous about this. I wanted to please her more than any other woman I'd been intimate with. I wanted her approval.

After we made love, I told her I loved her and she professed her love for me. We made love again. After it was over, we lay there, her head tucked under my arm. We were quiet for a while, and then she turned to face me with a serious look on her face.

"Frank, I'm worried about how this relationship is going to work."

"What do you mean, Darlene? So far, it's working out just great. I have no complaints."

"That's not what I mean. Your family is Italian and they're from New Jersey. They have roots in the community. You grew up in an all-white neighborhood. How are they going to take the fact that their son is in love with an African American?"

"I never gave that a thought, so I guess it doesn't matter what they think."

"It does, Frank. It matters. It's obvious. Your family is close, and I don't want to come between you and them. That's not the way to start a relationship."

I asked, "What relationship? You gave me a present and I took it."

She started laughing. "When is your birthday, anyway?"

"It's late November. I'll tell you when it gets close. And I'd like the same gift that you gave me tonight."

She kicked me.

"Ouch. What about your family? How will they feel about you seeing an Italian, white guy whose uncle is rumored to have ties with the Mafia?"

"I doubt that race would be an issue. Both my parents had careers, and we moved around a lot. We were used to being in a multiracial and ethnically diverse environment. My parents have friends from all over the world.

"My father's concern will probably be your character, your behavior, and possibly, your earning capabilities. You've heard the expression 'army brat'? Well, that's what I was for the first ten years of my life. My father graduated from West Point and my mother from Yale University. They met through mutual friends, right after my mother completed her doctorate in biochemistry.

"My dad was ten years older than my mother, and he was already established in his military career when they married. We moved so frequently that we never maintained a relationship with our biological families. It was not the life my mother had envisioned, and the higher he went up in rank, the less he was home.

"She may have had her education, but not the career she longed for. Finally, after twelve years of marriage, my mother told him she had applied for a professorship at Yale teaching biochemistry and that she had been accepted. She also told him that she and I would be moving within the next couple of weeks and hoped that he would join us. She wanted a home, a real home, and roots for her daughter."

"She stood up to him just like that? What did your father do?"

"He was stunned. He said, 'What can I say or do to change your mind, Veronica?' She said, 'Nothing. My mind is made up. Please say you'll come with us.' He said, 'You're willing to break up our marriage just for a career?' She said, 'Why couldn't I have both? You do.

"He walked out the door and did not return. We then moved to New Haven in August of 1988. My mother bought a lovely home not far from both our schools. My dad called me from time to time, but he never asked to speak to my mother. That Christmas Eve, there was a knock on the door. When my mother opened the door, there was Dad with so many gifts in his arms, you could barely see his face. He struggled to take off his hat. As he threw it in the hallway, he asked if he was still welcome.

"My mother pushed the door all the way open and told him, 'Always, my love.' So my mother went back to teaching and my dad would come home whenever possible. It was an arrangement that suited them; they were both able to be happy because they'd compromised."

"When can I meet your parents, Darlene?"

"My mother died five years ago."

I told her I was sorry and kissed her on her head.

"My mother was killed by a motorist. She had just parked her car, and she walking from the parking lot to the mall when a speeding car went out of control and killed her. That was the darkest day of my life."

This was the first time I had ever seen Darlene so vulnerable. We finally fell asleep with my arms still around her.

We got up extra early the next morning. I dropped her off at her place and rushed back to mine to change for work. I got there on time, business as usual. I went right to work on the Maude Smith case. I carefully read her deposition. On paper, her story was plausible for self-defense or by using the battered-woman syndrome, but we would need proof. Statements from any witnesses who could verify seeing or hearing her allegations, that her husband physically and mentally abused her, would be best. I made a list of everyone I would have to see, starting with Maude Smith.

I had to go over her statement with her. There couldn't be any loopholes in her testimony.

She also had to remember to tell her story in the exact same way each time she was cross-examined, or the prosecutor would tear her statement apart. I would need the name of her doctor. I had to speak to the housekeeper, nanny, neighbors, friends, and family—people she might have confided in. And I had to check the hospital to see if she had ever gone there for treatment. Was there any infidelity on either side? My first stop meant a trip to the jail where Mrs. Smith was being held until the trial.

Mark was there while she was being interrogated and for her hearing. He tried to get her out on bail at the arraignment, but Judge Markham said he would not give her bail because she was a flight risk. Mark and I thought it had more to do with the killing of one of their own, a judge. Finding an unbiased judge was going to be difficult.

I called the correctional facility to make an appointment for 11:00 a.m. Obviously, this was the first time I had actually walked into a jail to interview a client. When they brought Mrs. Smith in to speak to me, she looked surprised. She asked me where Mark was. I explained that I was Frank Scarpelli, Mark's assistant, and that I was doing the legwork for him. And he would be in to see her in a couple of days.

She smiled and shook my hand. "Nice meeting you, Frank. Please call me Maude."

Behind the smile, you could see the eyes of a terrified woman who was probably wondering how she got in this position. Maude looked younger in person than in her pictures. She was tall and slim with long red hair. Even without makeup, she was beautiful. And in a way, that was detrimental to her case. She was beautiful and rich, and no one would feel sorry for her. We had to prove our case.

"Tell me the truth, Frank. What are my chances?"

I told her she would have to discuss that with Mark, but I confided, "If everything in your statement is true and your story about the abuse checks out and if we can get you a female judge and a mostly female jury, I think you have a very good chance of being acquitted."

There was an actual sigh of relief on Maude's part.

I also stated, "I want to give you hope, but don't forget your husband's position in this community could make it difficult. But Mark is an excellent attorney and not without influence."

We started going over her deposition. Several times during my questioning, her eyes welled up and tears rolled down her face. Her statement was plausible. She killed him in self-defense, but we would have to let the evidence tell the tale. Her story never changed, nor did she contradict any of her statements. I tried to trip her up. I got the names of the people she thought could testify on her behalf. She said Mark had her telephone book, so I shouldn't have any trouble in contacting them.

When I left, Maude was still upset. As I was leaving, she asked how her son was. I told her we would find out and get back to her.

I returned to the office. On my way past Millie, she told me that Mark wanted to see me. She called him and told him I was back. He said to send me in. I was really taken by surprise because when I walked in, standing right in front of me was Mario Moretti, alias, Mark Moran, Sr.

I got very nervous and stammered when Junior introduced us.

"Frank, come on in, I want you to meet my father, Mark Moran, Sr."

"How do you do, sir? I have heard a great deal about you."

He replied, "I have also heard a great deal about you, Frank."

His handshake was firm for a man in his eighties. If my grandfather had not recognized him, I would find it hard to believe that at one time he was an Italian immigrant. The only distinguishable thing was his eyes. They looked the same as they did in that old picture my grandfather had of him—dark and cold.

"My son told me he is expecting great things from you." Then he then looked at Junior and asked, "What's the name of the new woman you hired?"

"Darlene. Darlene Banks."

"My son told me he thinks you will both make a distinguishable contribution to this firm and we're fortunate to have you."

"Thank you, sir. I appreciate Mark's confidence."

"He also told me your grandfather came in to see you and that he was taken ill. How is he now?"

It just now occurred to me. Had Mr. Moran Senior been in the office that day, he might have recognized my grandfather.

"He's getting better. Thank you for asking."

"Your grandfather, he's from Italy, isn't he?"

"Yes, he is."

He asked, "What part of Italy is he from?"

"Naples. In fact, my grandfather still has family there."

"That's a beautiful city. Have you ever been there?"

"No, sir. I haven't, but someday."

He just wouldn't let the interrogation go. "Scarpelli, I would imagine that's a common name in Italy?"

"I would assume so, sir."

"What's your grandfather's first name?"

"Frank. His name is Frank."

"I see. Your namesake."

It finally dawned on me why Pop lied about his origin. He wanted to find Mario before Mario found him.

Junior finally interrupted. I'm sure he didn't understand why his father was going on and on about my grandfather. He asked, "How are you coming along with the Smith case?"

"Fine, Mark. In fact, I just got back from seeing Mrs. Smith. My next step is to check her credibility and court records. But I was impressed with the fact that she stuck very close to her statement."

There was a pause in the conversation. It was time to leave. I told Mark Senior I had enjoyed meeting him and I left the office. Under my breath, I vowed to see him rot in hell.

When I got to my office, I made some notes pertaining to my visit with Maude. Before I knew it, it was getting late. Joan came in and asked if there was anything she could do for me before going home.

I told her no and that she should have a nice evening. "I'll be leaving shortly."

Darlene stopped in my office to say good night and asked if we were still on for Friday. I suggested we do something different.

"Do you like old movies?"

"I'd like that, Frank. I love old movies!"

"Then what do you say we break open a bottle of wine and I'll pick up some Chinese food or deli? You get to pick."

"Chinese food, shrimp and lobster sauce and don't forget the egg rolls."

"Chinese, it is. Bring your jeans or sweats or whatever is comfortable. I'll put on the fireplace. We'll gorge ourselves and watch a movie."

She smiled that broad smile. "Frank, that sounds wonderful—a relaxing night at home."

I got that stupid schoolboy feeling again. *Damn it.*

Chapter 26

Thank God it's Friday. I went through Maude Smith's list of names she gave me. I was trying to set up appointments with some of the people on the list. I needed to get some corroboration for a case of abuse. Between that case and reading briefs for next week's meeting, this week went fast.

I left a half hour before I was to meet Darlene in the lobby to pick up the Chinese food and a good bottle of wine. When we met at the first floor elevator, I had the food and wine, and she had a small duffel bag. We took the elevator to the garage where Junior happened to see us both getting into my car. He waived and so did we.

Darlene said, "Uh-oh the cat's out of the bag."

"It's no big deal. For all he knows, we could be going out for a drink."

She held up her duffel bag. We started to laugh. We were in such a good mood, we didn't even care.

After I parked my car in the garage, I took my seatbelt off and leaned over to kiss her. She pulled away.

"I've noticed that you don't like public displays of affection, do you, Darlene?"

"It's not that I don't like it, Frank. I'm just not used to it. I feel a little embarrassed by it. I guess it stems back from my childhood. Don't forget, my father was in the military and in the limelight throughout his career. He showed little emotion or affection."

"Well, I come from a family where even the men hug each other. We kiss when we come in and we kiss when we go out. It's probably a bit much. But I can understand how you feel. I'll try to watch it."

"No, don't stop, Frank. I don't want you to be like my father. That's one of the things I love about you. You're so different. You're so romantic. I like that. But I'm going to have to get used to it."

"That's why they call me the Italian Stallion."

"That still has to be proven."

"What about the other night?"

"Like I said, Frank, that still has to be proven."

"You know, it's a good thing I'm secure in my masculinity. You could sure deflate some insecure person's ego with that remark. But not me because I know I'm good. And no Chinese food for you."

Once we got into the apartment, we dashed to the bedroom and changed our clothes. Darlene put on her sweats and a tight blue T-shirt. I told her that she really didn't need all those clothes.

"Now stop that, Frank."

"You're right. Our food is getting cold. I put the gas fireplace on, opened a bottle of wine, put all our food on the coffee table, and put the disc in the DVD player."

"What movie did you get?"

"You'll see. And then her idol came on. It was Bogie in *The Big Sleep*.

Her eyes lit up and she smiled. We ate and drank while watching the movie. Darlene fell asleep on the couch just as soon as the movie was over. I didn't want to disturb her, so I decided to get some sleep myself.

I don't know what time it started. It had to be around 2:00 am, that's the time it usually started.

I was in the bushes, crouched down, hiding from the German Army that was on patrol. They were within two feet of our position. My heart was pounding. I could hear them hitting the bushes as they looked for the band of the underground resistance fighters. Finally, they passed and I turned around and looked for TC. He was crouching next to me, smiling.

"Hi, Frank. I brought you here to warn you."

"Of what? I'm doing everything possible. Everything you asked me to do."

"That's my point, kid."

"Kid? You're younger than I am."

TC laughed. "Had I lived, I would be eighty-four." He then got serious. "Listen to me, Frank. Once Mario gets wind of what's going on, he will set out to destroy you and your family. This man is a ruthless sociopath. Be careful. And there is something else."

I started to hear another voice from a distance, and I didn't know where it was coming from.

"Frank, wake up. Frank?"

I opened my eyes. It was Darlene. She looked scared to death.

She asked, "Are you, all right? You must have been having a nightmare."

I was stunned and sweating but managed to reply, "Yes, I was having a bad dream. I'm OK now."

"What was it about, Frank? Do you want to talk about it?"

"Darlene, I want to be very honest with you. There is something you don't know about me, and I guess now that the cat's out of the bag, now would be the time to tell you. But I must warn you. You're going to find the story I'm about to tell you is weird."

I proceeded to tell her when the dreams first started and how Dr. Bass had helped me in conquering my fears. How he'd made me address them by following the sequence of my dreams to the end. And of course, the horror was the massacre.

She sat there, stunned.

"I was afraid of what your reaction would be. That's why I never mentioned it before now."

"Frank, this is more than weird, it's unbelievable."

273

"Do you think I don't know that? I've had to live with this my whole life. But it's finally coming to an end."

"How could you know that?"

"I don't know how I know. I just do. The purpose of the dreams was for me to seek justice. At least, that's what Dr. Bass thinks. Once Mario is caught, it should stop. Look, I've almost accomplished what I was supposed to do. I know what you're thinking and I wouldn't blame you if you walked right out of my life. This sounds like I'm some kind of a weirdo."

"Does your uncle know?"

"Yes, I told him a couple of weeks ago."

"Did he believe you?"

"Not at first. But yes, he does now, especially after he spoke to Pop."

"Well, Frank, it must be so. This is too odd for anyone to make up."

She leaned over and she French kissed me passionately. I had no trouble responding. For once, she was the aggressor. This I liked. She was on top of me and took control. We started to undress each other. She wasn't rough, but she also wasn't gentle. It was a real turn-on. It was difficult to contain my excitement, but I held on until we were both ready. What a woman!

When it was over, I asked, "Where did you learn this?"

"Well, you see, Frank, I had this dream."

She made me laugh.

"You're really funny. Do you know that?"

We finally went up to the bedroom and crashed. Before I fell asleep, I was hoping to go back and visit with TC. He said he had something to tell me.

Maybe it will happen tonight? This was the first time I had looked forward to my encounter with him.

I drove Darlene home around nine o'clock the next morning. She said she had a luncheon engagement with some friend of hers from college. I suggested her leaving some clothes at my place, but she said it was too soon. I wondered if my nightmares had any bearing on her decision.

When I got home, I called my uncle to tell him about my encounter with Mark Moran, Sr. I also told him how Mark Senior questioned me about Pop's region of birth and his first name.

He questioned me on what I answered.

"I told him Pop was from Naples and his first name was Frank."

"That's good, but watch it, Frankie. This man is cunning. We have to work fast. Especially if he checks you out. Although there would be no reason to."

He told me he had some good news. It seemed Peter got his passport and will be landing in Newark Airport on Wednesday.

"That's great. They work fast in Italy."

"Not really. I had to pull a few strings."

"Like what?"

"*Madone!* What difference does it make?"

He hung up.

I decided to stay home and do all the stuff I hated doing but has to be done, cleaning, grocery shopping, washing clothes, dusting, and vacuuming. Before anything else, I had to get out and run. It was cold and it felt like it was going to snow. But the cold felt good, and I enjoyed being out in the fresh air.

After I got back from running, there was a message on my recorder; it was Darlene. It started with "Hi, Frank. I was thinking things over."

Here it comes.

"Very few things are out of the realm of possibility, so what I'm trying to say is . . . I believe in you and I love you, weird stuff and all."

Thank you, God.

I decided to let the chores go for a while and started studying for the bar exam. It was already November, and I hadn't even cracked a book open. The weather was lousy and this would be a good time to start. Plus, I would rather be studying than doing laundry.

I got my books out and started to take notes, but I couldn't keep my mind on my studies. I kept thinking about TC. I was wondering what he was going to tell me before Darlene woke me up.

I began to wonder if I could contact him without being hypnotized. I went to my bedroom, lay down on the bed, and made myself comfortable. I started to repeat, "TC, TC, TC."

Nothing. I started to count, "One, two, three, four, five."

Nothing. I got up, lit a candle, and put it on my night table. I just stared at it and tried to think of nothing. I cleared my mind.

Before I knew it, I was crouching down in the woods, but it was different. No one was there. It was quiet and I was alone. I stood up and looked around. There was TC, walking toward me and smiling, as usual.

He said, "This is a surprise. You actually came looking for me?"

"Tell me about it. You started to tell me something before I woke up. What was it?"

"I just wanted to tell you there is another way to identify Mario Moretti. Mario has a tattoo on his chest. It's two crossed saber swords about three inches in length. I just happened to notice it when we were at the cabin. Mario changed his shirt while we changed into the civilian clothes we were given."

I wondered why my grandfather never mentioned that. Then I got mad. "You know you could have saved me a lot of grief if you had told me that before. That information would have eliminated my grandfather."

I know that, Frank, but if you had eliminated your grandfather, you wouldn't have looked for Mario. The whole purpose for my visits was for you to find Mario Moretti. I don't have all the answers."

I woke up. I think I'll take a ride to New Jersey to see my grandfather.

I called my uncle's place. Aunt Dorothy answered. She said my uncle wasn't at home, but she and Pop were.

When I arrived at the gate, my aunt let me in. This time around, I was glad they had this protection. I didn't know if Mario would have the guts to try something here in the United States. My uncle was right; it's smart to take precautions.

My aunt was as hospitable as ever, but Pop still seemed frail. My only hope was that he would be able to make it through this whole ordeal. He came to meet me. He hugged me and asked me to tell him if I had any news. Not knowing what my uncle saw fit to tell him, I was reluctant to go into too much detail. I walked into the kitchen where there was coffee and cannoli waiting for me.

"Oh, boy, Aunt Dorothy, cannoli, my favorite, thanks!"

"I know that, sweetheart. You're very welcome."

We sat down and started to talk about Al's new baby and how he and Barbara brought the baby over to see everyone.

Pop said, "It's a beautiful baby. The new come in, and the old go out."

"Pop, please don't say that. You're not going anywhere."

"I am, my boy, but not for a while. First, I have to see Mario rot in jail for the rest of his life. That bastard!"

He was starting to get excited, so I changed the subject.

"So, Pop, I hear your friend Peter will be here next week. I bet you're anxious to see him."

"Yes," he replied, "I want to see Peter. It's been a long time. And this sweet woman, my daughter-in-law, is letting him stay here with me."

My aunt smiled at Pop and said, "Why not? We have plenty of room."

I was just starting to ask Pop about Mario's tattoo when my uncle came in. "Well, look who's here. Hi, kid."

My aunt immediately got up to get her husband a cup of coffee. My uncle smiled, walked over to her, and gave her a kiss on her cheek.

"Thank you, sweetheart."

I was wondering if it was just me who noticed they had a relationship that transcended just being a couple. My uncle sat down to join us.

I went back to asking Pop about Mario's tattoo.

"Pop, did you know that Mario Moretti has a tattoo on his chest?"

"I don't remember, Frankie."

My uncle said, "If you don't remember the tattoo, how did you remember his face?"

"His face is burned into my brain. Besides, I told you, he looks just like his father. Let me think. Don't bother me now."

We sat in silence while Pop stared at the wall.

"Yes, he did. That's right! He got that when he went to London to stay with his uncle."

I asked him, "What did it look like?"

"I think it was two knives?"

I said, "Close enough! They're crossed swords."

My uncle stated, "You should have told us, Pop. That's a great help in identifying him."

"Unless he had them removed."

"He could have, Uncle Frank, but laser removal has just been perfected within the last couple of decades. I doubt if he thought to have it taken off."

Pop said, "I forget sometimes. How much will you remember when you're eighty-three?"

We all laughed. I put my arm around Pop and told him that he was doing great.

Pop asked, "How did you know, Frankie? How did you know that Mario had a tattoo?"

278

"The same way I knew everything else about Mario Moretti. TC told me."

My uncle put his hands on his face. "Please don't start that crap again."

Pop asked me, "Who's this TC person?"

"No one important, Pop. I just wanted to know if he had any distinguishing marks and you said yes."

"Good, Frankie. Let's nail him."

Pop got up from the table. He said he was tired and was going to take a nap. My aunt asked him if he took his medication. He nodded.

My uncle confided that he was worried about him and told me that Pop was not doing well. He thought the only thing keeping him alive was revenge. That word struck a chord.

"In my dreams, every time I entered the church, the priest asked, 'What do you want?' and TC always said, 'Revenge.'" I told my uncle that Peter was also getting up there in age and that I was concerned that Mario's defense attorney could tear those guys apart.

He assured me that it wouldn't come to that.

"Mario is a fugitive with a price on his head. He's wanted in two countries. All we have to do is prove that Mark Moran is Mario Moretti. What surprised me is that egotistical bastard kept the same initials. He must have thought he was so clever, and that no one would ever find him. Do you realize that if you didn't find the gun and if Pop didn't go to your office, in all probability, Mario would have gotten away with this?"

"It's even stranger than you can imagine, Uncle Frank."

He said, "I don't want to hear anymore about that stuff."

My aunt chimed in. "What are you guys talking about?"

My uncle answered. "Nothing, sweetheart. Just how everything fell into place. Coincidences."

"I don't believe that for a minute, Frank. There are no coincidences."

He laughed. "Don't you start."

We all started to laugh. My uncle changed the subject.

"I really like your girlfriend. She's smart and gutsy. I like that in a woman."

"Good, because she's a keeper if she'll have me."

He asked, "What do you think your mother will say?"

"You mean about her being African American?"

"Yes, and the fact that she's not Italian."

My aunt asked, "Do you love her, Frankie?"

"Yes, Aunt Dorothy, I do. I love her very much. But we're just starting to get to know each other. For years, Darlene dated this guy she met at Yale University. A couple of months ago, they got engaged. Then, out of the blue, she broke it off. So we haven't been dating that long. But I think she's the most fascinating woman I have ever met."

"Frankie, who cares what anyone thinks? If you love her, go for it. When I started going out with your uncle, it was pretty much the same prejudices. I was Jewish, and Frank's whole family is Italian. My family wanted me to marry a Jewish doctor. No surprise there. And your family wanted him to marry a Catholic, Italian woman who could cook and have babies. When both families realized that nothing they said would change our minds, rather than lose us both, they accepted our decision. Your parents love you, and they won't risk losing you. They will accept your choice. Believe me."

I hugged her. "You're a wise woman. And you're right. If they don't accept Darlene, they will lose me because I won't risk losing her." I asked my aunt, "How does your family feel about Uncle Frank now?"

She smiled at him. "They love the way he makes me happy. And if I'm happy, they're happy. It will be the same for you and Darlene."

On the way home, I called Darlene. She didn't answer, so I left her a message.

"I received your message and I'm happy with your decision. Call me when you get in. I love you!"

No sooner had I left the message than my phone rang. I didn't even look to see who it was; I just assumed it was Darlene returning my call.

"Wow, that was fast!"

Jessie said, "Really?"

"Hi, Jessie, how's it going?"

"Everything is OK. I wanted to know how things were going with you and Dr. Bass."

"Great, it's going great. Thanks for recommending him. I think we made great strides and the end is finally near. I actually feel some kind of relief."

"That's great, Frank. I'm really happy for you. You haven't called me in a while."

"I know. I've been working on this case for my boss, and it occupies most of my time."

She paused and asked, "When am I going to meet your girlfriend?"

"Soon, Jessie, very soon."

"Great, you're a lucky guy. I hope it works out for you better than it did for me."

"Come on now, Jessie, life is a risk. Just because it didn't work out with him doesn't mean it won't work with someone else. There are a lot of men out there who would give anything to be with someone like you."

"Really, Frank? Do you know any?"

She put me on the spot. I thought of Norman Shires.

"Yes, there is this guy in my office. I'll talk to him. Maybe we could all go out for a couple of drinks."

Jessie perked up.

"What's he like?"

"I don't know. He's just a guy, an attorney."

"Is he cute? Does he have all his hair?"

"I don't know what a woman thinks is cute. He's thirty and, yes, he has all his hair. For God's sakes he's only thirty. He's kind of tall."

"He sounds OK, Frank. Let me know if he's up for it."

I told her I would. We said our good-byes and hung up.

Darlene and I connected for breakfast on Sunday, and later that afternoon I went to my family's house for dinner. I asked her to come with me, but she said she wasn't ready; she wanted to wait.

When I arrived, I got the third degree from the family. Everyone wanted to know what my girlfriend was like. I told them she was beautiful, intelligent, and the nicest person I had ever met.

My mother asked if she was Italian.

I told her, "No. She's African American."

It suddenly got so quiet you could have heard a pin drop.

Finally, I said, "Could someone please pass me the meatballs?"

My mother stated, "You know I'm not a prejudice person, Frankie, but if you two decide to get married, do you realize the problems you and your children will face?"

"Mom, this is 2006 and if we do get married and have children, I don't see a problem. And if we do have problems, we'll deal with it."

My father asked about Darlene's family and how I thought they would feel about me.

I told them, "Her mother passed away several years ago. And to tell the truth, I'm not sure her father will approve of me."

My mother got huffy. "How could he not?"

Spoken like a mother who loved her son.

We all laughed.

"Well, Mom, he might just want her to stay within her own class."

My mother nearly dropped her fork. "And what class is that?"

"Politically and militarily connected and well known in polite society. I'm sure you've all heard of him. His name is General Matthew Banks."

Everyone nodded.

"Well, Darlene's his daughter."

Not another word was spoken, except from Al. He asked me to pass the meatballs.

That evening my uncle called and asked me to meet him in the DA's office on Thursday at 9:30 in the morning. Michael Bonito would be expecting us.

Finally, the ball was starting to roll.

Chapter 27

When I awoke the next morning, I felt excitement. I could feel the adrenaline rush, and for a moment, I started thinking and evaluating my aspiration to be a trial attorney. *Maybe I'm on the wrong side? Making someone pay for a crime excites me. Maybe I should be a prosecutor? What am I thinking! This is not the time to make any major decisions. I still have to pass the bar. Come to think of it, Darlene and I should be taking it at the same time. How embarrassing would that be, if she passed and I didn't?*

As soon as I got to the office, I went into my office and closed the door. To my secretary and everyone else except Junior, that meant that I was busy and I did not want to be disturbed. I never told Darlene about my appointment with the district attorney. I didn't want her to be any more involved in this than she already was. She already knew too much.

I was especially concerned about last Friday evening when Junior saw us together in the parking garage. I would never forgive myself if any harm came to her because of my situation. And right now I had enough to worry about without worrying about her safety.

I went back to work and made several appointments to visit some of the people who might be able to corroborate Mrs. Smith's statement. It was quite evident that Judge Smith was not the nice guy he pretended to be, but a wife-beater and a tormentor.

This was not going to be easy. Her statement also indicated that in front of other people, he usually held his aggressive behavior inside until they were alone, which meant there were no witnesses. And according to Mrs. Smith he would punch her in the chest, stomach, and lower back. When dressed, there would not be visual evidence. I also realized that I would need a professional advisor on the symptoms of spousal abuse.

I approached Millie and asked if we had a psychiatrist on retainer for such evaluations. She said we did and gave me the name and telephone number of Dr. Willard Converse, a doctor who happened to have an office in our building. *How convenient.*

I called Dr. Converse and set up an appointment. I also had a thought; if the judge was that cautious in front of family and friends, he might not consider public places a threat? Perhaps his ex-wife and children could be of some help?

I called Maude Smith and asked her for the names of the local restaurants, pubs, and areas they frequented. She gave me a short list of their local itinerary. I walked into a restaurant called the Downtown Bistro.

I asked to speak to the manager. He walked over and asked if he could help me. I gave him my card and introduced myself as one of the defense attorneys for Mrs. Smith. He told me his name was Ryan Clark.

"I'll get right to the point, Ryan. Mrs. Smith said that she and the judge were regulars at the Downtown Bistro. I'm sure you know who they are. Would you mind if I asked you some questions?"

"No, I don't mind. In fact I'll be glad to help her out if I can."

"Great. Had you or your employees noticed any unusual behavior on the part of Judge Smith while they were dining?"

"What do you want me to say?"

"The truth and only the truth. Is there anything you could tell me that can corroborate her story that he was abusive? Did you ever notice any abuse or misconduct on the judge's part towards Mrs. Smith?"

"Yes I have. It's always busy in here, so I would pass their table many times during the evening. That man was a piece of work. He always had his teeth clenched, and he always seemed angry."

"Angry at whom? The service?"

"No, at his wife. She's a beautiful woman and men stared. But she never looked back. She always looked down. She was always afraid that he would create a scene."

"Why? Did he ever create a scene?"

"Yes, a couple of months ago, they came in and I gave them their usual table. She got up to go to the restroom and he followed her. I had to pass them on my way to the kitchen, and I saw him grab her arm. It looked like he was twisting it. She asked him to stop, that he was hurting her. And then she threatened to make a scene if he didn't. When he saw me, he let go and went back to their table like nothing had happened."

I asked if he remembered any other incidents.

"That night was the only time I saw him get physical. But he was always cursing at her. Saying that she was stupid. That she was getting fat and that he knew she was having an affair. You know, stuff like that. It seems the more he drank, the more abusive he got."

I thanked him and left.

I decided to go back to the building to see Dr. Converse. My conversation with him was quite shocking. I soon realized I had lived a sheltered life. I'd been punished from time to time with a swat on my butt when I deserved it. I never saw my parents hit or hurt each other in any way. They bickered back and forth until one of them stopped. It was usually my father. So I was surprised when Dr. Converse said that statistics show that 50 percent of all women have experienced some form of domestic violence from a spouse, partner, or a family member.

Dr. Converse said he would see Maude Smith as I had requested and evaluate her condition. He indicated that with all his experience, he was quite sure he could tell if she were lying. Furthermore, he could identify whether

Mrs. Smith had any symptoms of posttraumatic stress syndrome that sometimes accompanies abuse.

I decided that I would stop interviewing until Dr. Converse visited Mrs. Smith at the correctional facility. I went back to my office and put my notes on the case in my computer.

Darlene stopped in my office on the way to the lounge to get a cup of coffee.

"I'm also working on a case with Norman," she said.

"Great. What's it about?"

"One of our clients was picked up for indecent exposure in a parking garage. It's only a misdemeanor, but this is the third time he's been charged."

"You had better be careful, honey. If he takes a look at you, he might do it again."

She had a cup in her hand and she threw it at me. I ducked.

"You could have killed me with that."

She smiled. "If I wanted to kill you, I would have. And who knows? I still might."

I laughed. "I didn't know you had such a temper."

"I usually don't. I'm still not used to that New Jersey caustic wit of yours."

"OK, now that I know it provokes you to violence, I'll remember to keep it under control."

She smiled that sensuous smile of hers. "Don't stop now. I'm not only starting to get used to it, I'm taking lessons. And soon, Frank Scarpelli, I'll be able to give it back."

She walked out of my office, giving me a wiggly Marilyn Monroe exit.

It was funny. She was usually so sophisticated and understated. I started to laugh my head off. It was a playful side of her I hadn't seen before. She was full of surprises.

I suddenly realized how much I liked my job and the people I worked with. Maybe it will work out for them. Maybe they'll be able to wait out the bad publicity. Maybe they can change the name of the firm. I sometimes feel like I'm the traitor.

Chapter 28

It was Thursday. At 9:30 a.m., it would be time for Mario to get the shit kicked out of him. And I was glad to be part of seeing him go down.

I called Joan and told her that today I would not be coming into the office. She assumed I must be sick because she told me to eat some chicken soup and I would feel better in the morning.

According to my uncle, Pop's friend Peter was in culture shock. He'd never been out of Sicily before now. The energy and population of our area overwhelmed him. He spoke little English, but Pop was still able to translate. It must have taken a lot of hate or righteous indignation to get an eighty-four-year-old man out of his comfort zone.

I was to meet them all in the DA's private waiting room. The weather was cold but clear. The holidays were upon us. How fitting it was to have Mario behind bars at this time of the year. Christmas was just six weeks away.

When I got to the DA's office, they were all sitting in the waiting room, even John. I greeted everyone and introduced myself as best I could to Peter. My Italian was very rusty, to say the least. He stood, hugged me, and kissed me on both cheeks. *Oh yeah, he's part of the clan.*

Pop said Peter was thrilled to death because Frank bought him a cappuccino from Starbucks. He wanted to know if they were from Italy—even though he never knew anyone with the last name of Starbuck. We all laughed, including him, although I doubt he knew what we were laughing at.

Finally, we were told that Michael would see us, so we all filed into his office. He got up and shook all our hands. He went to my uncle to give him a hug, wanting to know how come he hadn't seen him in such a long time. He also wanted to know how Dottie and Robin were doing.

I was stunned.

He looked at me and said, "Hi, kid, how's it going?" Without waiting for an answer, he said, "What can I do for you, Frank?" He was referring to my uncle. "You sounded kind of secretive when you called. What's up?"

My uncle asked Michael, "Isn't your family from Sicily?"

"Yeah, my mother's people are Sicilians, but my father's family are from Rome."

My uncle went on. "We came here to get your advice on how or who should handle a warrant for the arrest of Mark Moran, alias Mario Moretti. The warrant stems from a massacre that took place in the Cathedral Monreale in Palermo, Sicily, in 1943 during WWII. Five soldiers were murdered, along with three civilians. Two civilians were wounded, including the priest who is now deceased. What we need to know is who has jurisdiction—New York, where he resides, or the Department of State because he killed five soldiers during the time of war? Oh, yes, and Italy also has a warrant out for his arrest and they will probably want extradition."

Michael sat dumbfounded. "I assume you have proof of these allegations?"

"Yes, we have the murder weapon with his fingerprints on it. These two witnesses said Mark Moran should have a tattoo on his chest that my father and Uncle Peter can identify as the man who massacred eight people and wounded the civilians."

Uncle Frank handed him a large envelope with all the evidence, including a report from a forensic specialist and the *Wanted* printout.

Michael called his secretary. "Marge, get Alvin Feldman in here. We need to take a statement."

Michael stated, "I know Mark Moran, Sr. I've never come up against him in a court of law, but I've heard he's a formidable opponent."

"His son, on the other hand, is smart but not nearly as ruthless as his father. In fact, Frankie here works for the firm."

292

"I'll contact the feds. They'll want him. But I want New York to get the collar and the publicity. So we're going to get out a warrant for his arrest and a search warrant for his office and home. We can take him into custody and hold him for the feds as a flight risk. He's a wanted man, but with all the evidence and witnesses, it gives them a solid case. He might have been able to have this overturned due to the fact he doesn't look anything like his picture. But seeing you have two witnesses and evidence, it looks like an open-and-shut case. Tell me, Frank, how did you get Mark Moran's fingerprints?"

"Luckily, they were on the gun."

"No, Frank. I mean *Mark's* fingerprints. How did you get a match?"

"That was no problem, Michael. I got it from the doorknob of his apartment, right out in the open."

Michael looked at him and laughed.

"Yeah, sure." He advised us, "Everyone should stay at Frank's house in New Jersey. It will be much safer staying there than in Manhattan. At least until he's arraigned."

I argued. "There is no way I'm going to let that creep force me to run with my tail between my legs. I'm staying in Manhattan. If need be, I'll stay at Darlene's place."

Michael was insistent. "I don't recommend that right now. I don't have the manpower to protect you."

"Come on, Michael. I don't need protection. He's an old man. I met him. What can he do in jail?"

The DA and my uncle looked at each other.

My uncle said, "Frankie, you're being stupid and foolish. I really think you should stay at my place until this blows over. I have some friends that will be covering my entire block."

Michael asked. "What friends? Do the police in Montclair know about your friends?"

"If New York doesn't have the manpower to protect my nephew, what makes you think a small town like upper Montclair does?"

Michael laughed. "Point taken, Frank."

"I think you're being overly cautious, Uncle Frank. There's no way he'll be allowed to make bail, especially once it hits the media. The feds will be jumping all over him. They might want to try him in a military tribunal. And don't forget, Italy also wants him. Mario Moretti is going nowhere."

Michael said that he wasn't really sure who had jurisdiction. He asked Alvin, the assistant district attorney, if he knew.

Alvin said he thought the U.S. government did.

"But the Italian government might want him extradited for the murders of the partisans. Who the hell knows? We never had this kind of a case before."

Michael told everyone go home and watch the news.

"But first, we will have to take Mr. Scarpelli's and Mr. Sorrento's statements. Also, I want Big Frank and Little Frank's cell phone numbers."

I glared at him.

He started laughing. "Just kidding, kid. A little DA humor."

"I didn't know district attorneys had a sense of humor."

Everyone started laughing except Peter. He didn't understand a word of what anyone was saying.

I had just left the building when I got a call from Darlene. She asked me what was going on and if I was really sick.

"No. I'm not sick. In fact, I'm just on my way to Starbucks. If I don't get a cup of coffee soon, I think I'll go crazy."

"Frank, talk to me. What's going on?"

"No, Darlene. I want you to stay out of this."

"It's too late, Frank. Don't shut me out. I'll be over right after work."

"No, Darlene, I have to be firm about this."

She started to laugh.

I didn't know what to say. That line always worked when my father used it on my mother.

"OK, Frank. If you don't want me to come over to your place, then I want you to stay at mine."

"No. I'm not going to let this asshole scare me. I think everyone is blowing this danger thing out of proportion."

"And you're not taking this seriously enough! What's the harm in being cautious?"

"Darlene, I don't want to talk about this anymore. I'll catch up to you in a few days. I'm sure the feds will pick him up as soon as he's arraigned. When the coast is clear and only when it is, I will call you."

"Frank Scarpelli, you are so stubborn."

She hung up. I thought, *I'm stubborn? What about you?*

After I had my coffee, I started walking around, looking in store windows and trying to think of what I would get everyone for Christmas. I decided to do some grocery shopping. The only thing in my refrigerator was cold water.

I got home a couple of hours later and put the TV on to watch CNN. I was starting to put the groceries away, all the while listening to the news. Then it came on. Breaking news: "Mark Moran, a prominent New York attorney, seems to have been living a double life. Mark Moran, Sr., is the CEO and founder of Mark Moran, Mark Moran, Jr., and Associates law firm. With a clientele that spans over three decades. Mr. Moran has been arrested for the brutal murders of eight people and two attempted murders in Palermo, Sicily, in 1943. Five of the murders were United States military personnel. Mario Moretti, alias Mark Moran, has eluded the Italian authorities and the U.S. government for sixty-three years. Mark Moran, Sr., claims it's a case of mistaken identity. The soldiers' names have been released: Lieutenant Harvey Bradshaw, Corporal Thomas Callahan, Private Leon Jones, Private Jerry Stein, and Private Ralph Watson. The Italian civilians were Angelina Sorrento, Mary Sorrento, and Anthony Pasco. Wounded were Father Michael Farrenti and Peter Sorrento. Our cameras are at the courthouse. We will bring you an update after the arraignment."

They showed Mark Senior on camera being brought in for custody. He made a statement to the press.

"I'm innocent. This is just a case of mistaken identity. I will be out shortly. I would expect nothing less than a formal apology from District Attorney Michael Bonito. Or I will sue him and the state of New York for false arrest."

I poured myself a double scotch and soda. That lying bastard! "Mistaken identity," my ass.

Meanwhile, Michael Bonito was also making a statement to the press.

"This is an especially heinous crime. A warrant for Mario Moretti has been out for over sixty-three years." He showed the *Wanted* poster and pictures of the soldiers who were killed. "I'm sure the families of these victims will finally be assured that justice will be served. We have an open-and-shut case against Mr. Moran. We have forensic evidence and witnesses to this massacre."

I lowered the volume on the TV. My cell phone was ringing. It was Darlene.

"Frank, the office is in chaos. Junior went down to the courthouse to help with his father's defense. They're going to try and make bail. Do you think he'll get out on bail?"

"I can't see how. He would be a flight risk, and the offense is premeditated murder. No way will they let him out."

"Frank, I have to go now. Please call me later and keep me posted."

Then my dad called. "Do you really think this was the right thing to do right now?"

"If not now, Dad, then when? There is no right or wrong time. That bastard killed eight people—in a church. For God's sake, Dad, he killed your aunt.

296

You think he should get away with this? Pop has been waiting for this day his whole life."

"I know, Frankie. You're right. It's your mother. She's worried about you."

Every time my father worried about any of his children, he blamed my mother. "Frankie, do me a favor. Come over and stay with us. She'll feel better."

"Thanks for the offer, Dad, but I want to stay here tonight. I'll stop by tomorrow."

He said, "You're going to have to look for another job."

"I know. I'll wait until the media blitz dies down."

"Son, do you need any money?"

"No, thanks, Dad. I've been putting some money away. I'll have enough for a while."

I changed the channel, but it was on all the channels. This was really news.

Last but not least, I got a call from my uncle.

"Get your bony ass down here right now!"

"Why? What's wrong? Is Pop sick?"

"What's wrong is your father. He's out of his mind with fear for your safety. Get down here now. I already sent John down to your place to pick you up and I told him to use force if necessary."

I started to laugh.

"Frankie, this is not funny. Mark Moran made bail."

A shiver went down my spine.

"What? Are you kidding? What idiot judge did that? He's a flight risk."

"Apparently, he had some connection with the judge. I don't know the whole story. John should be there soon."

"OK, OK. You people are so paranoid."

"And you're young and foolish. You take too many risks."

"I said OK. I'll just pack a few things and leave as soon as John gets here."

I heard a knock on the door.

"I have to go, Uncle Frank. Someone is at the door. It's probably John."

He started yelling, "Don't answer it until I call John on his cell phone."

I heard another knock and Darlene's voice.

"It's OK, Uncle Frank. It's Darlene."

"Don't hang up on me, Frankie."

I saw no reason to leave Darlene waiting at the door.

I yelled, "Just a minute, Darlene!"

I opened the door. A strange man was behind her.

He literally pushed her in. I dropped the phone and asked him, "What the hell is going on here? And who the hell are you?"

The guy slammed the door shut and announced, "I'm going to kill you and your girlfriend if you don't tell me where your grandfather and his friend are."

"I don't know where they are. All I know is that they're in protective custody. Go ask the DA."

"Listen to me, you wiseass kid. Don't hand me any bullshit. I don't have much time. Your uncle lives in New Jersey. You better tell me where he lives and how to get through his security system, or I swear I'll kill your girlfriend right in front of you."

"I don't know. Now you take your fuckin' hands off her, apparently you have no idea who the fuck you're dealing with."

He started to pull Darlene's hair. She screamed. He was hurting her. I had to stop him.

I grabbed her out of his grip and pushed her aside. We struggled for the gun and it went off. I don't remember feeling any pain. I fell to the ground. I couldn't move. I heard Darlene scream and then I heard another gun go off. One shot, two shots. I tried to get up but I couldn't.

298

Darlene was silent. I feared that Darlene was killed more than I feared my death.

I lay in a pool of blood, and then I saw a blurred face leaning over me. It was John's face.

He whispered, "Hang in there, Frankie. The paramedics are on their way."

I whispered, "John, is she dead?"

"No, she just fainted. Lie still. It's all over."

I vaguely remember the paramedics putting me on a stretcher and hooking me up to all kinds of gadgets. I also remember asking them if I was going to die. That was the last thing I remembered.

The next thing I recalled was: I'm standing in front of the church. TC is standing in front of those large bronze doors. He sees me, smiles, and starts walking toward me.

I ask, "It's over, isn't it?"

"Yes, thanks to you."

"No one is here. It's so quiet."

"I wanted to say good-bye, Frankie, and to thank you for all your help."

"I'm dead, aren't I?"

"No you're not. You'll wake up when you're ready."

I say, "Good-bye, Thomas Callahan."

When I awoke my thoughts were of Darlene. Was she really all right? I looked around and saw her sitting with my family. *My God, the whole family is here, including Jessie.*

I went to say, "What's up?" when I felt a sharp pain in my chest, so what I actually said was "Ouch."

Everyone looked up and came over to my bedside. My mother started to cry and my father and uncle looked like someone had kicked them in the guts.

"Mom, stop crying."

"I can't help it. How are you?"

I muttered, "Sore, very sore. Darlene?"

They all made way for Darlene to get close.

I asked her, "Are you OK?"

"I'm fine! You're the one I'm worried about." She started to cry. "You saved my life."

"No, I didn't. John did."

Her eyes welled up and she was sniffling.

"If you didn't act like the fool you are and pull me aside, he would have killed me to get you to tell where Pop was."

"I wasn't sure of what to do. He was hurting you."

She reached for my hand and started to cry.

I asked if John got in any trouble for shooting whoever the hell that guy was.

My uncle assured me he wasn't, that John had a permit to carry a gun and used it to save a life.

"He's not in any trouble."

I reminded him that he had a permit in New Jersey but not in New York.

"You know, kid, I could smack the shit out of you. You're near death and you're concerned about the damn law? Just to relieve your sense of justice, John has a permit to carry a gun in New York. He's a bodyguard."

I told him I was glad he did. He saved our lives and I was grateful.

My dad said, "All this happened because you're so damn stubborn and won't listen to anyone."

My uncle glared at his brother. My father shut up.

I could hear Pop in the background, asking if I was all right.

"Yes," my dad answered. "Thank God, he's going to be fine."

I asked my uncle how long I'd been unconscious.

"It's Sunday. You've been out for three days. You had a guardian angel looking over you, kid. That bullet grazed your heart. You're lucky to be alive."

"I take it this was Mark's doing?"

"Right after he was released from jail, he put out a contract to get Pop and Peter. But they didn't know how to penetrate my security system. So they went looking for you.

"Uncle Frank, can they connect Mark to me being shot and Darlene abducted?"

"No, not really. I heard about the contract through a friend. But don't worry about Mark Moran anymore. He's dead. He had an unfortunate accident."

I was about to ask what happened when the doctor came in and yelled at everyone for not telling the nurse that I was awake. He asked everyone to leave, that he needed to examine me. They all piled out.

The doctor asked me how I felt.

I told him I was in a lot of pain.

"I'm glad you're awake, Frank. You're lucky to be alive. If it wasn't for your age and the best cardiologist in this city, I doubt you would have made it. Right now, you need to rest."

That was the last thing I heard before falling asleep.

I don't know how long I was asleep. It could have been fifteen minutes or a full day. I only know that when I woke up, it was dark and quiet except for a nurse who was taking my blood pressure.

I asked, "Where is everyone?"

"The doctor advised them to go home and to get some rest. You're a brave young man, Frank Scarpelli."

"Why? What did I do?"

She smiled. "Did you also lose your memory?"

"I don't think so. Could you please turn on the TV? I'd like to see the news."

"I don't think so, Mr. Scarpelli. The doctor doesn't want you to get upset."

"Please, I wouldn't tell him. And please call me Frank. Nurse?"

"Nurse Baxter. OK, Frank, if you promise to try and eat something solid."

"What did you have in mind?"

"How about a nice bowl of chicken soup and some Jell-O?"

"Chicken soup? That's what you have when you have a cold. Fine, I'll eat the chicken soup, but forget the Jell-O."

After some stupid commercials, the news came on. It showed a picture of Mark Moran, Sr., and announced, "The funeral services for Mark Moran, Sr., who was out on bail for premeditated murder, will be held tomorrow at a small Catholic church in Long Island. The name of the church has been withheld. It seems Mark Moran was shot in a drive-by shooting, seconds after his son Mark Moran, Jr., had dropped him off at his home in Long Island. Mark Moran, Sr., had just been released on bail. He'd been accused of killing eight people and wounding two in the Cathedral Monreale in Palermo, Sicily, during World War II. The accusers say he is also known as the notorious Mario Moretti, who was a spy for the Hitler regime. The United States Department of State claims he should never have been released on bail. There will be a full investigation as to what authority Judge White had in releasing him, due to the nature of the crime.

"So far, there are no witnesses or clues to the car involved in the drive-by shooting of Mr. Moran. The police are asking for citizens to come forward if they have any information."

The news commentator went on as they showed a picture of the hospital.

"The latest report on Frank Scarpelli is that he is in stable condition. Buzz Dietz shot him at the Westward Building on Fifth Avenue. Buzz was holding Frank and his girlfriend, Darlene Banks, General Banks' daughter, at gunpoint when the gun went off, hitting Frank in the chest and nearly taking his life. An investigation is under way as to the motive for the assault. Buzz Dietz was shot and killed by a family friend who happened to stop by Frank Scarpelli's apartment and saw Frank and Darlene Banks being accosted. The police are also looking into the connection between his assailant, Buzz Dietz, and Mark Moran, Sr. Buzz has had two prior convictions of attempted murder and is thought to be a hired gunman. District Attorney Michael Bonito said, 'This is a bizarre twist of fate. Two suspects were killed prior to their trial. But you can be sure an investigation into the deaths of these suspects will be forthcoming.'"

I asked Nurse Baxter to shut the television off.

Nurse Baxter claimed, "This is nothing. You've been out for a couple of days. They had full coverage of you and Darlene the night they brought you in half dead."

"Well, I'm glad I was unconscious and didn't get to see it."

So Mark is dead, talk about coincidences. Thank God Pop and Peter are safe. That's twice Mario missed killing them. I don't know if Pop could have survived the trial. He is weak and the stress might have killed him. I was just hit with the realization that this was finally over. Uncle Frank said that they were going to give the reward money to Peter. He deserved it.

I fell back to sleep after my great dinner of chicken soup. I guess I was out for quite a while because when I looked at the clock, it was 10:00 p.m. I was in a great deal of pain, so I tried buzzing for the nurse. Nothing. I tried again and looked through the window to see if I could see her coming. All I could see was the shadow of a large figure of a man. I tried to yell, but I didn't have the strength.

As the shadow came closer, I asked him, "Could you get the nurse?"

It was a complete surprise to me when John answered, "What's the matter, Frankie?"

"John, thank God, please get the nurse. The pain is unbearable."

He walked into my room, put the light on, and said, "Hang on. I'll be right back."

A few minutes later, John was literally dragging the nurse into my room. He was so fast that she was out of breath.

"What happened here? I thought you died. This big galoot dragged me all the way down the hall."

I tried to laugh but couldn't. "I'm sorry, but the pain is bad. Can you give me something, anything?"

She looked at my chart and said, "You're due for a shot of morphine," and closed the curtain. When she was done, she opened the curtain, gave John a dirty look, and walked out.

He just shrugged his shoulders and laughed.

"I didn't even hurt her. She wouldn't come. She said she was busy."

If I hadn't been in so much pain, I would have laughed. What a sight!

"John, what are you doing here so late at night?"

"I came to visit you, but you were asleep, so I waited to see if you were all right."

"It's a good thing you did. Man, the pain is pretty bad."

John came over to me and sat down in a chair beside my bed.

"You scared the hell out of me, Frankie."

"Thanks to you, Darlene and I are still alive. You saved our lives. I owe you, man."

I held out my hand.

He pushed it away and hugged me lightly, knowing a good squeeze would probably send me into cardiac arrest.

I asked him if he would mind keeping me company for a while. He nodded. I thought this would be the perfect opportunity to ask him about himself and his family.

"You know, John, I know so little about you. What's your story?"

"I don't have a story," he replied.

"Everyone has a story. What was your family like? Do you have any brothers or sisters?"

"No. I'm an only child. My mother died a couple of years ago, and I live with my dad."

I started to pry a little more. "What made you work for my uncle? How did you get to know him?"

"I've known Mr. Scarpelli all my life. He and my old man were friends from the old neighborhood. You don't know much about your uncle, do you, Frankie?"

"Sure, I do. I've known him ever since I was born. What makes you think I don't know him?"

"Well, it seems to me you know of him and respect him, but no one in his family really knows him, except Mrs. Scarpelli."

The pain was finally subsiding and I was starting to get a buzz on.

"I don't know, John. I think I know my uncle better than you do. I know that no one dares double-cross him."

"No offense, Frankie, but I don't think you do."

"OK, John, tell me what I don't know about Uncle Frank."

"Do you or your family know how much he gives back to the community?"

"Yes, John, I know he's altruistic."

"I'm not just talking money."

"OK, so give me an example."

"All right, take my dad; he was a heavy-duty gambler. We lost our house, and we were always on the move. One step ahead of paying our monthly rent because he used every dime he had gambling. He was always waiting for that one big score. Then he got into the mob for one hundred grand and he didn't have a dime, let alone a hundred grand. So he got scared and took off. He just left us. My mother got a job in a grocery store, but she hardly made enough to pay the rent. The mob kept watching the house to see if he'd come home. Finally they came knocking on the door. They took one look at me and said, 'Come on, kid. You're coming with us.'

"My mother said, 'No, you can't take him. What do you want with him?'

"They said, 'Yes, we can. We'll hold him until your stupid husband comes back and pays us the money he owes us.'

"I was scared to death."

"How old were you, John?"

"I was a little over ten. My mother threatened to call the police. They told her if she did, she would never see me again. My mother must have called your uncle because he not only found my father hiding in some dump, he gave him the hundred grand to get me out. In a way, it was a good thing it happened. Your uncle told him if he didn't go to Gamblers Anonymous, the next time he'd let the Mafia kill him for being a coward and putting his family in jeopardy. My old man went for help, and your father gave him a job. Your uncle never spoke of it again, nor did he ask for the money back. He's helped so many people, I couldn't name them all."

"What about school? Didn't you go to school?"

"Sure, but you see how big I am. I got teased a lot when I was a kid. People thought because I was big, I was dumb. I was just a kid and the teasing hurt my feelings. So my mother, who was really smart, home-schooled me until high school. I had to take a test to get in. I did and I passed. I was at the same grade level as the other kids my age. On my first day at school, the coach passed me in the hallway. He took one look at me and told me to meet him in the gym at three o'clock. I did. He looked me up and down and said he finally got his linebacker. I was just what he was looking for. I joined the football team and I was good. I finally gained respect from my classmates. Those were the best four years of my life. After high school, I went to Chubb Institute in Jersey City to learn computer programming. It's supposed to be a hard course but I aced it."

"John, didn't you ever want to have a career besides being my uncle's bodyguard?"

"I'm not just his bodyguard. I'm his chauffer, I work on his computers, and I customize programs for his business. I'm with him on his business trips. I'm learning all about finance from the master. Your uncle is the master of finance. He should have articles written in magazines about him. Frankie, do you have a clue to how wealthy he is, how many important people he knows? Like politicians, judges, builders, architects, bankers, even in the movie industry. I could go on and on. He loans a lot of important people money, and they also invest in him. I have a great job, and he pays me well."

It was now time to ask the ultimate question about my uncle. The question I should have asked him but never had the nerve to.

"John, is my uncle in the Mafia?"

"I don't think so, Frankie. He doesn't hang with them or go to any meetings. He knows a lot of people in the mob. Some are his friends from the old neighborhood, and some are business acquaintances. Sometimes he finds them legitimate businesses to invest in. They trust him. He also knows how to keep quiet about their business dealings."

I asked him, "What if the businesses fail? Won't they come after him?"

"No, they're not stupid. No business venture is 100 percent guaranteed. Besides, it's a write off. They win either way. Your uncle is too smart to get mixed up in anything that could land him in jail. He doesn't have to. He's got all the money and power he wants without them. Take your school, for instance."

"What school? You mean Harvard?"

"Yeah, Harvard. Look how he helped you in school."

"What the hell are you talking about?"

"Oh, you didn't know about the donation?"

"What donation?"

307

"Forget I said it. I spoke out of turn."

"Oh, no you don't. What the hell are you talking about? I got excellent grades on my own. No one bought my grades. I worked my ass off in school."

"Don't get excited, Frankie. I shouldn't have said anything."

"Well, you did. Now tell me what the hell you're talking about."

"Your uncle was really proud of your grades. When he heard you wanted to get into Harvard, he gave a large donation to the school in good faith. It's difficult to get into Harvard even with excellent grades. No one in the family was an alumnus. But he knew plenty of people who were. When he's grateful. He gives."

"He didn't pay for my grades, did he?"

"Of course not. You can't bribe a school like Harvard. And he wouldn't do that anyway. He just wanted you to be remembered as an alumnus."

"Holy shit," I said, "I had no idea."

Then I remembered when the dean came over and congratulated me. *That's how he knew me.* I started to get really tired, but I wanted to hear more about John.

"Do you have a girlfriend, John?"

"No, I get all stupid around girls. Don't get me wrong, I'm not queer or anything. I'm such a big guy, I'm afraid I'll hurt them."

"Don't put yourself down. You're such a nice guy I can't imagine a woman not wanting to date you."

"Come on, Frankie, look at me. You're a good-looking guy. You don't know what it's like to be afraid to go up to a woman and ask her out."

"Are you kidding, John? No one wants to date a nerd, someone who has their nose in a book all the time. That's all I did all during high school and college. So when I met Darlene, I went spastic. I could hardly speak to her."

John saw how tired I was getting. "I'm going now, Frankie, I'm glad you're going to be OK. I've already talked way too much."

"Thanks for coming, John. And you were right. You do know my uncle better than I do. But thanks to you, I now know him a lot better."

He smiled that toothy grin and left.

The next morning, the doctor came in and said if I kept improving the way I was, I would be able to go back to my normal way of life.

"But you can't go back to work for at least a month."

"That's OK, Doc. I don't have a job anyway."

I asked him if this injury would change my life as I knew it.

He said he expected a complete recovery and I could leave the hospital in another week if I promised to take it easy. No jogging, no exercise, and no sex for at least a month.

"What! No sex?"

"Especially no sex, Frank. After your final exam, I'll tell you when you can resume your normal routine. In fact, today you sit up and tomorrow you get on your feet for just a few minutes. Every day, we'll increase you're up time until you get your strength back. Right now, you're on a restricted diet. But in a couple of days, you can go back to a normal diet."

As he was starting to leave, he said, "Believe me, Frank. I'd like to get you out of here before your pain-in-the-ass family arrives."

I laughed. "I know what you mean, but aren't I a lucky bastard to have them?"

He agreed. "You are lucky to have such a close family in this day and age."

One by one, they all came in smiling because I was sitting up. My aunt came in with a box of candy and my mother brought flowers. It wasn't until that time that I noticed my room was full of flowers. There were flowers everywhere.

I asked, "Where did all these flowers come from?"

My mother read me a few of the cards. "This is from your office. This one is from Nate's Deli. This one is from a Dr. Bass. And this one is from a Theresa Callahan Sullivan. Who's she, Frankie?"

"I don't know a Theresa Callahan Sullivan."

And then it hit me, TC. Thomas Callahan. *It must be a relative.*

"Mom, can you read me the note."

"May God bless you and heal you, Frank Scarpelli. I want to thank you and your courageous family for finding my father's murderer. I can now have closure, knowing that justice has been done, and now my mother's soul can rest in peace. I'm forever, in your debt, Theresa Callahan Sullivan. (215) 555-3363."

I asked my dad to dial the number for me. It rang quite a while, and I was about to hang up when a woman answered.

"Hello?"

"Hello, this is Frank Scarpelli. I would like to speak to Theresa."

"I'm Theresa. Frank, are you all right?"

"The doc said I would be soon."

"I just got back from church, Frank, and the whole congregation was praying for your recovery."

"I appreciate that. Thank everyone for their prayers, and thank you for the flowers."

"It's me who should be thanking you for finding the man who killed my father and his friends. It's like a miracle. How did you ever find him?"

I wanted to tell Theresa that it was her father who found me. I wanted to tell her that he was finally at peace. But how could I? Besides, she probably wouldn't have believed me.

She said, "If my mother were alive, she would have been so pleased that there was finally closure. All those years she wondered who could have done such a terrible thing, especially in a church. And most of all, she wondered why. Why weren't they taken as prisoners?"

"I'm sorry to hear about your mother's death, Theresa. When did she pass away?"

"Ten years ago. She and my grandparents raised me after my father was killed. My mom went to school in the evenings, got her bachelor's degree, and became a teacher. This way, she could have the summers off. She taught school for over thirty-five years."

"It sounds like your mother never remarried."

"No, she never did. She never got over my father's death. I didn't understand at first, but as I got older, I understood. My dad was her one and only love."

"What about you?"

"Oh, I married a fine Irish cop. His name is Robert Sullivan, and we have two children, Thomas and Anna. And I already have three grandchildren. I don't want to tire you out. Thank you for calling me. And may God bless you, Frank Scarpelli."

I started to get all choked up. I guess it was the drugs. Everyone asked who I was speaking to; I told them it was an old friend's daughter.

My mother said, "Darlene will be here around ten o'clock."

"Well," I asked, "what does everyone think of my lady?"

Everyone gave a nod and a smile of approval.

To my surprise, my mother said, "I do like her, Frankie. And for what it's worth, you have my blessing. Darlene did not leave your side for one moment. I'm sure she loves you very much."

"Thanks, Mom. That means a lot to me. How do I look? Do you think I should shave?"

My father spoke up.

"Frankie, you almost died. Darlene is just happy you're alive. I'm sure she doesn't give a damn if you don't shave."

I heard the clicking heels of a woman. I thought it might be Darlene, but it was Jessie. She came over and kissed me on the cheek.

"I'm so glad you're OK. When are you going to introduce me to your girlfriend?"

"You know you're nuts, don't you? Can't it wait until I'm just a little better?"

She laughed. "I'm just busting your chops, Frank."

"I know that, Jessie. When aren't you?"

"Come on, Frank. Don't tell me Darlene doesn't tease you. What fun is that?"

I just looked at her and gave her the Scarpelli evil eye. I didn't like where this was going. It worked. She actually shut up. I should have done that a long time ago.

John left to drive Peter to Kennedy Airport. Peter's mission was over, and he wanted to go home. In fact, half the town was going to greet him at the airport. The bells of Cathedral Monreale would be ringing in his honor. I was glad Pop had a chance to see his old friend before his time ran out.

I happened to look up and through the window of my room that faced the corridor; I could see Darlene walking with a very tall, distinguished-looking man who looked somewhat familiar. As they got closer, I could see it was her father, General Matthew Walker Banks. I got a little nervous; I wasn't sure if I was up for this.

She walked in and greeted everyone. Then she came over and kissed me on the cheek. I pointed to my mouth.

She shook her head and whispered, "Behave yourself. I'm so happy to see you sitting up, and I would like everyone to meet my father, Matthew."

He went around shaking hands. He then came close to my bed and shook my hand lightly, so as not to disturb the IV and all the other tubes in my arm. He expressed his wish that we were meeting under better circumstances.

"But I had to come here today to thank you for saving my daughter's life."

"Thank you, sir, but I feel guilty for putting her into that situation."

"She told me the whole story, Frank. How you insisted on her staying out of this until it was safe. I know my daughter and I think you should know that my daughter is stubborn and bull-headed."

"Dad, I think Frank already knows that."

He went on. "But I must confess. My daughter is very much like me. Thank God she has her mother's looks."

We all laughed.

I was speechless. He was as he looked, pleasant, controlled, and he had a presence. All eyes were on him.

General Banks stayed for twenty minutes and then excused himself. He had a plane waiting to take him back to D.C. As he was leaving, he told me to take care of his pigheaded daughter, that she can get in all kinds of trouble in a city like New York.

I tried to reach out and shake his hand. Trying to extend my hand was very painful, so I just told him that it would be my pleasure.

One by one, everyone started to leave, including Jessie, but not before kissing me on the mouth.

Darlene arched her eyebrows and said quietly to me, "When everyone leaves, we have to talk about Jessie."

"Sure, honey, I'll tell you almost anything you want to know."

"I really appreciate your family leaving so we can be alone."

She pulled her chair close to my bedside and we held hands.

I looked at her and confessed, "Do you have any idea how scared I was? I thought that nut would kill you. And do you want to know what else is scaring me? How much I love you."

"I do know, Frank. I felt the same way when you got shot. I thought you were dead." Tears starting rolling down her cheeks. "If you hadn't pulled me out of his way, he might have killed us both."

"I didn't do anything Bogie wouldn't have done."

She smiled, kissed me on the lips, and started to cry.

"Honey, please don't cry. The doctor said I'm going to be fine. Is John going to be all right for shooting that Buzz character?"

"Yes, after they took you to the hospital and revived me because I'd fainted, I can't believe I did that."

I patted her hand. "That's OK, honey. Don't forget, you're the weaker sex."

"Don't you patronize me, Frank Scarpelli. Seeing you lying on the floor, bleeding to death, scared the hell out of me. So as I was saying, after I was revived with some smelling salts the paramedics had given me, I went with John as his unofficial attorney to interpret the statement he would have to sign. It was all settled. John won't face any criminal charges.

"You know, Frank, after the operation was over, the doctor informed us that you were still alive but it was touch and go. And it might be days before he knew if you would survive. They put you into a private room in intensive care. The doctor then told us all to go home and come back the next morning; that you would most likely be unconscious for at least forty-eight hours. But John was so worried that someone else might try to kill you that he stood guard outside your door all night until we all came back the next morning. He's a good and loyal friend. Once Mark was killed, we all started to relax."

I felt somewhat relieved.

"So John couldn't have killed Mark? He was here with me."

"No, Frank, he couldn't have. No one knows who shot Mark. In fact we may never know."

"Is it just me, Darlene? Doesn't this have the earmarks of a Mafia hit?"

314

"Michael doesn't know for sure. There is no evidence linking organized crime to the shooting. Does he care? I don't think so.

"OK, now that we're alone, tell me about Jessie."

"Jessie is a very good friend of mine, and I hope she will be yours too."

"She doesn't act like just a friend, Frank."

"You're right. She was a little more. She was probably to me what Bruce was to you."

"Are you sure it's over between you two? It didn't seem that way? The way she kissed you . . ."

I laughed. "I think that was more for your benefit than it was for mine."

"Oh, I see. She wanted to make me jealous."

"Last month, I told Jessie that I was seeing you and it was serious. That meant our physical relationship was over. But our friendship wasn't. After all, we've known each other since we were in high school. She actually broke up with me and she was right. We had different agendas. Besides, we were just kids."

Darlene leaned over and kissed me lightly on my lips. "I can live with that. You know, Frank, now the both of us are unemployed, with all this publicity, no one working for the firm will have a job."

"I know and I feel bad about that. I really do. But with your credentials, you won't have any problem finding a job in Manhattan."

"The same goes for you, Frank. Chances are we won't be working together."

"Why? I hope you're not planning on moving out of New York."

"No. I wouldn't leave here. I wouldn't be able to keep an eye on you and that All-American-looking blonde cheerleader."

"I'm glad, Darlene. I hate commuting."

"All kidding aside, Frank, I've been thinking about changing my vocation. I'm pretty sure I want to get out of the private sector and apply my legal expertise in law by working for the district attorney."

"Why would you want to do that? The money's lousy compared to private practice."

"I'm thinking maybe I would prefer helping the victim and their families by putting these criminals away and getting them off the streets."

"Does this decision have anything to do with what happened to us?"

"It probably does, Frank. We were victims and I felt vulnerable and scared. Take a man like Buzz Dietz; they keep letting him out."

"True, but now they have the 'three strikes you're out' law, and not everyone who walks in our office is guilty. There are a lot of innocent people who are accused of a crime. And there are also circumstances when a crime is committed. Perhaps it was the only solution to survive, such as self-defense. Take the case I'm working on now. Mrs. Smith said she killed her husband in self-defense. I didn't have time to fully corroborate her story of abuse, but if she had been beaten and abused by her husband and she found the opportunity to save her own life, it will be the prosecutor who will try to give her life for premeditated murder. Truthfully, my gut feeling is she's innocent."

"That's true, Frank, but what about the case when you know your client is guilty? Do you want to be responsible for putting them back on the streets?"

"You know, honey, I'm sure all attorneys have to struggle with this. In the United States, everyone is entitled to a defense and I don't have to tell you they are innocent until proven guilty. If the prosecutor does his homework and has enough evidence, the jury should find him guilty. I guess we just have to choose sides. If you do decide to work in the prosecutor's office, there is a good possibility we will be adversaries in court."

She smiled. "I realize that. May the best person win."

She finally brought up the subject of the nightmares. "Frank, do you think the nightmares will leave you now?"

"Yes, I really believe that I've seen the last of TC."

"Why do you think you had those terrible dreams for such a long time?"

"I'm not sure. My gut feeling is that Dr. Bass was right. It could have been divine intervention or however you want to define it. Maybe Mario had to pay for his sin against humanity. 'Vengeance is mine, saith the Lord.'"

"Frank Scarpelli, that is a very spiritual analysis. I didn't know that about you."

"I know. I don't know what to think. Look at me; I'm alive. The doctor said he couldn't understand how I survived. Some things like my dreams are just as unexplainable."

I was stunned when Mark and Tim Moran walked into my room. They seemed somber, but who wouldn't be? They went through the same hell my family had gone through. They not only lost a father, they had their lives and their careers turned upside down.

Mark asked, "How are you feeling, Frank?"

"I've felt better. How are you guys holding up?"

They replied almost in unison. "We could be better."

Then Mark spoke, "We came here to tell you how sorry we are for all that's happened to you, Darlene, and your family."

I asked how their families were doing. Tim said his mother was taking it pretty badly, but she never in her wildest dreams thought that her husband was capable of committing those horrible crimes. Apparently, he had a dual personality, a respectable attorney living a proper conservative lifestyle and, underneath, a psychopath and a criminal.

Junior said, "My father was not an easy man to live with. He had fits of temper, but he never physically hurt us. He just set our standards so high that it was impossible to attain them. My mother finally told us that we were adopted.

It seems Mother couldn't have any children, so my father went to a friend of his who owned an adoption agency. His friend told him of a woman in New York state who became a diabetic after the birth of her second child. They were very poor and she was ill. We were very young when we were adopted. Tim was only a couple of weeks old and I was two when the Morans adopted us. Right now, our only concerns are for our families. Our mother needs care, not to mention this has made her a social outcast. I guess now she really knows who her friends are. After all, it brought shame upon the Moran name. And it's sure to affect the firm, but we're sure that in time people will forget and life will go on."

I was really starting to feel bad for these guys.

"I'm sorry that you and your family became the innocent victims. Mark, Tim—there is no way you're to blame for your father's actions. But what made you tell him that I was involved with Darlene? If he didn't know, he never would have used her to get to me."

Mark said, "I didn't tell him. The night I saw you and Darlene leaving work, my father was in the backseat of my car. He saw you."

Tim said, "Frank, we want you to come back to your job when you're well."

"Are you kidding? After all that's gone down, you still want me to work for you?"

"Yes," Tim stated. "It makes good sense. The vendetta between our families is over, and none of it had anything to do with us. This bad publicity will kill us. People will eventually forget, but in the meantime we won't survive the fallout. We'll have to close down. Our clients will probably leave. Everyone in our office will lose their jobs. They are good and competent people; we've been like a family. My father may have started the business, but Mark and I have doubled the business since he retired. If you come back, our clients will stay. Without you, we can't survive. What do you say?"

"I had no quarrel with you, but won't I be a reminder of this whole mess?"

Mark answered, "What my father did was horrific and we're mortified, but it was his doing, not ours and certainly not yours. Business is business. You need to learn the business, and we're willing to give you that opportunity. Although, I know with your credentials, you could get a job with just about any upscale firm. But we're expanding and promotions will be made, along with pay raises. Keep in mind you'll get no special favors. You'll have to earn it. By the way, we have already taken legal steps to change the name of the firm. It's now M. Moran, T. Moran, and Associates. What do you say, Frank? Is it possible to put the past behind us and start a new year in a new firm?"

I looked over at Darlene. She smiled and put her thumb up. She liked the idea. I was going to ask for time to think about their proposal, but the truth was I liked the location and the staff. I also thought Mark and Tim were pretty good guys for bosses.

"OK, I'll come back."

As best I could, we all shook hands to seal the deal.

After everyone left and I was alone, I thought about all I'd been through in the past five months. What a hell of a roller coaster ride. But in spite of everything, I wouldn't have missed it for the world. My nightmares are gone. I have fallen in love for the first time in my life. I feel I've grown and matured from this experience. Right now, life is good.

Oh shit, here comes the pain again. Crap, it really hurts. I hit the buzzer to call the nurse, as usual no response. Where is that damn Nurse Baxter when you need her?

I started yelling, "Nurse. Nurse, if you don't get your ass in here, I'm going to call John. Then you'll be sorry."

Chapter 29

I was finally released from the hospital, but not after getting a lecture on staying home and taking care of myself. I was told not to go back to work for at least a month. My mother wanted me to go to New Jersey to recuperate, but that was out of the question. I told her I would rather stay at my place and study for the bar exam. And that's exactly what I did. What else could I do?

On the way to taking our bar exams, Darlene and I were competitive and quiet, each of us wanting the other to pass. On the other hand, both of us wanted to outsmart the other. I sure as hell didn't want Darlene getting a higher grade than me. As it turned out, we were as close in our test scores as we were academically in our respective schools.

I would never admit it to her, but I was damn glad I scored a few points higher. I know it sounds petty. She's as smart as me, but she's also condescending. I didn't want her lauding it over me for the rest of my life. And I knew she would. Me, on the other hand, I'm a lot more humble.

Although our relationship had been going great, she refused to move in with me. It seemed she preferred her independence. If I didn't know her like I do, I would say she wasn't sure she loved me. But I know she does. And she's smart enough to want to make sure that we can stand the test of time. Forever is a long, long time.

As soon as Darlene got her license, she called Michael Bonito, the district attorney, to tell him she was interested in working with him. As soon as there was an opening, she would like to be considered. Michael told her she was in luck. Jennifer O'Keefe, one of his top prosecutors, was leaving to go into private practice and he needed a replacement.

Darlene assured him she could handle the job. He reminded her she wouldn't be making the kind of money working for the state that she would if she stayed in private practice. Two weeks later, she was working for Michael Bonito and enjoying every minute of it.

I would have liked for things to stay the same, both of us working for M. Moran, T. Moran, and Associates. I used to like running into her office whenever time allowed. I was also not looking forward to us being adversaries. I wasn't sure any relationship could take that kind of punishment. But we'd find out when that time came. We all hear a different drummer, and I think her decision was commendable.

There is nothing like a tragedy to put things into perspective. After my mother got to know Darlene, she really liked her. She began to admire Darlene for her activist modern approach to self-awareness and what her role was as a woman—much to the chagrin of my father.

A funny and strange thing happened at one of our Sunday dinners. My father kept asking my mother to get him this and that. After we were finished eating and still talking at the table, he asked my mother to get him another cup of coffee.

She looked right at him and said, "Al, get up and get it yourself. I just spent hours cooking this dinner."

We all looked at each other, not knowing what to expect. My father looked at my mother and started to laugh. I mean, really laugh. My brother, Al, asked him if he was all right.

"She's right, Al. I can get up and get it myself."

We all started to laugh. My mother looked at Darlene and winked.

I leaned over and whispered to Darlene, "See what you started, trouble-maker."

She smiled, "Frank, I never said a word."

And then she started to snicker at her own private joke.

Pop took a vacation and went back to Sicily to visit Peter and his family's gravesite. We all tried to talk him out of it, but he said after all these years it was now time to put the past behind him by facing it. He planned on staying a month.

They never caught the person who killed Mark Moran, Sr., and no one was surprised, including the district attorney.

I kept my promise to Jessie and fixed her up with Norman; so far, so good. They're really hitting it off. Darlene is not thrilled about that situation, although she tolerates Jessie. They're as different as night and day. Occasionally, we double date and its obvious Darlene and Norman are not comfortable with the bantering that goes on between Jessie and me. It's that sister-and-brother thing we have going.

I finally went back to work and it is great to be back. Everyone greeted me when I walked in. Joan, my secretary, had even stopped off to get me a Starbucks coffee before coming to work. I told Joan she was going to spoil me.

"No, I won't because as soon as you're back to normal, you can get your own coffee."

I wasn't in the office ten minutes when Mark came in. He shook my hand and told me it was great seeing me looking so fit. He congratulated me on passing the bar exam with such high scores. I told him that was also a complete surprise.

"Not to me," he remarked.

I asked Mark the outcome of the Maude Smith case.

It seems Maude lied to Mark and to me. She was having an affair, and she had intended to leave Judge Smith as soon as the separation papers were filed. Maude swears he did abuse her and that she did have to fight him off in order to save her life. Mark had Judge Smith's ex-wife's statement, accusing her ex-husband of being a brutal and sadistic man. She also stated that the day he left her for Maude was the happiest day of her life. She confided she was too afraid to leave him.

After hearing the numerous statements confirming the abuse, Michael Bonito relented and offered her a one-time deal rather than taking it to court and having all these witnesses come forth discrediting a New York judge. Mark also reminded Michael of how this would play in the media.

Maude walked away with justifiable homicide. After Maude walked a free woman, Michael leveled with Mark.

"None of us know and can't know what really happened in that house. If the guy was the bastard people said he was, he deserved it. But if you ever tell anyone I said that, I'll deny it."

After Mark told me the story, he headed for the door. I called his name and he turned to face me.

"You're a good attorney, Mark. You're damn good. There's a lot I can learn from you."

"Thanks, Frank. I appreciate that."

He then walked out the door, leaving me to tack up my newly framed license on the wall of my office.

Phenomenon: (n) A fact or occurrence that can be perceived or observed.

A rare fact or occurrence that occurs.

An extremely outstanding or unusual person or thing.[*]

Supernatural occurrences have been documented since time began. But because it cannot be substantiated, it leaves doubt to the doubters of this world, and to the believers, an unsubstantiated mystery.

---

[*] Source: Webster's Dictionary.